PART 1

VIEW THROUGH A GLASS EYE

C.W. Reed lives in Whitby. He is married with grown-up children and is also a grandfather.

LOOKING GLASS

In the north-east town of Margrove, eighteen-year-old Alice Glass is reunited with former schoolmate Elsbeth Hobbs: shy, pretty, and from a privileged social background. Alice is rescued from her life in a small terraced house when she and Elsbeth assist in the wartime evacuation of schoolchildren to the Yorkshire Dales. Here she is caught up in the mystery of foreigner Gus Rielke's nefarious connection with farmer Bob Symmonds. Her admirer, Davy Brown, a labourer on a nearby estate, helps her in her investigation. But it is the truth about Alice's unacknowledged feelings for Elsbeth that brings about the most startling consequences . . .

Books by C. W. Reed
Published by The House of Ulverscroft:

TO REASON WHY
TIES OF BLOOD
ALL MANNER OF THINGS
THE FOOLISH VIRGIN
SEASON OF SINS
THE DECENT THING
SILK STOCKING SPY

C. W. REED

LOOKING GLASS

Complete and Unabridged

ULVERSCROFT
Leicester

First published in Great Britain in 2006 by
Robert Hale Limited
London

First Large Print Edition
published 2007
by arrangement with
Robert Hale Limited
London

British Library CIP Data

Reed, C. W. (Colin W.)
Looking glass.—Large print ed.—
Ulverscroft large print series: romance
1. World War, *1939–1945*—Evacuation of civilians—
England—Yorkshire Dales—Fiction
2. Young women—England—Yorkshire Dales—Fiction
3. Large type books
I. Title
823.9'14 [F]

ISBN 978–1–84617–825–2

Published by
F. A. Thorpe (Publishing)
Anstey, Leicestershire
Set by Words & Graphics Ltd.
Anstey, Leicestershire
Printed and bound in Great Britain by
T. J. International Ltd., Padstow, Cornwall

This book is printed on acid-free paper

1

'Come on! Up you get, you lot! Be quick!'

The three Glass girls groaned and whimpered and grunted to consciousness as their mother scooped up their little brother from his nest of blankets in the shake-me-down at the foot of their bed. 'Come on, Algy, chuck! Wakey-wakey, pet. It's them bloomin' Jerries again. Up you come!'

She disappeared through the door, clutching the five-year-old to her soft bosom, while his three elder sisters disentangled themselves from the venerable double bed. Or rather, two of them did. Thirteen-year-old Ethel and ten-year-old Doreen were already obediently up on their sleepy bare feet, tugging woollen shawls around their shifts and shuffling off after their mother. Eighteen-year-old Alice Glass stretched her limbs in the unaccustomed space of the warm sheets and hauled the blankets back up over her.

'Come on, our Alice!' Ethel reprimanded over her shoulder as she left. 'Hurry up! I can hear the guns going off.'

'Oh, leave us alone. Them buggers aren't daft enough to waste their bombs on this dump. I'm stopping here.' She rolled over deliberately, presenting the hump of her shoulder towards her departing siblings to emphasize her defiance.

How many times now had the sirens disturbed their night's sleep? At least five times in the past week, and never a bomb dropped in anger. Not on them, anyhow. The poor buggers in London were getting it in the neck. And maybe towns further up the coast, like Newcastle, or Middlesbrough. But not Margrove. Even Jerry didn't give a toss about *this* dump, and who could blame him? Nobody else did, herself least of all!

She couldn't wait for them to bring in the call-up for women. In fact, if she had her way, she wouldn't have to. She'd already tried to make enquiries about joining up. She fancied the Wrens — the uniform was the best of the lot, she thought — not that such things really bothered her, she hastened to assure herself. Most of her mates made her sick, with their constant jabber about clothes and hairstyles and make-up and all that stuff, their noses always in the latest magazines or dashing off to the pictures to gawp at the latest Hollywood glamour pusses. She wasn't like that at all.

And boys! God! They were even worse, made her hackles rise, the big-headed, mucky-minded lot! Like her brother George. She could hear him coughing and grumbling as he clattered downstairs. Typical! I'm off my arse so let everyone know about it! Sixteen, and he spent more time tarting himself up in front of the mirror than any lass, with his hair cream and his spot cream and God knows what besides. And those mucky magazines he thought he had so cleverly hidden away from everybody. She'd drop him right in it one of these days if he wasn't careful.

Why should he have the luxury of a room to himself? *She* was the eldest, damn it! She was a grown-up now, old enough and fit enough to go off and fight for king and country — and here she was still sharing a bed with two others, and with little Algy sleeping at her feet. It wasn't right!

'But you're a girl, love!' Her brain viciously mimicked her mother's reasonable tone. 'You can't have George sharing a room, can you? He's a young man now.'

By God! I wish *I* were an' all! she reflected bitterly. She was more than half-serious, too. They had all the luck. Even God had favoured the menfolk, she thought, with mutinous blasphemy. They didn't have to go through half the things lasses did, and she didn't have to review all of that in its messy and ignominious detail, did she? No! She'd always envied the fellers, even as a kid. When she was young, she'd felt more affinity with the boys and their rough-and-tumble world. Tomboy, they called her, and they were right. She could always keep up with them in most games, including thumping one or two when they called for it. Then, as she grew into her teens, she began seriously to envy them, and to feel more and more at odds with her own sex. Just lately she'd become sick of the whole caboodle of them, lasses and lads! She couldn't be doing with either, she reckoned.

The rapid bark of the AA-gun battery on the nearby rec ground forcibly disturbed her gloomy introspection. It was followed by her father's angry tone. She guessed he had been about to ignore the nightly interruption, but at the rising crescendo of martial activity discretion had got the better part of valour — or sloth — and he had decided to cram with the others into the tiny sloping cupboard under the stairs.

'Alice! Get yourself out of that bed now or I'll drag you out myself! Get a bloody move on!'

With a theatrical sigh she flung back the bedclothes and scrambled out. 'Shouldn't you be out firewatching?' She snatched her shawl, draped it over her shoulders and followed him down the dark, narrow staircase.

'You're getting too big for your breeches, my lass! But you're not too big to feel the back of my hand, lady, so just watch your mouth, all right?'

Let him just try it, and she swore she'd be off, straight out that door and never come back. Last time he'd really skelped her had been more than three years ago, when she was just about to leave school and she'd refused to take a job skivvying for one of them posh families up near the park. She could hardly sit for three days and her backside had been all the colours of the rainbow — but she hadn't taken the job! Instead she'd landed herself a job at the co-op stores just round the corner, where she'd done probably just as much scrubbing and sweeping and dusting as she would have done up by the park, and for just a few pence more. But at least she didn't have to slave day and night, only from half-seven in the morning till six — and Saturday afternoons and Sundays off! Wasn't she the lucky one? Who said the war was a disaster? If the Jerries hadn't been trying to bomb them out of house and home she'd have sent Adolf a thank you note! For her it seemed more like a

God-sent opportunity to escape the drudgery and dreariness that made up her life in the happy home of 19, Maudsley Street, and she was determined to seize it, come what may.

The cupboard under the stairs was sardine-packed, with the six bodies already in occupation. The high, narrow shelf stacked with boots, shoes and other paraphernalia restricted even further the minute space available. Her mam and dad took up the area immediately inside the door, where there was the most headroom — a person of medium height might almost stand upright there — then the ceiling sloped steeply, following the inclination of the stairs, so that where Ethel, Doreen, and the somnambulant Algy were squeezed, there was room only for them to sit side by side with their knees drawn up and heads bent chestward. It reminded Alice of that book at school, about her namesake, and that drawing of the great gangling girl jammed in a house where her head was wedged in the bedroom and her arms and legs poked through the windows. She could do with a drop of that magic potion now, to shrink her, Alice thought, as she attempted to fit herself around, between and beside all the limbs and projections smotheringly surrounding her.

'Get your fat backside out my face!'

snapped her brother, giving the offending part of her anatomy a vigorous dig with his fist.

He had taken the third and last of the low wooden stools placed there for these emergencies, and Alice was forced to half kneel and sprawl over the extended legs and cold bare feet of her sisters. 'Keep your hands to yourself!' she snarled, aware of the indignity of her position, and transferred her verbal attack to her father, unseen behind her in the fetid darkness. 'Why don't you put in for one of them Anderson shelters? We could have had one ages ago.'

'They're not giving them away free, you know!' came the fiercely defensive answer. 'Not if you're in work, anyhow. Anyways, where would we put it in here?'

'There's always the yard!' Her voice tailed off. What was the use? But then she couldn't help letting the words burst from her. 'God forbid we spend money, just to save our lives, eh? If this keeps on I'm going to start going across to the shelter in Lister Road.'

'No, you are not, my girl! The things that go on over there! Gambling and drinking, and swearing. And a lot worse besides!' Fred Glass added significantly, and Alice gave a sarcastic bark of laughter at the novelty of her father's tone of moral outrage. She could smell the whiff of stale beer breath which betrayed his evening visit to the Black Horse — a visit he rarely missed, unless he was on the late shift at the steelworks, in which case he usually managed to get two or four in before his labours, when the pub opened its doors at eleven a.m.

To Alice's contempt and secret dismay, Maggie, her mother, decided to weigh in on behalf of her husband. 'Hey, we haven't got money to chuck away, young lady! There's enough to do to keep house and home together and put food on the table as it is. And we don't exactly live off the fat of the land on what *you* chip in, either!'

Why, Ma? Why? Alice screamed in silent protest. Dad spends more on his booze and the horses and the dogs than he gives you to feed the family. Why do you stick up for him, let alone put up with him? Why on earth did you get yourself lumbered like this? Married at eighteen, five kids and a miscarriage somewhere along the line, living in a dump like Maudsley Street, outside lav, back yard like a prison exercise yard, back lane, walls practically with mushrooms growing out of them, make do and mend, hand-me-downs, scratching about like chickens to survive?

No! Alice swore yet again. Not for me! Never! All at once she felt the thick air choking her, she had to get out. She squirmed and wriggled round, barged past her muttering brother. 'Mind. I need the lav. I have to go!'

'Use the po, for God's sake! It's down there, by the door, only don't knock it over.'

'No! I have to go.'

She groped through the room and the back kitchen, drew the bolt on the back door. The September night was cold, she felt it through the thinness of her cotton shift, felt the cold striking up through her feet from the concrete of the back yard. This bloody blackout! Not even the glow of the streetlamps to give faint illumination any more, and the stars were hidden by the cloud. She fumbled with the sneck, slipped in to the chilly little cubicle of the lavatory. She hitched up her shift and felt the cold thin wooden rim as she lowered herself on the pedestal. She might have been lying about her desperate need for the netty, but she could always squeeze a few drops from her bladder. And she wasn't going back there in a hurry. She'd rather freeze to death, German bombers or no.

The guns seemed to have quietened down again, and there weren't even any searchlights probing the sky. She wondered how the Jerries could see their way with all this cloud about. How did they know where to drop their bombs? Maybe that was why they seemed to scatter them around in such funny places. Nothing on Margrove so far, in spite of the steelworks, which everyone had said would be a prime target straight off. You'd think they'd stick out a mile, with the furnaces and cooling towers and everything. Mind you, they'd covered one of the sheds with green and brown — camouflage, they called it. That had been one of George's first jobs when they took him on last year: helping to paint the roof, and deck it out with false trees and bushes. Daft! her da had said, but who knows? Maybe it looks real enough from the air.

Oh God! She hoped she'd be able to get away soon. They were taking women into all kinds of jobs now — the railways, buses. Even on the land. Her dad kept going on about trying to get her into the canteen at the works — he claimed he had been influential in getting George taken on, and that he'd be safe from call-up, even though it wasn't an apprenticeship but just a labouring job. 'Reserved Occupation'. The way her dad rolled it off his tongue you'd think it was the highest honour in the land. Well, she was more than ready to do her bit! Couldn't wait, and the fact that it seemed she would have to made it all the more galling. There was still no sign of the government bringing in the Registration Act for young women, even though the war was one year old.

She had felt so hurt and deflated when she'd gone down to the town hall and enquired about the Women's Royal Naval Service. All those embarrassing questions, and the forms to fill in. 'I'll do anything!' she offered desperately. 'I don't mind!' But they'd politely declined her offer. Turned her down, though they tried to take the sting out by saying she could apply again, later. She would be nineteen in December.

She shivered, felt the cold spreading through her frame. She might be a bit on the short side, and quite stocky for a girl. But she was fit and strong. She'd had plenty of practice at grafting at work, and at home. And she meant it. She was ready to do anything — just as long as she didn't have to do it in Margrove and its dreary little terraces! She shifted a little, felt the coldness and the hardness striking up. *There's a blue ring round my arse, Virginia!* as her dad was always singing. Fancied himself as one of them Hollywood crooners — he would sit out here for hours, bawling away bold as brass, and studying the form from his racing pink. She squinted up through the darkness, could just make out the sheaf of papers fastened by their string and looped to the nail driven in the door. Plenty of reading material here, though you might find the story cut off in mid-stride by Doreen's scissors. That was her job now.

Alice smiled in the dark. She remembered when she used to have that job, how she used to enjoy sitting at the table, scanning the old newspapers and magazines before cutting them up into those neat squares and poking the holes through the top corners with a meat skewer. She was good at reading at school. Miss Laverton always used to get her to read in class, and to the little-'uns in the corner of the hall if it was a rainy dinner time. The smile faded, her mouth reset itself in its grim, thin line. She'd been as good as Elsbeth Hobbs, her big rival in Standard Five. All those fluffy golden curls, so fine and soft compared with her own tight, unruly fair mop. And a damn sight cleaner, too! And those great big baby blue eyes, that soppy grin; her protruding little rabbit's teeth. Clean frocks, lovely clean white ankle-socks, shiny new shoes. Going off to college now, she'd heard. Elsbeth had gone into the scholarship class, of course, at eleven, away to the Girls' Grammar. Nothing but distant nods, a snooty half-acknowledgement whenever their paths crossed — which wasn't

14

often, even in a small town like Margrove. And why should they? Maudsley Street and the surrounding warrens might be no more than two miles distant, but the big houses with their fenced-off gardens around the park were a world away.

There'd never been any thought of Alice sitting the scholarship. Miss Laverton, for all her faith in Alice's ability, hadn't even suggested it. When the almost-eleven-year-old herself had brought it up at home, her dad had hooted with derision. 'Ooh! Fancy yourself as Lady Astor, do you? They'll be having you on the wireless next!' End of story.

Reflections on her schooldays reminded her of the morrow. She would be setting foot inside Lister Road again — at least in the infants' department — for she had been inveigled into taking young Algy, embarking on his first day, no doubt the start of an illustrious scholastic career. Poor little bugger! Alice had had to ask for time off, claiming her mother's illness. She had arranged to go into work at ten o'clock, much to the disgruntle-ment of Mr Johns, the manager — Little Hitler, as he was referred to, though not in his presence, by most of his staff.

Really, Mam was getting worse and worse. She practically wore a groove in the uneven pavements as she did her slipper-shuffle round to Wilson's the corner shop, or the co-op stores, or the jug and bottle of the Black Horse to get a jug of ale. Apart from this well-worn route she went nowhere. She'd even given up the Saturday-night outing to the best room of the pub, which at least had involved getting into a corset and putting on stockings and shoes and a hat, instead of the eternal headscarf wound round her curlered, mousy, thin hair. Why the curlers? What for? She never took them out — unless maybe she did so late at night, turning into a voluptuous temptress in the sanctity of the front bedroom for Fred. Swiftly Alice shied away from such indecorous and downright uncomfortable speculation.

Poor little Algy! He was in for a shock tomorrow all right. There'd be some bawling and screaming, she suspected, and maybe a bit of kicking as well. But the staff of Lister Road would soon knock the rebellion out of them, literally, if necessary. Except, she thought defiantly, they had never quite succeeded with her. There was still a bit of rebel preserved within her, and she was glad of it.

'Hey up, our Al! Have you fallen down the bloody hole or what?'

George's voice from the back door abruptly

16

terminated her philosophic mood, and she stood, massaging feeling back into her frozen and grooved behind. 'Don't get your knicks in a twist!' she called out. 'I'm on my way! And I'm straight off to bed and all, all clear or no all clear.'

★ ★ ★

Alice's predictions about Algy proved all too well-founded. She had felt sorry for him as his clammy hand had clutched hers, his little face pinched, a map of worry creases, his eyes out on stalks, gazing round the fearfully large world of Lister Road Junior School's cavernous hall, while she stood before the desk and gave them the necessary details. But then when Alice, encouraged by the fact that he had recognized a few familiar if equally anxious faces, gently disengaged his tight grip from hers and said, 'Right! I'm off now, our Algy. You'll have a lovely time here, all sorts of new things for you to do. And look. Tommy Sanderson's here. And Sally, too. You can tell us all about it this afternoon. And don't forget Doreen's here and all. And Ethel up at the big school. You'll see them at dinner-time!' he stared at her in crumpling horror, before flinging back his head and howling at this frightening betrayal. 'Come on. I told you

you'd have to stay!' Alice argued helplessly.

Even those of his contemporaries who were being brave felt their courage ebb. Eyes filled, lips quivered, and thumping chests heaved. A few began to join in Algy's heartfelt and highly audible sobs.

'Now now! Stop that at once!' Miss Clarke, the head of the junior school and overall commander of this morning's operation, showed her authority. Her hair was a pepper-and-salty grey, the rolls of sausage curls made it look like a barrister's wig, and would have been set off nicely by a square of black cloth. The crisp no-nonsense of her piercing tone suggested much more might follow. It choked off the wails in mid-flight. Algy sniffed and spluttered and swallowed his grief. 'Miss Peterson! Take these new ones off to the class. Keep them busy. We'll send the rest along as we finish them here. Off you go, children. Quick march!' And march they did, Miss Peterson looking almost as cowed as her flock of infantile charges.

The sooner she got out of there the better, Alice decided. As she turned thankfully to escape, she stopped in her tracks and stared in surprise. It was like having a dream broken. There, one of the little group of staff standing by to help, was Elsbeth Hobbs, fluffy blonde hair and baby-blues as china doll as ever, pretty as a chocolate box, in a long-sleeved blue jumper, over which peeked the dainty lace-fringed collar of her white blouse, dark, narrow skirt and school-marmy lisle stockings and lace-up shoes. Even these last two items could not take away from the attractiveness of the whole picture.

Their eyes met. It was clear from the enchanting hint of a blush on Elsbeth's fair cheeks that she recognized Alice. Her eyes widened even more. 'Hello there!' She smiled tentatively.

Suddenly Alice had a vivid memory of the last time they had met in this louring tower of a Victorian building, when she had been the ringleader in a boisterous send-off she and some of her classmates had arranged for the lucky scholarship winners. One of her more spectacular contributions to the festivities had been the jug of water she had poured down the back of Elsbeth's neck. 'How do. What are you doing here? I've just been bringing our Algy — my little brother.' She gave an embarrassed laugh. 'You saw. You haven't . . . ?'

'Oh no. It's my first day, too. As a matter of fact. I'm starting here. Teaching. Unqualified.'

'Oh! I thought — I'd heard you were going to college.'

'Yes, I was. I mean I am. I *think*!' She gave

another nervous little giggle. 'Things are a bit tricky. I have a place. For next month. But things are a bit messed up. You know. The war and everything. Not sure what's going to happen. So someone suggested I start here, for the time being. They'll be short of teachers, I expect.'

The poor girl looked ill at ease. Perhaps she was remembering the icy water down her back, too. 'That's dead funny. I mean seeing you like this. Today. I was just thinking about you last night. While the air-raid was on, as a matter of fact.' She chuckled, glanced around her. 'The good old days, eh?'

'Oh yes. I should say so!'

Her gushing tone, and her educated accent, its lack of regional twang, instead of grating on Alice's nerves, as it might well have done, made her feel sorry for the girl. She was obviously doing her best to sound matey. Making the effort. She was a good looker all right. A bobby-dazzler, George and his mates would say. Her teeth. They looked cute, just one of them sticking out just a teeny bit. Not really. It just sort of showed a bit more when she smiled. Had she had them done? Alice wondered. 'Our Doreen's here, in Juniors. Standard Four. And Ethel.' Alice jerked her head upward to indicate the senior school, which occupied the two upper floors. 'She's in Big School. She's thirteen now.'

'Gosh! So many of you!' The colour heightened in the pretty face as Elsbeth realized her remark might give offence. She began to make incoherent noises of apology, which Alice laughingly waved aside.

'You'll see more than enough of them if you stay on here. Let's know if any of them give you any bother.'

'Oh, I'm sure they won't. I'm only with the infants, in any case. But I'll keep an eye out for your brother . . . ' She fumbled for the name, and Alice supplied it.

'Right then, I'd better go in case he catches sight of me again and starts blubbing. Nice to see you again. And good luck.'

Elsbeth joined in her hearty laughter. ''Bye. I'll see you again, I expect.'

Outside in the yard, Alice glanced up at the towering face of red brick, with its tall, narrow, segmented windows. Each little square had its X of pale tape, to prevent injury from flying glass in the event of a bomb blast. The railings had been newly removed from the walls surrounding the perimeter of the playground in the desperate hunt for metal to supply the munitions factories. It looked so solid, this gloomy edifice, blotting out the sky almost. Generations of kids had streamed through its doors,

21

played in this yard, screamed with relief to fight through the gate to the real world again. It looked as if it had been here for ever.

But nothing lasted, especially now. At the pictures last week, she'd seen on the newsreel the blazing fires down by the docks in London. Buildings as huge as this gutted, flames raging through their glassless windows, walls folding and collapsing in a heap of dusty rubble. Mr Churchill giving his two fingers, puffing at his cigar, all those pinnied housewives in turbans, curlers, no teeth, grinning away and patting him on the back.

'Fight them on the beaches!' Her father's voice was rich in sarcasm. 'And him and his mates'll be half-way to bloody Canada before a shot's fired, you mark my words!'

And I don't think you'll be in the front line, either, Dad! she thought now, as she hurried along Maudsley Street before she dashed in to change and get off to work. There was only her mother in, and there was a pot of tea warming on the hob. 'Come on, love. Have a quick cuppa. Tell them there was a big queue. Ten minutes won't hurt.'

She told her mother about Algy's tears. 'He wasn't too bad, though. A few of them were bawling but that Miss Clarke soon put the fear of God in them. They went off like mice.' For some reason she couldn't understand,

Alice found herself reluctant to talk about Elsbeth Hobbs, and made no mention of her. But, as she went upstairs to change into her work things — from shabby to rags! she mocked at herself — Elsbeth continued to occupy the centre of her thoughts. 'Gosh!' She savoured the word, the way Elsbeth had said it in that toffee-nosed voice of hers, and she chuckled aloud. Well, kidder, I don't envy you this morning. I wouldn't even swap my lousy job for yours right now. Wiping snotty noses — and quite probably wiping cacky bums and all, if my memory serves me right. How long will you stick at that, my cute little Elsbeth?

It struck Alice with sudden force. That's exactly what the girl was, cute! And she felt all at once tenderly protective of her, and hoped all would go well on this her first day. You soppy cow! she scolded herself equably. You'll be wanting to say sorry for tipping that water down her back next!

2

'There's a young *lady* asking to see you.' Mr Johns emphasized the classification in order to indicate just how unlikely he considered it in juxtaposition with the 'you'. 'Five minutes, mind. I don't know what you've been up to but I won't have it interfering with your working hours. You've had enough time off lately,' he added, even more maliciously. Clearly, he was not going to forget easily the 'half the morning' she had taken to see her little brother into school, nor the fact that she had returned a full ten minutes after the ten o'clock deadline.

Alice was working out the back as usual, in the cavernous storage area, weighing out the sugar from the grey-white mountain and bagging it in the blue bags. Mr Johns let his booted feet crunch with deliberate loudness in the grains scattered about the wooden floor. 'And get this floor swept as soon as you come back. We'll be having more mice than ever, at this rate. Don't leave it till you've finished. Keep doing it.'

Better than rats like you! Alice thought, but her mind turned to the more absorbing question of the 'young lady's' identity. What on earth was he on about? She didn't know any young ladies. She gave a swift tug at her headscarf and adjusted her grubby overall as she followed him through into the shop front. The counter ran almost the length of the shop, and Alice scanned the customers on its other side hastily. A slim figure stood just inside the door, at first just a silhouette against the light it admitted. Alice's heart gave a thump as she recognized Elsbeth Hobbs.

She lifted the heavy counter-flap and hurried towards her. 'What's wrong? Is it our Algy? What's happened?'

'No, no, it's not Algy. He's all right.' Elsbeth glanced about her. 'Can you — is there somewhere we can talk?'

'Outside. Come on.' Alice caught hold of Elsbeth's arm, steered her through the narrow doorway into the busy street. 'Let's walk a bit.' She linked her arm through the other girl's and headed off along the pavement. 'I can't have long. The manager'll have a fit. He's a right ba — so-and-so!'

'It's just — I thought it would be better if I saw you — came to see you. Miss Laverton suggested it. She's still there, you know. She remembers you. She sends her regards.'

'What's it about?' Alice demanded impatiently. Already she could sense Elsbeth's diffidence, her reluctance to broach the reason for her visit.

'It doesn't really involve me at all. But it's — well, I said I knew you. It was Miss Laverton's idea that I should come and see you. Before they contact your parents, at home.'

'What the hell *is* it?'

Elsbeth blushed. The curling lashes flickered as she cast her eyes down, away from Alice's piercing glare. 'It's your sister. Doreen. The one in Standard Four. There's been some trouble. Some money's been taken. From another girl in the class. Doreen — and some others. They've been taking money from her.'

'What? Money? Who is it? Who's this lass with the money?'

'It's not a lot, apparently. Just a few pennies. Her parents give this girl money, to buy things from Barnes. Sweets or fruit or stuff. Penny carrots — you know.' She hesitated a little. 'But they were a bit too rough with her. In the toilets. She got into a bit of a state. Hysterics and so on. And it all came out. Miss Clarke, the headmistress, was up in arms. Everything's a bit fraught anyway at the moment. You know they're evacuating some of the children? I don't know if any of yours — your sisters — are involved?'

26

Alice grunted, shook her head. 'Mam's not keen on letting them go. But what's all this about our Doreen? What's happening?'

'As I said, it was Miss Laverton's idea that I should come and seek you out. You could maybe break the news to your parents. Talk it over with them.'

'Dad'll bloody well kill her!' Alice spoke almost to herself, then caught the dolefully anxious expression in Elsbeth's ingenuous blue eyes.

Elsbeth nodded sympathetically. 'That's what Miss Laverton said. The trouble is, the girl's parents are making a bit of a fuss. Talking about going to the education committee.'

'Listen! They'll get their precious bloody money back, if that's what they're worried about. No fear! They can have it out of *my* wages. I get my pay-packet on Saturday night. They can have it first thing Monday morning. Or I can take it straight round if they like!'

Elsbeth's face was still pink, her manner even more constrained. 'Well, I don't know. I don't think the money's the issue. Apparently the girl's been more and more upset. At the intimidation, the bullying. She even wet herself the other day.'

Well, she was in the right place, in the lavs! Alice thought callously, then had the grace to

27

feel ashamed. Suddenly it occurred to her that part of Elsbeth Hobb's embarrassment might stem from the fact that she could well sympathize with this feeble little victim. Alice was uncomfortably stirred by memories of her own and her mates' treatment of Elsbeth and other 'posh-'uns', as they contemptuously dubbed them. Incidents besides the jug of water down the neck were recalled. In fact, Alice was sure she could see the ghostly remnants of such wariness even now in the pretty girl's demeanour towards her.

'Perhaps you could come up to school, have a word with Miss Clarke? Miss Laverton was saying — there might be no need to inform your parents — ' the blush intensified — 'unless of course you think they ought to know. Miss Laverton said she'd speak in support . . . if you agree.'

The glance Elsbeth gave her, the anxiety on the pretty face, impressed Alice. There was no need for the girl to associate herself with this at all. She had taken the time and trouble to get herself involved, when she might well have said, nothing to do with me! and left it at that. Alice caught hold of her arm again, and reached out and captured her hand. It felt cold in the cloudy September afternoon. She held it in both hers, squeezed tightly. 'Hey! Listen! I'm really grateful. I mean, you going to all this trouble for us. Thanks very much. You've been ever so good.'

Elsbeth's face was flooded tomato red, and she looked both pleased and thoroughly flummoxed at the same time. 'Oh, not at all. I mean, I'm only too pleased to help out.' She smiled shyly. 'After all, we're old school-chums, eh?'

Not quite! Alice thought, remembering her own cruel delight in giving this quivering little creature a good soaking. But she beamed back at her, still holding on to that dainty hand. 'No, I mean it. You're a brick. Now, when can I come up to school? Tomorrow?' She pushed away thoughts of Little Hitler's ire. 'If you — '

'You could always telephone,' Elsbeth began and saw the embarrassed reluctance on the open face, the instinctive shake of the head. 'Or perhaps I could suggest . . . after school would be best. Say four o' clock? Tomorrow? If it's not convenient I could ring you here — at work. If you don't hear from me, we'll leave it at four. I'll keep an eye out, see you in the yard.' She paused, blushed again. 'If you want,' she ended shyly. 'Or not?'

'Oh yes! That would be great! If you can be bothered. I'd better go. Otherwise Little Hitler'll be going off his rocker. Ta-ra — Elsbeth! And thanks again!'

The sunny smile enveloped her. 'It's nothing, really! 'Bye, Alice. See you tomorrow.'

* * *

Mr Johns's rocker started to sway perilously as soon as Alice returned to the shop. He was busy with a customer, but he cast a swift, glowering look in her direction as she sidled past. 'I'll be with you in a minute, Miss Glass.' And two minutes later he was, beside the diminishing sugar mountain. 'What was all that about?' he said, without preamble.

Mind your own bloody business! Alice was tempted to say it, could almost feel the words trembling to burst from her lips. 'Family business,' she muttered surlily, and before he could launch into a diatribe, she added brusquely, 'I'll probably have to finish early tomorrow. Half three. Unless there's a telephone message comes for me.' She nodded back towards the glassed-in hen-coop that represented 'the office', and looked as though it was stuck on to the wall at the top of a short flight of creaky wooden stairs.

Little Hitler's red face transformed to a shade closer to puce. 'Telephone messages, is it? Time off, is it? I don't think so, *Miss* Glass! You're a junior assistant here, not the

30

flaming manageress! We're not here to run a personal message service on your account. And any family problems will have to be sorted out in your own time, if you don't mind! And if there's any more of this attitude from you you'll be out that door for good. Is that clear?'

Alice fought to keep her temper from erupting, the effort compressing her lips until they almost disappeared. The tips of her ears felt as though they were blazing, but she managed to say nothing. She was still sweeping and tidying up out back at half past five, when the store officially closed, and Mr Johns came through with the cash and the 'divvy' tickets, and headed up the creaking stairs to have his usual half-hour's dalliance with Miss Burton, clerk, cashier, and goodness-knows-what besides, as far as Mr Johns was concerned, despite the engagement ring on her finger and his wife and two children waiting at home.

Rumours among the shop-girls and van-men were rife, and scandalously exaggerated, Alice thought in her less prejudicial moments. There was *something* between them though, she was convinced. The busty, attractively curvy Jean Burton normally treated the shop girls and the storemen and drivers with cold and obvious disdain — like dog muck on the pavement, or worse, on her shoe, Alice thought. Whenever Little Hitler appeared on the scene it was like Cinders, you *shall* go to the ball. Eyes flashing, carefully permed head tossing, apple-red cheeks and grinning chompers, nostrils flaring — she did everything but paw the ground, the big, randy mare! And he was no better! Eyes all over her. You could almost hear the buttons pinging and zips sliding and elastic twanging in his nasty little thoughts. Betty Avery reckoned Miss Burton had already put off her wedding because of Johns — like most firms, the co-op didn't employ married women. 'She must need glasses, eh, kidder?' Betty had sniggered. 'Still, ten out of ten for her guts, eh?'

There was no sign of Doreen when Alice got in soon after six. 'Poor bairn's upstairs in bed,' her mother told her when Alice grimly enquired. 'Feeling sick. She hardly ate any tea. See if she wants anything when you go up.'

'I will. I'll sit and have a chat with her,' Alice promised. 'When I've had a wash.' George came through from the back kitchen wearing only vest and drawers, and with a towel slung round his neck. 'For God's sake!' Alice snapped, by way of greeting. 'Do you have to? You're getting a big boy now!'

'Aye. You've been peeking, have you?'

'Shut your mucky mouth and get some clothes on before our Ethel sees you. Enough to put her off for life!'

'What? Like *you*, you mean? Time you were finding out what little boys are made of, isn't it? I don't see the lads exactly queuing up to walk out with you.'

Alice was filled with a murderous desire to smack the grin off his spotty face, but her mother cut into her spluttering rage with practised ease. 'Now pack it in, you two. I've enough on me plate with the young-'uns and your da. You go and get your wash,' she commanded Alice, 'and you get away and get some clothes on, our George. Alice is quite right. It's not decent. You're a grown man now. Time you started behaving like one.' Alice's sarcastic bray of triumph followed him as he headed for the narrow dark of the passage and the staircase.

Alice wondered if Doreen had somehow learned of her older sister's visit to the school. Was that why the little madam was keeping out of the way? Well, if it was, Alice decided, she could stew in her own juice a while longer. After she had washed her face and arms and upper body in the chill of the back kitchen but in mercifully piping hot water from the copper her mother had lit earlier, she slipped her arms into her vest and petticoat again and draped the towel shawl-like over her shoulders to make herself decent. She sat and ate her tea, lingered over her second 'cuppa' before she finally headed for the staircase, by which time George was safely out of the way, out to see his mates. Her dad was not yet in from the Black Horse, where he would still be sitting, or standing, in the grime and stale sweat of his long shift at the steelworks. Ethel was away out, too, in spite of the pitch black, black-outed night, doing what thirteen-year-old lasses did, Alice recalled with the lofty contempt of her five-year seniority.

'I hear you're not well, Doreen, love. What's the matter, pet?'

She was sick all right. Sick with fear. The face looked pinched, the complexion sallow. The eyes were huge as she peeped over the sheet and blankets drawn up to her chin. Like an elf. As delicate as Ethel, with those big eyes and heart shaped faces. Why couldn't I have come out looking like them? Alice wished, and immediately dismissed it as foolishness. She'd be looking a lot sicker in a minute! Alice swore to herself.

In response to the treacly tones of sympathy, Doreen gave a smothered, martyr's sigh and turned on her back. 'I feel awful, Al. Real bad. I don't think I'll be able to go to school tomorrow.' She gave another sigh, and Alice watched the dark eyes fill with tears.

You should be on the fillums, kidder! she applauded silently. Aloud, she said, 'Where does it hurt? Come here. Show me.'

'Oh, I dunno. All over, really.' The husky voice quivered, and the tears were clinging to the dark lashes. She half-raised herself, as Alice gently eased back the bedclothes, slipped an arm round the thin frame, drawing it out from the covers.

'Mebbe I can help you. Take your mind off it, like.' She was sitting beside her on the bed, and had half-drawn the unsuspecting victim on to her lap. Now, with lightning speed, she flipped Doreen over across her knee, hauled up the shift, and gave her a ringing, open handed slap on her warm, skinny buttock.

Doreen yelped and squirmed, and Alice pinned her down, and struck once more, leaving a second crimson branding. 'You'd best shut up!' she hissed, 'unless you want Mam and Dad to know what a thieving, robbing little tart you really are!' The message got through, and Doreen clawed at the corner of the sheet, stuffing it hard into her mouth. The pink heels flailed in the air as Alice's stinging palm descended in a further rapid tattoo of blows until the haunches were as hot and red as Doreen's tear-soaked face. When the blows ceased, the thin frame twisted round, the face was buried in the pillow to muffle the sounds of her weeping.

'You bitch!' she spluttered at last, lifting her tragic face, and kneeling to glare at her attacker, unmindful of the indignity as her hands busily massaged her bum under the disarranged shift.

Alice felt the muscles of her cheeks tugging towards a smile, which she sternly suppressed. 'Ha! You don't mind dishing it out, do you? But you don't like it when somebody bigger picks on you, do you?'

'Elsie Peel's bigger than me! She's a great fat cow!'

'Aye, but not bigger than you and your mates, is she? Proud of yourselves, are you, making her pee her pants with fright? And robbing her as well! Taking her money off her. You can end up in gaol for that, you know!'

The pain and indignity were forgotten. Doreen's eyes were wide with fear again. 'It was only for a laugh, at first. We never meant owt, honest! How do you know, anyway?' She shot a frightened glance towards the door, remembered Alice's warning. 'Mam and Dad — they don't know.'

'Not yet,' her sister answered threateningly. 'You can thank your lucky stars Elsbeth Hobbs is there. Working in the infants. She's a mate of mine. She came and told me at work. I have to go up to school tomorrow. See Miss Clarke. And Miss Laverton. See if we can keep it from going any further. You could get taken away, you know! This kid's folks are hopping mad. Poor little bugger's been terrified of you and your gang. How much have you taken from her?'

Doreen began to cry again, struggling to keep it quiet. She shook her head. 'I dunno. It was just tuppences and that. I don't know. It's been going on a while.'

'You'll end up in one of them homes. For wayward children.' Alice saw the look of undisguised horror on the young face, and she reached out her arms as Doreen gave a desolate wail and hurled herself into the shelter of her elder sister's embrace. She pressed her wet cheek against the softness of Alice's bosom. Alice's hand came up, cradled the dark head, and rocked her like a baby. 'All right. There there. I dare say it'll be all right. I'll sort summat out tomorrow.' The tears changed to sniffles, then sighs, and Alice released the woebegone figure. 'By heck, you'll owe me for this, though, our Doreen. It'll take you the rest of your schooldays to pay me back — especially if I have to fork out for your robbing and all!'

*   *   *

Alice had her own battle to fight before she could take up arms on behalf of her sister. She had half-hoped there might after all be a telephone message to delay the meeting at school. She even went as quietly as she could up the creaking stairs at the end of the half-hour lunch-break and tapped on the glass door of the cubby-hole office. 'Yes?' Miss Burton asked, pointing her splendid bosom at Alice. It seemed to inflate even further to match the disdain on the handsome features.

Alice reddened. 'I was just wondering. Has there been any telephone message for me? Alice Glass,' she supplied.

'Ah yes!' It was clear that Miss Burton was responding to the name rather than the question. Obviously, Little Hitler had filled her in with all the details of the latest clash. 'No, there's been no message. We don't encourage staff to use the store as a service for personal matters,' she added frostily, as Alice was about to turn away.

'No, I don't blame them. I wouldn't want every Tom, Dick and Harry tittle-tattling over my private affairs. Would you?' Alice was rewarded by the spots of heightened colour on each of the immaculately made-up cheeks, and clattered back down the stairs in triumph.

But she grew increasingly nervous as the next hour ticked by with remorseless slowness. Her body ached at muscles tight with tension, and she could feel a clammy sweat and a bilious weakness increasing as zero hour approached. At three o' clock she went out into the shop, to beard the lion in his den. 'I have to leave at half past, Mr Johns. It's me mam. I told — '

'And I told you, Glass, that you couldn't have the time off. There's nothing further to say. You must sort your personal problems in your own time — '

'It's just this once. It can't be helped. I have to go.'

'And I say you can't. That's the end of the matter.' He turned away, glancing ostentatiously towards the customers, who were being attended to further down the store.

'I'm off then. Cheerio.'

Alice heard the door swish to behind her as he followed her through into the gloom of the rear. Interested faces glanced towards him, then away again, studiously absorbed in any task that would keep them within earshot and vision. His fleshy face was red now, his eyes bright. 'You walk out that door, girl, and you needn't bother coming back. Except to collect your dues. And there won't be a reference to go with them.'

She was trembling, but she prayed he wouldn't notice. She unbuttoned her overall, hung it on the peg and took her shabby overcoat. 'Can't be helped. I told you. This is urgent.'

'How long have you been here? Three years, is it?' She nodded. 'You're being very foolish, my girl. You know that, don't you?'

She nodded again. She had a sudden premonition that he was reluctant, that he didn't want this final confrontation. That if she turned on the tears, came over the poor little girlie, all weak and cuddly, if she begged him, she might yet get away with it. She imagined his hands round her, soothing her, there there, having a quick feel . . . 'Yes, I know, Mr Johns. I must have been, *very* foolish, to put up with this place for three years. Good riddance, I say!'

She slipped on her coat, while he was still spluttering, unable in his wrath to form a coherent sentence. She turned in the doorway, stared back at all the staring faces and let a grin spread over her face. '*Sieg heil!*' And she was out, gasping as though she'd run a race, half-laughing, half-crying in the sultry autumn afternoon.

Elsbeth was waiting at the school gate,

looking worried as usual. Several of the juniors were still streaming out on to the street. There was no sign of Doreen. 'She's inside,' Elsbeth said.

Alice caught hold of her arm as they moved to enter the building. 'I'm sorry, Elsbeth. To come like this. In my work things. But I daren't go home and change. Mam would have wanted to know what was going on.'

Elsbeth blushed guiltily. 'You look fine!' she said, with false assurance. 'They'll understand.'

Whether they did or not, it all went well — eventually. Miss Laverton's warm greeting and firm handshake went a long way towards helping Alice to feel slightly less nervous, and Miss Clarke, the headmistress, for all her merciless appraisal of Alice's unkempt and shabby appearance, had already made up her mind, having taken the veteran Miss Laverton's advice, that the affair should go no further. She had appeased the angry parents of Elsie the victim, and now brought the miserable Doreen, alone, to endure, in front of Alice and the small group of teachers, a last withering denunciation for her crimes which reduced her once more to a soggy, sobbing bundle of penitence. 'We estimate that about one shilling and sixpence in all was extorted. If that could be reimbursed we can draw a line under this sordid little business. *I hope!*' she suddenly bellowed at Doreen, who literally wilted before the blast, and blubberingly avowed her determination to be angelic from here on in.

'All's well that ends well!' smiled Elsbeth Hobbs a little later in the now deserted school yard, while Doreen stood, eyes fixed firmly on her dirty, worn shoes, the old piece of sheet that served as hankie held to her still damp face.

Alice thought of her own exit from work earlier and nodded unenthusiastically. 'Aye. I suppose so.' Wait till Dad finds out tonight. Or should I wait till tomorrow? Till I've been back to the stores. Mebbe I could try again — one last appeal to Little Hitler. Throw myself on his mercy? Let him . . . let him what? Have a feel? Pinch my bum? She shivered in genuine and deep revulsion. She remembered her final gesture of the heel-clicking Nazi salute, and the muscles of her cheek did not resist this time: she gave her wide, infectious grin, and revelled in Elsbeth's glowing response.

She took hold of the girl's hands, both of them, and gave a last enthusiastic squeeze. 'Listen, I can't tell you how truly grateful I am for bothering the way you have.' She jerked her head back in the direction of the building they had just left. 'If it hadn't been for you, goodness knows what would have happened.' She released the soft hands and gave her young sister a vigorous dig in the shoulder. 'And you can say thank you and all! You could have ended up in a kids' gaol — or at the least you wouldn't have been sitting down for a week if our dad had got to hear of it.'

The teary face lifted, and Doreen thought of the vivid red imprints of Alice's palm on her still tender behind. You didn't do so bad yourself! But wisely she kept silent, except to give her best sackcloth-and-ashes smile and murmur softly, 'Thank you very much, Miss Hobbs.' She even remembered to sound the aitch.

3

Alice had been looking, and feeling, extremely woebegone since she had entered the co-op and been ordered curtly to report to the office. The other girls had obviously been warned to show the circumspection afforded in earlier times to bell-carrying lepers, though there were several sneaky glances of muted sympathy as Alice passed through their midst. Now, at Miss Burton's incisive tone, Alice put on her brashest, brassiest, devil-may-care grin. 'What? You think I'll be blubbing to get away from this dump? I should cocoa!'

'There's a lot worse jobs than this, my girl!' Miss Burton permitted herself a ladylike sniff. 'I suppose you'll be rushing off to one of those factories?'

Alice's grin widened. 'Mebbes! I might see you there one of these days, when this women's call-up comes through. Unless totting up Stores' divvies is a reserved occupation now! Although I think you'll do better in the Land Army — on the farm.' With all the other cows! she thought but did not add.

Jean Burton's face was florid, the bosom

positively heaving in swollen indignation. 'You'll be no loss to us, I can assure you! Now. Here's your envelope. Paid up to date, minus the sick club contribution. And there's an official letter of dismissal. Mr Johns likes to do things by the book. Head Office has been informed. There's no reference, of course. And please don't ask any future employer to contact us.' She gave a sarcastic snigger. 'You'd be well advised not to. If you'd just sign here.'

Up yours and your white mice! Alice's mood of chirpy defiance lasted all of five minutes after she had shaken the co-op dust from her worn shoes, by which time her feet were treading the cracked pavement of Maudsley Street once more. Her mother was waiting in No 19, the blackened kettle was steaming on the hob, the teapot ready to receive its boiling contents. 'Got your money, love?'

'Aye.' Alice tipped her wage packet from the larger envelope, opened it up and tipped the money on to the wooden tabletop. Quickly she set aside a shilling and sixpence. 'Someone I've got to pay back.' She did not explain further, and her mother did not pursue the matter. She was glad enough to receive Alice's contribution earlier than usual. Sufficient unto the day . . . Maggie agreed

45

with the Good Book on that one. She'd deal with Fred's rage with his eldest child and her wilful loss of a thoroughly respectable job when he returned that evening. There would be quite a few hours before that event took place, for he would not deprive himself of his usual stopover at t' Black 'Oss on his way home. 'A man's got to put some liquid back in him after the smelting. Sweat gallons you do at that game!' She shouldn't really begrudge him, she supposed, they worked like blackies at the works. It never stopped and times had never been so good, God forgive her for saying so, but it was true. Which was why it dismayed her so that he should take on as he had last night and bawl and shout at Alice for getting the sack.

She'd tried to tell him, the lass would find something soon enough. Alice wasn't afraid of hard work, either, and she'd always been as good as gold when it came to handing over her wages. She kept hardly anything out, spent next to nothing on clothes and fags and gadding about — not like the other lasses. But even that didn't suit his nibs — he was always going on about her. 'There's summat wrong with her. She never goes to the rink or any of the dances. Never gets dolled up, or has her hair done. If she wasn't fair-haired she'd look like a bloody golliwog!'

There was no satisfying him. Mind you, it was true, in a way. She ought to be taking more of an interest in herself, getting out a bit, meeting up with lads. At her age . . . at her age Maggie was pregnant and terrified of her own father and happy as Larry that Fred was man enough to own up to the wrong he'd done her and marry her, before she was hardly showing. Would she wish that on the lass? Maggie's conscience was uncomfortably stirred at her thoughts, and she pushed them determinedly aside, and reached for the pot. ''Oway, lass. Sit down and have a cuppa. It's nice to have you home, and somebody to chat to during the day.'

★ ★ ★

Two days later the whole town was absorbed, thrilled, and terrified with the sensation of the first bombs to fall on Margrove. The enemy had been aiming for the dock area — one missile had struck very close to the Coal Dock, blowing up the railway tracks and scattering pieces of fragmented wagons over a considerable expanse. Several others had detonated a couple of hundred yards further from their target, destroying entirely an ugly old pub, the Jolly Sailor, and demolishing three of the row of Victorian terrace houses adjacent to it, and causing varying amounts of damage to the rest of the dwellings in Mains Terrace.

Estimates of human loss fluctuated widely. 'Thousands' was reluctantly put aside for 'hundreds', then 'scores'. When people's responses were sobered, the real loss, modest as it was, was shocking enough. Most of the inhabitants of Mains Terrace were in the communal concrete block of a shelter meant to serve the whole neighbourhood, and were unscathed. The landlord and lady of the Jolly Sailor and several regular customers — nothing was said of the thriving tradition of the 'lock-in', which had meant that at least fifteen clients were still on the premises in the early hours when the raid occurred — were dug out, shaken but intact, from the solid cellar beneath the smoking pile of bricks and shattered timbers. But an old lady and her married daughter died in the house next door to the pub. The husband and three children had gone to the communal shelter, but the infirm old lady always insisted she would be content to die in her own bed. Little knowing that her wish was to be so soon granted, her daughter volunteered, or insisted, that she would stay by her side. 'Nowt ever happens, any road!' she averred, for once mistakenly, and thus left a grieving widower and three

48

offspring. And in the house next to them, the protection of the under-the-stairs cupboard had proved drastically inadequate for a mum and dad and three of their four young children, the only survivor being the baby of four months, found wailing thinly in a wooden drawer serving as cradle, miraculously saved by a tiny, precarious cave formed by collapsed masonry and the hunched body of his mother amidst the destruction.

Alice succumbed to the morbid interest so many others displayed, and walked the two miles down to the coast to join the crowd who gathered to stare from behind the ropes rigged up by the civil defence lot at the wrecked buildings. There was practically nothing left above ground level of the Jolly Sailor, which made it seem even more miraculous that seventeen or so people had climbed out uninjured from the pile of bricks and blackened timbers. But next door, the front of the house had been swiped away to leave the interior exposed. It reminded Alice of a wonderful doll's house she'd seen in Dunn's shop window one Christmas when she was a kid. You could see into all the tiny rooms, upstairs and down. There'd been a little dining table and chairs, set with miniature dinner things; a carpeted staircase, and on the upper floors a proper bathroom, with white tub, and a bedroom with a brass-railed bed and even a little guzunder underneath.

But there was nothing pretty about this real, lopsided, smashed house. The bedroom floor tilted crazily, its floorboards jagged where the rest was missing. The bed — what was left of it — was stood practically on end down below, in what once had been the front room. 'That's where the old woman was,' some ghoul said, from behind her somewhere. 'Her and her daughter. Must have fell right through. What was left of them.' Alice suddenly wanted to turn round and scream at him. Haven't you got no respect? She felt deeply ashamed all at once, her face red, and she pushed her way through the people pressing in on her, and hurried away.

Dad was on late shift, so she wandered about down town, through the indoor market, stuffy under its glass roof. 'Bloomin' dangerous, that lot,' folks muttered, their sense of apprehension sharpened all at once by the raid. And Alice noticed how many persons were carrying their cardboard gasmask boxes over their shoulders, though the sirens had hardly ever gone during daylight hours since that first morning a year ago, when war had been declared. And that had been a false alarm — or some sod with a wicked sense of humour!

Her calculations proved correct. By the time she got back home her father had already left for his customary 'jar' in t' Black 'Oss before work, so she spent a peaceful and even pleasant dinner time, with mam and the girls. Doreen was still subdued and almost fawningly subservient towards her. Alice was surprised to see her glance furtively about her in the kitchen and then start pulling faces to indicate she needed a private communication with her eldest sister. Alice followed her in to the yard.

Doreen came out of the lavatory and hastily handed over an envelope, with a wary glance towards the back door and kitchen window. 'Here! Take this! It's from that posh lass. Miss 'Obbs. Says I had to give it to you. She got me at playtime. Was asking — about you, and what had happened and that.' Another anxious glance houseward. 'Don't let Mam see it!' she pleaded.

Alice slipped through the door into the vacated stall. She slid the bolt home and sat down on the wooden seat to read the note.

Dear Alice,

I was so upset to learn from your sister that you have lost your position at the shop, all because of your concern for Doreen and her predicament.

Alice whispered the syllables of the last word slowly. What's that when it's at home? Her and her fancy words! But she smiled almost with pride.

I feel awful because I'm really responsible for it, having suggested you come to the school. Is there anything I could do — perhaps have a word with your superior or someone? Explain the circumstances to them. Surely they would be more sympathetic towards you?

In any case, I would really like to see you again, if only to say sorry. And to have a longer chat, about the old days and things. Could you possibly meet me after school today, say at four? Or if not send a note via Doreen to say when would be convenient. Miss Laverton tells me by the way that she's behaving like an angel (Doreen that is!) and is as good as gold.

I do hope you can make it. I'm so looking forward to it.

Best regards,
Elsbeth

★ ★ ★

Alice watched the slim figure come through the green door into the playground. Elsbeth was wearing an elegant tweed coat, tied tightly at the waist, with a pretty little woollen tam, complete with pompom, perched aslant on her golden head. The pair of matching knitted gloves made Alice acutely conscious of her own red, work-coarsened hands, and she resisted the sudden urge to thrust them into the spacious pockets of her own far older and shabbier winter coat, in a muted check, which had once reached almost to her ankles when she had herself been a pupil in the senior school upstairs at Lister Road. Now it scarcely reached her knees and didn't quite hide the hem of the dark-grey skirt which peeped beneath it. Or the sturdy, pale, stockingless calves showing beneath *that*. It was chilly enough for such garments on this late September day, but the wide and open smile of pleasure which lit up the pretty face brought a corresponding inner glow to its recipient.

'Hello there! I'm so glad you could make it. How are you?' Elsbeth Hobbs strode forward, hand outstretched. The beaming grin was replaced by a wide-eyed look of dismay and a curl of down-turned lips. 'Oh, but I'm so sorry to hear about your job. I feel terrible! You must let me help — I mean, if there's anything I can do . . . '

She linked arms with Alice and they swung

away through the outer gateway into the drab road. 'I was thinking we might go somewhere. For a coffee — if you've time?' Once more that ingenuous, anxious look of appeal, and Alice grinned back brightly.

'I've got plenty of that now that I'm a lady of leisure. Not like you poor working lasses, eh?' As she saw the returning look of concern on Elsbeth's features, she squeezed her arm more tightly. 'Hey, howay, man! It's not the end of the world, is it? I was sick of that place any road. That old devil of a manager was driving me batty, I can tell you.' She chuckled. 'It was a relief to be able to tell him what I think of him at last!'

'I thought maybe the Regent?' It was quite a popular, even fashionable, café on York Street. Too 'posh' for Maudsley Street folk, though Alice had been a customer there occasionally when she was feeling flush. 'We could go home for tea' — in the fractional pause that occurred here Alice had the ungenerous thought: But I'm not good enough for that, then dismissed it with swift shame as Elsbeth continued — 'but mummy would be there, and maybe my brother, and she'd be wanting to talk. I'd rather have you to myself!'

Alice, still trying to deal with her reaction to the word 'mummy', and the inner hoot of scornful laughter it raised, was bowled over anew at the ingenuous enthusiasm of the last sentence and, again, her own glowing reaction to it. 'Right enough! I'm all yours, kidder!'

'And the treat is on me, I insist! After all, *I'm* the working girl here!' She giggled, returned the squeeze.

'My! You'll make a good school marm, I can tell. A right little bossy boots already!'

Most of the afternoon tea ladies had already left, and there were plenty of empty tables, the only occupants being sober-suited business gentlemen, and a couple of self-conscious lads in ugly-looking, raw new khaki. Their red faces looked briefly alight with interest when the girls entered, until Alice returned their glance with a bold and hostile stare, before choosing a table as far as possible from them. 'It's getting terrible these days,' she grumbled. 'These lads in uniform. They don't even try to hide it any more. What they're thinking. Mucky minded lot. Seem to think it's a lass's duty to drop her drawers for them as soon as they look at her!'

She saw the tide of embarrassment sweep up the pretty features, and Alice groaned with genuine remorse. 'I'm sorry, love. I'm not fit to take anywhere, am I? I'm sorry — '

'No, no! It's all right. You're probably

right.' Elsbeth jumped in quickly, as though apologizing for her own sensitivity, and the awkward moment passed.

The waitress came, and Alice could not help admiring Elsbeth's poise as she ordered a pot of tea and a plate of scones. Such events were a rare enough treat for Alice. It was, she thought sadly, a timely reminder of the social gulf between them.

'It's very good of you. To bother about me, I mean,' she said awkwardly, after the waitress had returned with their order. 'But you mustn't feel bad about me job. Like I said, I was fed up of the co-op anyway. And they'll be starting this call-up business soon, maybe. I've already tried to put me name down for the Wrens but they said I have to wait. I'll find summat, don't you worry.'

'But I can't help feeling responsible. And all because you were helping out.' She reached across the table, put her hand over Alice's clenched fist.

'You've got lovely soft hands.' Alice had spoken without thinking. She saw the colour again mounting up from the throat. Now she shared the lass's embarrassment. 'Take no notice of me. I say some daft things — whatever comes into my head. I just meant — well, you *are* a bobby-dazzler, you know.

You must know that. No wonder them soldier lads are gawping!'

'Stop it! Don't tease!'

But she wasn't just putting it on, fishing for compliments, the way most lasses did. She really was upset, and Alice was contrite. 'What's going to happen with you, do you think? About college and all that.'

'I was hoping to take up a place, but I don't know now. The term's been delayed. And my parents aren't keen for me to be away just now. 'Specially now that the air raids have started. It's really bad down south. Far worse, Daddy says, than they're letting on.'

'I know. Wasn't it awful? Did you hear? They bombed the palace, even. Me da said the royal family wouldn't be anywhere near, but he was wrong. The king and queen were right there. I saw them on the pictures. They were going round talking to people. Looking at all the bomb damage. I think they're really brave.' She bit into the dry crumble of her scone, and the crumbs fell from her lips. She chuckled as she wiped at her chin. 'They won't use up their sugar ration on these, eh?'

Rationing had begun at the beginning of the year, with bacon and butter and sugar. Meat rationing had come with the spring, though for families like the Glasses, it hadn't made much difference, for the cheaper cuts were still readily available in quantity. Then, just recently, in the summer, it had been extended to tea, fats, cheese, and jam. The grocers themselves were responsible for doling out foodstuffs like eggs — one per customer per fortnight. 'Unless you're in the know and can slip a few bob extra!' Fred Glass said cynically. 'Business as usual. One law for the rich . . . ' Alice hated his worldly cynicism, but she had to admit there was a new code going around, which she'd learnt from the co-op. 'Any AUC?' customers would increasingly mutter. Anything under the counter.

'How do places like caffs manage?' she wondered now, embarrassed yet again by her gaffe of pulling a distasteful face at her scone, when it was Elsbeth's treat.

Her companion shrugged, murmured some innocuous reply. Clearly, she had other things on her mind. The baby-blues fixed on Alice with that solemn, half-anxious, half-pleading expression. It still came under 'cute' in Alice's book. 'Listen.'

Again, that typical hesitation, until Alice wanted to say, Come on, lass. Don't fanny about. Spit it out. But she didn't, only waited, smiling back at her.

'I wonder. If you like . . . we're going to be

moving. The school. As many as we can, from the juniors and the infants. With the raid on Mains Terrace. There'll be other raids, they say. Because of the steelworks — and the docks. I've got to go with them. There's a place in the Dales. Just a bit inland. Howbeck. It's such a pretty village. There's a small school. And they're allocating us the village hall as well. The children will be billeted around.'

'Sounds fine.' Alice's grey-blue eyes narrowed. There was more. Still she waited.

'Well, I was wondering . . . *we* were wondering . . . Miss Laverton was saying . . . '

Her again! Alice thought. She really must remember me all right! What have I done to deserve all this?

' . . . we'll need some auxiliary staff. Someone to help with the kiddies, see they're settled, happy. To help . . . ' The blush started to rise again, up that pretty throat. 'With meals — the dinners, keeping the place tidy, helping with the little ones.'

'A skivvy, you mean? Sort of cleaner, like?'

'No! Well . . . er . . . sort of, yes.' Elsbeth's face was glowing now. 'But more than that! Someone who'll really help, make the children feel more at home — a friendly face . . . '

'And a strong pair of arms, eh?' Alice was teasing, but she couldn't help it, she enjoyed it, and she was way ahead of the struggling girl. 'And you think I'd suit, eh? Having just lost me job?'

'You don't mind? I mean, my mentioning it to you? It was just a thought. I don't know about wages and that sort of thing.'

No, of course not. I don't suppose it would matter to you, either, ducks. But the reflection didn't annoy Alice, as it might have done if anyone else had been sitting opposite. 'Do you reckon they'd have me? Would I stand a chance of getting it?'

'I'm sure you would! Certain of it!' Her eyes shone, her features were alight with her pleasure.

Alice warmed to her enthusiasm, was a little startled by it. 'I reckon you're turning out to be my guardian angel, Miss Hobbs.' Now it was Alice's turn to feel a little constrained, but she made herself go on. 'Why? I mean, why bother about me? We were never mates, were we? Back at Lister Road. You were one of the toffs. Still are!'

Beacon time again in the pretty face. The long, light-coloured lashes fluttered, closed down a little, hiding the blue for an instant. Then they cleared, the shy gaze came up to meet Alice's steady look. 'I always — was

60

envious of you. You never — you weren't scared of anything. Or anyone. Not like me! I was frightened of most things — especially you!'

'Oh God! Don't!' Alice laughed deprecatingly. 'I was a little thug, wasn't I? Me and Sally Chalmers. Remember her? We were worse than our Doreen and her mates. Hey!' Her eyes probed Elsbeth's with searching mischief. 'You never wet your drawers, did you?'

'No. *You* did that, when you tipped that jug of water over me. Soaked me — right through!'

★ ★ ★

'Eeh, no. I couldn't let our Algy go. The poor bairn! He's only five, bless him!'

'But I'll be there with him, Mam! We'll find a place for both of us. I'll be with him, night and day. Mebbes Doreen and all — we can all be under the same roof. In any case, it's only a small place, is Howbeck. I'll be there for both of them, at school and all. And it's only an hour away on the train from Middlesbrough.'

Alice knew her mother was weakening. She would finally surrender and allow her to take Algy along with Doreen to Howbeck. The deaths of the parents and their three children in Mains Terrace, with the baby the only lucky, or some would say luckless, survivor, had shaken everyone in the town, and the ranks of the evacuees from Lister Road had swelled proportionately.

As for her father, though he had raised his usual vociferous objections, in reality Alice believed he relished the prospect of three fewer bodies about the house, especially when one was herself, and the others his two youngest offspring. Her wage would be less than she had earned at the Stores, by a full three shillings a week, but board and lodging would be paid for, so she would still be able to send something home to contribute to the household she would no longer be part of. That had gone quite a long way towards taking the sting out of Fred's objections.

Alice started work the day after her interview and acceptance, even though she would not be on the education committee payroll until the Lister Road evacuees were established in their new abode. She didn't mind. She was glad to be involved in the hectic preparations for the departure. The senior school upstairs was not to be part of the move, and Ethel maintained a scoffing contempt for the exodus. She even caused Algy a great deal of grief by frightening him with tales of the terrors of the countryside and the dangers it posed, like massive charging cows and biting horses and pigs that could gobble you alive, until Alice stopped her taunts and Algy's tears with the threat of more immediate physical violence which would descend on her if she didn't 'put a sock in it!'

At last, labels were written and tied round scrawny, scruffy necks, the strings of gas-mask boxes were draped over narrow shoulders; carrier bags, and, in a few instances, cardboard suitcases, were clutched in sweaty hands, and the exodus began, with fast beating hearts and trepidation probably as great as that of the hosts of Israel who followed their bearded, staff-wielding patri-arch out into the wilderness. Miss Laverton had no beard, but, newly promoted to Acting Head of the uprooted branch of Lister Road, she cut a suitably magisterial figure in a thick, heathery suit and a hat like Robin Hood. And she could certainly wield a stick with vigour, as many miscreant, stinging palms had learnt over the years of her benevolent despotism in her small kingdom.

4

Alice and Algy were billeted with a family who lived about half a mile from the village itself, near the top of the steep slope which formed the northern side of the valley, along a narrow rutted lane known as Howbeck Side. How Backside, as Alice irreverently christened it in her mind. Mr and Mrs Aygarth had three young children of their own: a nine year-old girl, Rebecca (Becky), another just a year older than Algy, Maureen, and a third, the pride and joy, a two-year-old son named Malcolm, after his father.

Mr Aygarth worked with his father and brother on the tenant farm. The small piece of land stretched away behind the farm buildings. They had a herd of milkers and a much larger flock of sheep, which grazed up on 'the tops', as the expanse of moor which extended almost to the coast was known. Algy's face had blanched at the first mention of cattle, but Alice had gripped his hand in tight warning. He was slightly reassured later, when he discovered that the Aygarths' cottage, one of several such dwellings widely spaced along Howbeck Side, was comfortingly distant from the main farmhouse, the pasture and the milking-shed.

Alice tried to tell him how lucky they were. That first day had seemed endless. The excitement of the initial early morning bus-ride, the train journey and arrival at the small country halt, soon faded, as the arrivals were marshalled into the village hall, and the process of 'pick-your-evacuee' began. Like cattle themselves, the children stood, or sat on hard wooden chairs, in the centre of the bare room, while these hard-eyed, grim strangers circled, peered, and in some cases poked at them, before making what seemed always to be their reluctant choice.

'We'll try to keep you together,' Miss Laverton reassured Doreen. 'With Alice and Algy.' But Doreen proved lacking in familial *esprit de corps*. Or perhaps she still felt the weighty shackles of indebtedness towards her elder sister and believed it would be wiser to put what distance she could between them. After a long interval, when more than half the children had been placed, an imposing, smartly dressed lady of advanced middle age and with a distinctly refined accent, gazed with approval at Doreen's delicate budding beauty, only to turn away on ascertaining that the winsome figure was one of a trio.

Treacherously, Doreen seized her chance. 'I don't mind, miss!' She was addressing the stranger, as well as Miss Laverton. 'I mean, going on me own. Be easier. And I'm a good girl, miss. I know how to do things. I can help round the house, look after myself.' She widened her eyes, put on her best, solemn, waiflike expression.

Miss Elizabeth Ramsay's spinster heart was touched. The gel would clean up nicely. And those eyes, that elfin little face. Reminded her of dearest Daisy. Faithful little companion for so many years, now laid to rest behind the lavender hedge. The sweetest little pooch ever to grace God's earth. 'Yes. Very well,' she announced, with the rich satisfaction of knowing she was doing the Lord's work. 'I'll take this one.'

Alice was mightily relieved when the Aygarths agreed to house her and Algy. 'We're not very grand,' Eileen Aygarth said readily, but her grin and her fresh face looked open and honest. 'You'll have to share with your little brother, but I'm sure you'll fit in well. We've got three bairns of our own, so one more won't mek any difference, eh?' She reached out and ruffled Algy's already tousled hair. 'You'll have a great time with our Becky and Maureen. We'll have to teach you how to milk t'cows, won't we?'

66

Alice squeezed Algy's sweaty hand convulsively and prayed he wouldn't burst into tears. 'It's very good of you, ma'am.'

Eileen gave a snort of surprisingly girlish laughter. 'Eh! We'll have none of that, tha knows! We're not gentry. It's Eileen. And my man's name is Malcolm. Big Malcolm cos Malcolm's me youngest's name and all.' She studied Alice critically, still with an infectious grin. 'You look like a good strong lass to have about the place. If ever you get fed up of working with t'chool, you can help out on the farm. You look like you'd tek to it real well!'

The cottage was, as Eileen had said, not 'grand'. Bits had been tacked on over the years and generations. The original walls were of thick stone, as could be seen from the frontage, where the windows were set in recesses of almost three feet, and reminded Alice of ancient castles and the like. Extensions had grown to the rear and to the side of the original design, again on a two-storey level, so that there were now four bedrooms, and, a luxury bordering on decadence in Alice's admiring eyes, an indoor bathroom with claw-footed tub and piped hot water. No more pails of water carried from the copper out back at No 19, and the galvanized iron bath in front of the kitchen range, with Dad and George banned from the scene during the girls' weekly bath night and the additional fail-safe of the wooden clothes horse draped with a sheet to ensure decency.

Both Alice and Algy had the opportunity to enjoy these exotic ablutions on their first night in their new home. 'We're well in here, eh, Algy?' She grinned as he sat splashing between her legs in the tub. He smiled back. He had been greatly relieved at the reassuring length of the neat rows of vegetables which stretched from the rear of the building, and the total absence of any of those fearsome cow shapes. But he was reserving judgement after the less than welcome snarling from two black-and-white collies, and Becky Aygarth's casual advice to 'watch that Geordie. He's not above having a snap if he thinks he can get away with it, and his teeth are bloomin' sharp!'

Almost a mile away, in a double-fronted, ivy-covered house with Georgian windows, and a geometrically designed garden, behind brick walls and an imposing set of iron gates, which had thus far evaded the greedy search for 'scrap' to turn into weapons of war, Doreen was savouring a similar novel experience of bathing in a room designated solely for that purpose, but on a more elegant and modern scale than that in the Aygarths' cottage. She wasn't sure who had been more embarrassed at her being seen in her 'birthday suit', she or her hostess, but Miss Ramsay stalwartly overcame her own diffidence to stay and oversee Doreen's cleansing, and even to assist in the shampooing and rinsing of Doreen's brown locks.

'I don't have a full-time maid, I'm afraid,' Miss Ramsay awkwardly confessed, pinking slightly from shame rather than her endeavours. 'I have a cook who lives in the village, and Milly, a daytime girl for the household chores.'

Doreen, eyes screwed tightly shut against the flowing suds and the water poured from the jug, nodded wisely and wondered what on earth 'chores' were.

Alice was back at the village hall at eight o' clock next morning, with Algy in tow. 'I thought I'd better bring him with me. I didn't want to leave him up there on his own.'

Under Miss Laverton's capable sergeant-majorship, the teachers from Lister Road, together with a handful of village women, set about transforming the hall into another schoolroom. Alice had scarcely time to exchange more than a greeting with Elsbeth, who, blonde head hidden in a green knotted turban and slim form wrapped in a paisley-pattern pinafore, was ready to do her enthusiastic if inexpert bit. Swept, scrubbed, and partitioned off into sections, the hall was ready by mid-morning to serve as schoolroom to the infant classes and the first year of the junior school. The others, who included Doreen, would be accommodated in the village school itself, 200 yards away, across the humpbacked stone bridge crossing the 'Beck', the shallow, fast-running River Howe.

The tiny 'kitchen' area of the village hall was scarcely adequate for the preparation of the midday school dinner that Alice and two other local servers were responsible for providing, especially given the vagaries of the portable stove brought in to cope with the new regimen. Alice was surprised, and a little alarmed at first, to find that the two village women seemed quite willing to surrender any claim to authority and defer to her, despite her youth and inexperience. But she knew how to cook. The years as eldest sibling in the Glass household had ensured a sound if basic culinary expertise. With the encouragement of Edith Bowen, the qualified infant teacher, and Elsbeth, together with the brief gung-ho, head-popping-round-the-door visits from Miss Laverton, who was managing to give the impressive impression of being in at least two places at once, the meal, of mince and a form of dumpling made from potatoes, carrots, cabbage and mash, appeared on the two long trestle-tables set up when the desks had been pushed aside, and only twenty-five minutes late.

'Excellent! Well done, ladies!' Miss Laverton swallowed stolidly from her minuscule portion, then disappeared 'up the road', to the village school proper, to see how her other charges were faring.

'Algy! Use your spoon!' Alice admonished, and hovered about the little ones' table to see that some rudimentary form of order was maintained and that everyone was fed.

Hands and faces were washed, and trips to the outside toilet behind the building were organized and supervised, then, at last, both Alice and Elsbeth had a respite, their first chance to have a real chat since the previous day.

'What's your digs like?' Alice asked. They were glad to be out in the open, even though the day was blustery, with high-riding white clouds and fitful bursts of sunshine. She knew Elsbeth was staying in the pub, the Oddfellows. 'Just temporarily,' Elsbeth had said, with that customary hint of apology in her tone. 'Till I find somewhere.' Miss Laverton had booked a room there, too. Alice wondered if the veteran teacher had been entrusted by Elsbeth's folks to keep an eye on their daughter for them. Alice was sure that the education committee would not be picking up the bill for their stay.

'It was a bit noisy,' Elsbeth confided. 'From the bar, I mean. They seem to do a roaring trade.' They had linked arms and headed round the margin of the small pond, towards the inn. 'I'll show you my room.' Elsbeth's voice lowered. 'And we can use the toilet while we're there.' The toilets outside the village hall lacked appeal after the visits of thirty plus youngsters.

There were several lunch-time drinkers at the bar, and they all called their good-days as the girls passed by the open door to the stairs. Elsbeth's room was small, the walls whitwashed. Thick beams crossed inches above their heads, and, where the single bed stood in one corner, the ceiling sloped, slightly unevenly, downward. A small window looked out over a grassy orchard inclining down towards the river. Elsbeth pulled a face. 'Bit of a poke-hole!'

'It's lovely!' Alice breathed. Imagine! she thought. Having a room all to yourself! But she was glad to have Algy's warm, unconscious little body to snuggle up to, on their second strange country night, even if he sighed, and kept squirming restlessly away from her under the thick blankets and heavy eiderdown. Alice envied him his sleep.

Despite her long, exhausting day, she could not drop off herself, and she lay reflecting on how alien this new world was, for her as well as the kids she was helping to look after. For a start, there was the foreignness of the country dark. So deep a silence, and what noises there were mysterious, impossible to identify. Rustles and movements, the sounds of animals. She heard a sudden, sharp cry, like a scream, that made her heart race. Then footsteps, a kind of tearing and chomping, and a shrill, drawn-out wail which she thought at first was a baby crying. Only when she heard the longer, deeper bleats did it occur to her that these were the sounds of the sheep, which wandered everywhere around the village and its environs, right alongside the houses. 'Don't bother with lawn mowers round here!' someone told her. 'Just leave t'gate open and sheep'll have grass like a billiard table in five minutes. Only trouble is, the beggars'll have all your plants and all while they're on.'

And, of course, for only the second time in weeks, no air raid siren to disturb the night. Though, still fretfully awake at midnight, Alice heard a distant rumble, which she thought might be thunder, until a brief flurry of regular pulses helped her to identify gunfire. She eased herself up out of the warm bed, and poked her head through the thick blackout curtains. There was the slightest flicker of redness on the horizon towards the coast. The war was still there, but it was a long way away, only the faintest echo, the merest ghost of the aftermath of horror she had witnessed in Mains Terrace.

★ ★ ★

As they got on with the business of settling in, organizing school and dinners and the difficulties of pastoral care for the fifty-odd youngsters who had been uprooted and dropped into a world different in almost every way from their lives at home in Margrove, Alice and Elsbeth, though they saw each other every day, had little time for talk or shared reflection, a fact Alice was regretting more and more as the days passed. Algy, with his big sister comfortingly on hand even during school hours, and the diversions of new playmates and substitute siblings in the Aygarth children, adapted quickly to his new life. Alice sometimes envied him his ability to do so. But then it was easy for kids, she soon decided. She saw examples every day how most of the Margrove children took to their new life. Far easier for them than it was for the adults.

For the first time in her almost nineteen years, Alice felt truly grown up. It hadn't happened, as she had thought it would, when she had her first period. She had felt, startlingly, more like a kid than ever, when, after the storm of tears, she had talked about it for the first time with her mother, and revealed the abysmal extent of her ignorance. 'Is that it then?' she had sniffled with relief. 'It's over now?' And her mother had stared at her open mouthed before bursting into peals of incredulous laughter. It was only after Maggie had recovered that a desolate Alice had learnt that this seminal moment was something she would have to endure time and time again. 'Unless you're up the spout. Carrying.' Her mother had hefted her own belly in illustration. 'Why the hell do you think they call it the 'monthlies', you daft ha'p'orth?'

It hadn't happened when she had left school and started work, either. In fact, work at the co-op was like school, but without the pleasure of laughs with your mates. There were still loads of older folk to tell you what to do and to cuff you round the earhole if you didn't do it right. True, you got paid for it, every Saturday, but then she had to take her wage packet home unopened and have her 'pocket-money' doled out to her as though it were a generous gift from her parents. And the threat of the 'back of a hand' if she voiced any serious objection.

But now she was on her own, away from the nest, just what she had been wanting for so long now, and she had the war to thank for it. She hadn't thought of this as a proper job at all, just as a heaven-sent opportunity to escape from Maudsley Street. It was Miss Laverton who had pulled her up short, made her think again, at the end of their first week in Howbeck. She had told the children to play out in the yard for an extra half-hour after dinner on the Friday while she held a 'staff meeting'. Alice and the two local dinner assistants had just finished wiping down the long tables and dismantling them and were hastening towards the exit when Miss Laverton called them back. 'Where do you think you three are sloping off to?' she said jocularly. 'Sit down please, ladies. If anybody is an essential part of our team here it's you three. I'd like to put it on record now, what a splendid job you've done. We couldn't manage without you.'

'Hear hear!' The small group of teachers were vociferous in support. Alice reddened with embarrassed pleasure. It was good to be appreciated. She was surprised at the surge of pride she felt, followed by the sobering reflection that she was, after all, engaged in a worthwhile task, however much it involved mop and bucket and peeling spuds.

She wished she could find more time to spend with Elsbeth Hobbs. It was through Elsbeth that she had landed this job. She had been so friendly since their paths had recrossed, not at all the 'right little toff' Alice had thought her for the past ten years. She was a sweet kid, with no side to her at all. It was funny. For all her education, and her posh voice and gorgeous looks, she seemed somehow much younger than the three months which separated her from Alice, in whom she brought out a protective tenderness.

Alice was a little uncomfortable with this attraction of hers to the pretty girl, she felt a reluctance even to examine it too closely, yet it was there, and she savoured it to herself, also. She found herself watching out for the slim figure, and the quick leap of appreciation sight of her brought. Several times she thought of going down to the village in the evening, dropping in on Elsbeth as if by chance at the Oddfellows. What was wrong with wanting to be with her? They were friends, weren't they? But then, Miss Laverton was there. Elsbeth probably spent her evenings with the older mistress, preparing schoolwork, having their tea together. Or dinner — that's what the posh folk called their evening meal. And what would Alice talk to her about, if they did meet up? What was on the menu for school *dinner* tomorrow? What the hell could she chat about with a lovely, clever girl like Elsbeth Hobbs?

It was Elsbeth who voiced the very sentiments Alice had been hugging to herself. 'Look. We really must get together for a talk. A proper chat, I mean. Can you get away in the evenings? We could fix a time. Have you heard? We're moving. Miss Laverton and I.' She gave an impish little grin and gave a theatrical flourish of her hand. 'Up to the Big House, no less! We've been offered rooms there. Pretty grand, eh?'

The 'Big House' was a term almost universally used in Howbeck to refer to Howe Manor, modest enough as mansions go, with the restrained late-eighteenth-century elegance of a gentleman's country house, set in a spacious walled garden on wooded slopes on the opposite side of the valley from Howbeck Side. From the Aygarth cottage you could see the chimneys and a corner of the grey crenellated roof peeping through the surrounding dark foliage.

Mr Aygarth senior, still taking an active part in farming the family land in spite of having recently celebrated his sixty-ninth birthday, was a mine of information to the curious Alice. 'Squire now is Mr Denby. His father, Sir Eric, bought the estate nearly forty year ago, in 1904. Been goin' down the drain ever since, if you ask me!'

Denby Estates was the Aygarths' landlord, as it was for practically all the farms along the length of Howe Dale. 'The old lords of the manor were the Ansells. Been round here for generations. Way back to King Charles and the Civil War. Proper gentry. Sir Eric was nowt but an incomer. Made his money through weapons — armaments and all that. And the last squire — Sir Arthur Ansell — he was fair strapped for cash. I remember him well. Right temper on him. He'd send his groom or his keeper after you with a whip if he thought you weren't showing respect. But he knew every one of his tenants, and he'd get round and see them all himself. Not leave it to his agent like this lot! But he was a terrible man for the bottle. His wife left him and cleared off to London. She hadn't given him a son, neither. Only a couple of lasses, daft as brushes. Spent all their time abroad or down in London. In the end the old man just got fed up. Sold up and off.' Mr Aygarth growled and spat sizzlingly into the kitchen range fire. 'Sir Eric was never a countryman, though. Not proper. Liked to play at it. And his son's no better. Plain *Mister* Denby, just like me. Not even a sir, and never will be.'

'There's a couple of our teachers moved up there,' Alice told him.

'Aye. Well, they've already got a girls' school staying in t'Big 'Ouse nowadays. One of them posh private schools come from down south somewhere. So likely your lot will feel at home, with their own kind, like.'

Alice had noticed the gaggle of uniformed children around the village occasionally, in their black winter hats and gymslips and black stockings. You could tell they were from some private establishment, even before you heard their cut-glass accents. Oh, I say, Priscilla! Just like Elsbeth, Alice thought guiltily, but then she would admonish herself. She can't help the way she talks, can she? It's only the way she's been brought up. Alice had assumed these privileged kids were from some local boarding school, and she was surprised to learn from Grandad Aygarth that they were evacuees, just like the Margrove kids. Well, not quite, mebbes, she thought wryly. At least Elsbeth would feel more at home, up at the Big House, with that lot.

One thing had puzzled Alice. What on earth had Elsbeth been doing as a kid, stranded in a dump like Lister Road Junior School? Surely she should have been running about in one of them swanky places like this bunch who had been billeted in Big House? And in one of their snatched after dinner conversations in the village hall she had, with customary brusqueness, asked her.

As so often, Elsbeth prefaced her answer with one of her pretty pinkings. 'My brother — the older one, William — was already at prep school. Boarding school,' she explained at Alice's blank look. 'Daddy couldn't really afford to send me as well. My other brother, Rob, was just a toddler, but he'd have to be sent to school, too, eventually. We weren't all that well off, really.'

Alice knew that Elsbeth's father owned Hobbs & Sons Printers. Like many inhabitants of areas like Maudsley Street, Alice had simply believed that the world was divided into two classes — money folk and the poor.

Elsbeth was still wearing her shy confessor's smile. 'They did send me to Rosebank, the kindergarten up on the Dalby road, but then I had to go to Lister Road when I was eight. You remember? I didn't come until standard three.' The rosy shade deepened a little. 'Then I got the scholarship and was at the high school when the business started to do really well, and Daddy expanded.' She paused and went on in something of a rush. 'In the last couple of years things have got more and more — well, better. Lots of contracts, from government. With the war coming . . . '

'Good old Adolf, eh?' The mocking words were out before Alice could retain them. 'Hey, just kidding! It's good. Not just for you, I mean. It's like doing your bit, isn't it?' She had seen the flash of hurt in the blue eyes, and was relieved to see the look of gratefulness which replaced it. And getting rich in the process! Wisely, Alice kept this last uncharitable thought to herself. 'What's your brother doing?'

Elsbeth's tone changed to one of pride now. 'William's in the army. He's down south. Near Salisbury somewhere. He finished college early in the year. He was in the OTC — Officers' Training Corps. He's still doing his basic training with the infantry. Then he's going to specialize in Signals, I think. Rob, the youngest, he's still at school. Near Harrogate. He's only fourteen.'

For all the time they spent in close proximity, such brief moments were all they managed to exchange in their busy routine. Brief, but precious to her, Alice was coming to realize more and more. She had had little real contact with people of her own age since leaving school. Largely through her own choice, she had to admit, for as she advanced through her teenage years, she had found more and more how little she had in common with them, especially the members of her own sex. Daft, 'fripperty' things, they were, all talk of boys and tarting themselves up, and mucky, whispered sniggers. It wouldn't do for her at all.

Now, she realized that her existence over the past three years had been a lonely one, in spite of the three-to-a-bed and scarcely ever a moment of solitude unless you were locked in the bum-freezing netty. What was it about Elsbeth Hobbs that made Alice feel close to her? Want to be close to her? You're mad, lass! she kept telling herself. You're about as close as chalk and cheese. The best-looking lass round these parts, off to college, already knows more than you'll ever know. A young lady, that's what she is! She's off another planet. Belongs up there at the Big House, with her squires and her long-legged, toffee-nosed school chums. How could she be best mates with a mop-head with a voice like a navvy and arms to match, who'd look like a clown with a smear of lipstick across her gob and a dab of rouge on her cheeks, and feel just as daft?

5

Another two weeks passed before the girls managed to organize some uninterrupted leisure time together. Weekends were as busy as weekdays for the small staff of Lister Road. Miss Laverton had not flattered or exaggerated when she described Alice as a key member of the team. The acting headmistress was fully conscious of her new responsibility towards her children, and that included watching over them on Saturdays and Sundays in their new and very different environment. Alice was busier than most on her behalf.

'I want you to get round as many of their digs as you can,' Miss Laverton told her confidentially. 'You're closer to them than any of us are. I mean with being Doreen and Algy's big sister and not being one of us dreaded *teachers!* We've got to really watch out for them now. Most of them have never been away from home for more than a night or two at the most. And you know how different things are here. They'll probably let on things to you they won't ever mention in the classroom. It's a big job I'm asking of you, I know that. To be big sister to *all* of them, not just your two. You'll have to be careful. Be as subtle as you can, but try to see if they're being treated properly. Looked after as they should be. I know it's not much, but these people are being paid something for putting us up.'

She was right. It was a big job, and Alice found she had hardly any time to spare for herself — or her friend. But at last, one Sunday afternoon, Alice hurried through the cold drizzle of late October down the hill and over the humped bridge, then out of the village and up the southern slope of the valley to the stone pillars of Howe Manor, recently denuded of the heavy, spiked iron gates. She had arranged to meet Elsbeth at three. They had planned to follow the path of the beck eastward, and have a really good country walk before returning to the manor for tea, in Elsbeth's room. But Alice was half-hoping they would stay indoors. Her only decent pair of shoes were leaking through into her clean grey ankle socks — she hadn't wanted to wear her workaday boots, they hardly constituted 'Sunday best'. And, in spite of the umbrella Eileen Aygarth had lent her, she could feel the damp through the shoulders of her winter coat.

The muddy puddles at the bottom of the

drive changed to drier, scrunching gravel as she turned the bend to the impressive façade of the house, with the circular rose-bed in front of the worn steps. Alice was nervous. It felt wrong to be approaching the grand main entrance. She ought to have been making her way round the side of the building, through a wooden door she could see in the weathered bricks of the wall stretching away to her left. But this is what Elsbeth had told her to do, with that little grin of hers. 'Of course come through the front doors. You're not a tradesman. You're my guest!'

Alice was relieved to see Elsbeth talking to a small group of uniformed girls, just inside the glass doors of a kind of big porch — bigger than the parlour of 19 Maudsley Street. Most of them looked as old as she was, but they murmured politely, in response to Elsbeth's farewell, ' 'Bye, Miss Hobbs.'

'Hello, Miss Hobbs!' Alice grinned at her, and Elsbeth clutched at her, gave her a brief hug.

'Don't! They make me feel as old as Methuselah.'

'Get away!' She released her and stepped back in amused admiration. 'Wow! Very nice, kidder!' She was referring to the dark-brown slacks Elsbeth wore, with a thick knitted, oatmeal jumper. The tailored trousers had knife-edge creases, and the court style shoes that peeked out beneath them were of the softest burnished leather. 'Really! You look so smart. I feel a right scruff.' She glanced round her. They had moved into the entrance hall, where other groups of girls, all in the same dark gymslips and stockings, stood around chatting. Alice could feel curious eyes on her. She felt even more conscious of her shabby appearance, as Elsbeth led her up the wide stairs, which divided to left and right, on to railed galleries. Elsbeth linked arms, steered her to the right hand corridor. 'This wing's the school. Our rooms are on the floor above, with their staff. The girls' dorms are up there, too. Old servants' quarters. Same as ours.'

The noise from the pupils at their Sunday 'make and mend' could be heard all round them, only slightly muted when Elsbeth closed the door of her small sanctuary. There was a thin rug laid over the centre of the uneven, creaking floorboards. A single bed stood against one wall, whose faded paper showed old water-mark stains of ancient damp. The narrow little window looked out on to a section of the walled garden, now turned over, like most available patches of land, to growing vegetables, and beyond that a strip of green parkland, with clusters of venerable trees, whose leaves showed the varying shades of autumn. Black branches were beginning to appear, the grass dappled with the constant shedding.

A curtained-off rail had been fixed in another corner of the room to act as wardrobe. The only furniture apart from the bed was a scarred chest of drawers and an upholstered chair with scratched wooden arms. 'This is where some poor maid must have slept.' Elsbeth smiled apologetically. 'You can have the chair if you want, but the bed's more comfortable.' She sat and leaned back against the wall, patted the coverlet at her side. 'I think we'd better hang on. See if it stops raining, eh?'

Alice settled companionably beside her, stretched out her pale legs. 'Those slacks look smashing. It's great, being able to wear trousers, eh? They've given me a pair of workmen's overalls to wear, up at the farm. I think I might start wearing them for work. Do you think Miss Laverton would allow it?'

'Why not? I mean, you're not teaching, are you?'

'It's so much easier wearing trousers. And a damned sight warmer, now that the weather's turning nippy, eh?'

'I'll pop along to the galley. There's a little kitchenette place at the end of the landing, that's what we call it. It's hardly bigger than a cupboard, but we can boil a kettle there, and there's crockery and stuff. I'll make us a cuppa.'

Elsbeth seemed a little nervous, and Alice wondered why. 'You needn't rush for me. It's not that long since we ate.' She patted her stomach, and rolled her eyes. 'Talk about being well fed! Them farmers don't want for nowt! I'm going to be as big as a barrage balloon if I keep eating so much.' Why did Elsbeth seem so on edge? 'Hey, listen! We're mates, aren't we? Good friends, like?'

'Of course we are.' Elsbeth pinked a little, as usual, but she looked pleased, nevertheless.

'Well then, do us a favour, will you? Call me Al. That's what my mates call us.'

Elsbeth's face registered her surprise. 'But that's a boy's name! And Alice is so pretty.'

Alice grunted in distaste. 'Aye! For a — well, somebody like you, mebbe! But I'm not exactly a glamour girl type, am I? I've always hated it — my name. So if you're my pal, call me Al! Hey! I'm a poet! Anyways, I always wished I was a lad. They have a much better time than us lot.'

'I'll try. But it sounds so funny. Al!' She tried it dubiously, her face screwed up. Then she seemed to come to a sudden decision. 'Right! We are pals, aren't we? You said so. So promise you won't be offended. Right-oh?'

Alice stared up at her, mystified, shook her head. 'Don't be daft. What's wrong?'

'You know I popped home last weekend?' Alice nodded. Elsbeth drew the faded curtain aside and unhooked some clothes hanging on the rail. She laid them on the bed, then opened the topmost drawer of the chest. She took out a neatly folded pile of garments and laid them beside the others. 'You promised you wouldn't be mad.' Alice was staring at her. 'I've been going through my wardrobe. Mummy said she'd chuck some of it out if I didn't make room. I've got far too much.'

Her nervousness was making her talk quickly, with a gushing eagerness. 'We're nearly the same size. I'm an inch or two taller, and a bit skinnier. But these — well, if they're any good, I'd like you to have them. They're no use to me, and . . . well, I brought them for you. To see if you'd like them.' She picked up a smart belted winter coat, in a deep mulberry. 'Try it on. You could always take it up an inch or two if it needs it.'

Alice could feel her face growing warm. She stared at the clothing beside her. She saw some delicate looking underclothes. A matching set of pink vest and knickers, of the finest wool. There were satin shoulder straps, and the garments were trimmed with embroidered lace; several pairs of woollen stockings and a shiny, lace-edged pair of step-ins; some blouses and two thick winter jumpers. Alice looked up at her, saw the tension in Elsbeth's face. 'I can't take these,' she whispered, her throat suddenly feeling tight.

'I knew you'd be like this!' Elsbeth's voice was high, wretched with her embarrassment and dismay. 'You said we're friends — '

'Aye! That's right! I'm not a charity case, you know!' It came out fiercer than she had intended. She saw Elsbeth flinch, as the colour flooded her features.

'I never — I didn't mean . . . ' She wrung her hands together, in what struck Alice as a thoroughly theatrical gesture. 'I just wanted you to have them! I've got more stuff than I need, and . . . and . . . I wanted to give them to you. A present. For my friend!'

The voice quavered, the blue eyes fixed on hers, filling with tears which threatened to spill over. 'And now I've spoilt things. I'm sorry, Alice! Please! Don't be angry with me?'

She looked so woebegone, standing there, her hands clasped in front of her. Alice felt the tears pricking at her own eyes, felt exasperation and tenderness all mixed in a swirl of emotion. 'You don't have to give me things, to be my friend.' Her voice came out as a low growl.

'I know. I just wanted to. I'm sorry.' A little

sigh caught in her throat.

Alice sprang up, and reached for her clumsily, flung her arms round her and drew her in close. Chins hooked over shoulders, cheeks nestling, they hugged each other. Alice could feel the thin frame against her, smell the sweet fragrance of the soft hair brushing her face. Felt the wetness of Elsbeth's cheek. 'You daft ha'p'orth! Don't upset yourself. I'll take them then. And thank you. They're beautiful. I've never had nowt like them.'

'Oh, thank you, thank you!' Elsbeth squeezed her, planted a wet kiss on her cheek.

Alice's heart was racing, she was over-whelmed by the great surge of excitement and joy she felt. Head spinning, she let go of the girl, stepped back, full of Elsbeth's sweetness, her fragrance and beauty. 'God! What you blubbing for? You're still as soppy as ever you were. It's a good job for you I can't get my hands on a jug of water, or I'd give you another soaking, I swear I would!'

'You're just an old bully!' Elsbeth laughed. Her eyes still shone with tears. She reached out, caught hold of Alice's hand and tugged her towards the door. 'Come with me while I make us tea. Then you can try them on. There's a siren suit among them. They keep you lovely and warm. I'm going to wear mine in bed when the cold weather comes.'

Alice freed her hand from Elsbeth's grip as they left the room. She felt shaken, and suddenly deeply unsure of everything around her. She was shocked at this new uncertainty, and even more shocked at her fierce exaltation when she had held the lovely form so close, the desire she felt to do it again.

★   ★   ★

'Hullo dere! Liddle Doreen's big sister! How are you den? Warm enough, yeah? Doreen is helping me wid de garden. We make de fire before dark, yeah? We don' want de bombers seein' to drop de bombs on us, yeah?' The big laughter boomed out, at fitting volume for the bulk of the figure facing Alice.

His name was Gus Rielke, the 'Gus' short for Gustav. He was known to the villagers as the 'Big Swede', though everyone acknowledged that he was Norwegian by nationality. Norwegian, Swede, they were all the same. Foreigners. And exotic fish to be landed in Howbeck. He had arrived in May, about four months ahead of the Lister Road evacuees, an escaped war hero who had fled the German occupation of his country in his fishing-boat, along with his colleagues, all of whom were now enlisted in the British Forces. He, himself, much to his bitter regret, had sustained injuries during the escape which had rendered him unfit for active service. After failing to find work, again due to his incapacity, at his trade as fisherman, with the neighbouring north-east coast fleets, he had wound up in Howbeck. He had been taken in by the generous landlady of the Oddfellows, where, in return for his room and board and a very modest stipend, he worked as pot-man, cellar-man, and general factotum for Mrs Vera Rhodes, the licensee, whose husband, a member of the Territorial Army since '36, had been mobilized at the outbreak of hostilities, sent to France and taken prisoner during the retreat to the French coast.

There were many unkind, smutty souls who sneered that Gus's handyman duties extended far beyond the cellar and the bar, but not to Vera Rhodes's face, for she was quite capable of defending her own honour, however dubious it might be. Besides, it was not sound politics to upset the keeper of the only pub within five miles. He helped and eked out his limited means by odd-jobbing elsewhere, hence his presence this chilly, damp November Sunday morning in Miss Ramsay's garden.

A thick, seasonal mist hung about the valley as he raked the leaves into dank, black heaps on the lawn and dragged the lopped branches and stray twigs into a wigwam pile, which he was shortly hoping to ignite. 'She's a good liddle worker, yeah?' He nodded, grinning at Doreen, who beamed back, her face peeping like a squirrel from its drey in her grey Balaclava. She was wearing a mackintosh which she was rapidly outgrowing. Between her wet mittens and the sleeves a pale stretch of thin wrists was exposed, while the hem ended way above the knees, to reveal the wrinkled bagginess of grey woollen stockings, much darned, and overlarge rubber boots.

'God! What a sight you look! On a Sunday and all!'

Alice frowned at her, and Doreen pulled a suitably dissenting face. 'What do you expect? Me to mucky me best clothes doing this?' She gestured about her, and made an explosive sound of disgust. 'Miss Ramsay said I should help Gus. She's off to church.'

'You should've gone with her!'

Doreen made an even louder and ruder noise. 'I don't have a load of swanky stuff to tart meself up in, do I?'

The expression and the colour of Alice's features showed the hit had found its mark. Alice was very conscious of the smart new winter coat, the fine stockings, and the other unseen garments she was wearing. Especially under the scrutiny of those crinkled piggy eyes and the leering smile of the man opposite her. Some girls, and women, said he was handsome. Alice didn't agree. That great bulk didn't impress her and the red features were too open, coarse, while the pale blue eyes seemed cold, distinctly lacking in any real feeling. Except a hint of something that made her feel uncomfortable and ashamed, an indecent feeling, as though he was imagining what she looked like beneath her clothes.

Even his heavy accent annoyed her, with his 'v's for 'w's, and his 'd's for 'th's. She had heard the wicked gossip about him and Vera Rhodes, and she was inclined to believe it. Well, she was welcome to him. She was another hard faced, brassy cow. Mutton desperate to be lamb, as Mam would say.

'Just popped in to see if you fancy coming up to the farm after dinner?' she said, smothering her irritation with her young sister, and trying pointedly to ignore the grinning bulk of Gus. 'You could stay and have some tea with us. Algy would be pleased. So would Becky and Maureen.'

'We're going to have a fire.' Doreen nodded at the pile of brushwood. 'Miss Ramsay said we could. I want to stay and help Gus. It's instead of Bonfire Night on Thursday.'

'You can't have bonfires. Not now. You'll have the wardens after you.'

'I know that!' Doreen answered scornfully. 'That's why we're doing it now. We'll get it blazing. Then we'll have to put it out before dark. Won't we, Gus?'

He nodded. His narrow slits of eyes were still fixed firmly on Alice. 'You can stop and watch. We can't ask you to help, yeah?' He turned, winked at Doreen. 'She too much of a lady in dem nice clothes.'

Alice continued with her effort to ignore his presence. 'Haven't you got anything you should be doing indoors? Like getting the dinner ready? Setting the table for Miss Ramsay or summat?'

Doreen blithely shook her head. 'Naw. She won't be back for ages yet. She goes off for coffee with the vicar and some of the other toffs after church. Any road, Mrs Addis left it all ready. We only have a sandwich. We have *dinner* tonight,' she said grandly, full of airs and graces.

Alice gave a derisive grunt, and made to go. 'Mind you don't set fire to yourself. You'd make a good guy looking like that.'

'Don't you worry. I take good care of her, yeah? We good friends.' As Alice began to move off, he came across to her. 'Hey! Why you not come in the Oddfellows for drink one night? You big girl now, yeah? Lady.' His laugh boomed out. 'I buy you drink. You very nice-looking.'

That message was there, in the eyes again, and Alice felt an inner shiver of revulsion. Her cheeks were hot. She strove to find a cutting riposte. 'No, thanks. I don't frequent public houses.' There! That was a posh word, 'frequent'. Elsbeth would be proud of her. The Big Swede probably wouldn't have a clue what it meant. 'Tara, Doreen. Be good, won't you? See you tomorrow.'

The hollow boom of his laughter followed her down the broad path to the gate. She could sense his gaze steady on her back, and she was almost angry with herself for dolling herself up in all her new, second-hand finery.

She mentioned Rielke round the Aygarths' table when they had finished their midday meal, and were sitting back in leisured ease, the children having been released to go back to their various outdoor pursuits. 'What's he supposed to have had happen to him? There doesn't seem a lot wrong with him, from what I can see. He works on a lot of folks' gardens. Helps out all over the place.'

'Aye. He certainly pulled his weight with getting the harvest in,' Malcolm Aygarth said, leaning over to knock his pipe out on the fender of the big range. They habitually ate round the big old table in the kitchen, unless they had company or were celebrating some special occasion. 'Summat to do with his hip, they reckon. Still got a bullet or a bit of shrapnel in it. Jerries fired on their boat. He doesn't like to talk about it. Not like some. He doesn't go round bragging. He certainly doesn't let it stop him getting on with things.'

It was clear that Malcolm Aygarth thought quite well of him, and Alice decided she had better hide her own feelings about the foreigner.

As though she could detect Alice's ungenerous opinion of Gus Rielke, Eileen Aygarth added, 'You don't want to take no notice of some of the gossips round here. You know. About him staying at the Oddfellows.' She glanced round significantly, to make sure none of the children was within earshot. 'There's some awful narrow-minded folk around village.' She nodded emphatically, and lowered her voice. '*Mucky*-minded, too.'

'Well, some people are bound to talk,' Alice offered hesitantly. 'I mean with her husband being away, a POW. And him staying there, under her roof. Why didn't he find somewhere else to stay?'

'He's working for her, isn't he? Board and lodging are probably part of the arrangement. It's a big enough place. Sharing a roof doesn't mean sharing a bed, does it?'

Spots of colour had appeared on Eileen's cheeks, darker than her already ruddy country countenance. Alice remembered she had made her customary attendance at the Methodist chapel that morning. Must have rubbed off on her, all this love thy neighbour, Alice thought ungraciously. She couldn't keep from speaking out. 'Aye, it's a big place. She didn't offer to have any of our lot, though, did she?'

'Well, a pub isn't exactly an ideal place to bring little children to, is it? And as I recall, she did put up that headmistress, and your mate. The bonny lass. Elsbeth, is it?'

'They were paying guests! And they were only there a couple of weeks. Till Squire Denby offered them a place up at Big House.'

'What's wrong? Have they said anything — about what went on there? Did they see anything untoward?'

Her tone was sharp, and she sat forward with new alertness. How's your Christian charity now? Alice thought with mean amusement. 'No, nothing,' she admitted. 'It's just . . . I dunno. He seems a bit odd to me.'

Eileen relaxed, gave a knowing smile. 'You know your trouble, my girl? You don't get out enough. Young lass like you. You should be getting around more. Dances, that sort of thing. I bet your friend Elsbeth is fighting the lads off, eh? You should make more of yourself.' She looked appraisingly at Alice. 'Do something with your hair. Soften those curls, grow it a bit longer. I mean — you look really nice today, with that jumper. And a bit of make-up. You don't make enough of yourself. There's a village hop week after next. You've never been yet, have you? It's good fun. You meet some lads, have a dance. You never know your luck! What do you reckon, Malcolm?'

Alice was a little shocked at the depth of emotion Eileen's gently teasing remarks were arousing. Especially that crack about Elsbeth having to fight the lads off. Why should that upset her so? Eileen was right. Anyone as beautiful as Elsbeth must have loads of admirers. Probably half the village lads drooled over her. Suddenly Alice recalled the look in Gus Rielke's piggy eyes, and the shiver of revulsion it caused her. She imagined similar looks directed at her friend, and felt herself tighten with disgust, and anger.

She pushed back her chair and stood abruptly, struggling hard not to let her inner turmoil show. 'I can't be doing with all that daft carry-on. I'd better go up and get out of these glad rags then, before I drive half the men folk of Howbeck mad with passion!'

6

The Reverend Michael Beardsley's voice dropped from the piercing half-chant he used for delivering prayers to the deep, plum-rich, syrupy tone he employed for less elevated matters. 'So, children, remember. God is on our side, and as long as we obey His commandments He will not fail us. The army of Pharaoh against the Children of Israel could not prevail; nor the Philistines against Samson; nor the giant Goliath against David. But remember also — ' the long forefinger was raised, hung like a sword over his sniffling, coughing and shuffling little audience — 'God sees everything you do, hears everything you say, the smallest whisper. He knows every thought you have. So be good. And I'll see you all in Sunday school. No shirkers, mind. I'll be checking the attendance. Goodbye, children.'

' 'Bye, sir!' they chorused, with loud relief, and the din rose that marked the end of Friday-morning assembly, until Miss Laverton's voice rose to quell it, and the piano jangled out a march to speed the departure of the senior classes from the hall, on their way up the hill to the school proper.

Alice pondered the vicar's words as she helped to drag out the partitions which divided the room into the two classrooms for the infants, then heaved the low two-seater desks into place. *All* the commandments? What about 'Thou shalt not kill'? She'd never been to Sunday school, not even the chapel lot, but that was one she could remember. And they'd all just been praying that we would kill more Jerries than they could kill of ours, so that we'd win the war. And the Jerries were no doubt saying their prayers, too, for it to be the other way round.

Seemed like God was paying more attention to them than us for the moment. True, Hitler hadn't invaded, like everyone had feared, but he was doing his best to bomb us all out of our homes first instead. They'd even bombed that big church in London, but the vicar had made out that it was a miracle that it hadn't been flattened. The cathedral at Coventry hadn't been so lucky, though, and there'd been raids on Liverpool and down south at Bristol. And now the Eyeties had joined in, so we had to fight them as well, abroad. At least that Yank Roosevelt had got himself elected again, but what's the point of being friendly to us if you're just going to sit back and watch us getting hammered?

The rest of the morning sped by as usual for Alice, as she and the two local helpers prepared the midday meal. 'Should be a fish day!' Annie Hogan, the older of the two village helpers said, as she competently set about skinning the first of the three rabbits destined for the pot, while Alice and Jess Corbett peeled the heap of vegetables for the stew.

Jess's elbow dug surreptitiously into Alice's arm. 'Now then, Annie. We're not all left-footers, ye know.'

'Don't you start, Jess Corbett! Bloomin' chapel folk! Don't forget, we were the *first* Christians. You heathen lot!' She was turning the fur, peeling it like a glove from the gleaming pink flesh.

'That's me!' Alice cut in cheerfully. 'That's *my* religion. Heathen! Here, let me have a go with one of them — what is it you call 'em? Conies, is it? My da can skin them fast as anything!'

The refugees from Lister Road were almost as familiar as their village counterparts with the taste of rabbit meat, for even in Margrove it had long been a cheap alternative to other animal flesh. There was very little left when the meal had been finished. Both Edith Bowen, the qualified infants' teacher, and

Elsbeth democratically pitched in with the washing up and the clearing away of tables and benches to prepare the room for the usual Friday lunch-time staff meeting. 'We'll have to be quick,' Miss Laverton told them, with a wary eye on the weather. The early December day was mild enough temperature wise, but gloomy, with low, scudding clouds, threatening rain on the wind. 'It's all right,' she said to Annie and Jess. 'You two can cut along. There's not a lot to get through and nothing to bother you with. Thanks again, ladies.'

Alice was wondering whether she should leave, too, but Miss Laverton discreetly signalled for her to stay. The reason for her discretion became apparent as soon as the two helpers had departed. 'It's rather a delicate matter,' she said to the handful who had remained. 'It's about the James Gang.' The humorous reference to the three brothers, Alfred, 11, Norman, 9, and Frank, aged 6, rarely failed to draw a chuckle or at least a smile, but the look on their headmistress's face did not warrant a light hearted response. She nodded at Edith Bowen. 'Miss Bowen tells me Frank's been behaving badly. Far worse than usual, with tears and temper-tantrums at the slightest excuse. And the eldest, Alfred, is downright rude and surly these days. Not that he's ever been very talkative, but it's far worse. I had to use the stick on him for his rudeness yesterday. I tried to get him to talk afterwards, but he just clammed up. I'm worried. I know we were glad to keep them together, and we thought we were very lucky to find someone to take all three, but now I'm not so sure.

'They were never exactly like new pins even at home, but they're looking scruffier than ever these days. Elsbeth was saying young Frank is positively whiffy, isn't that right?' Elsbeth pinked as she nodded her confirmation of this observation. 'High Top Farm is about the remotest billet of all. And it's by no means luxurious. But that's no matter as long as our children are being well looked after. A little hardship's no bad thing for forming character.'

Aye, that's easy to say when you're living up at t' Big 'Ouse! Alice thought, but without any real malice. Now Miss Laverton was looking directly at her.

'Alice, you've been there, haven't you?'

'Yes, miss. Just the once and that was a while ago. It's a fair hike all right. No wonder they call it High Top! That's just what it is. Two mile out on the moor. It's a mile from the Whitby road, along a cart track. I only met *Missus* Symmonds. *Mister* was out and about somewhere, but it's a rough old place as far as I can tell. Not that I had much of a chance to have a look round. She wasn't what you'd call a friendly soul. But I *did* get a look at where the lads are sleeping. Big bare place, but not bad. Over this back kitchen place. Two of their own kids sleep in there an' all, but there's room enough. Mrs Symmonds said it was warm as toast in the winter when the fire was on downstairs. There's a chimney-breast runs up through the bedroom. Let's hope she's right. The walls were all rough stone, like some blinkin' old castle or summat.' She paused. 'You want me to go and tek another look, miss?'

'Would you, Alice? I'd really appreciate it. I'd go myself, but I don't want to raise any suspicions, especially if there's nothing wrong out there. If you're not sure about anything, anything at all, I'll be out there like a shot. And we'll have the James boys out of there, too! There's something not right, I can feel it. It'll be sheep only up that high, I guess. They don't make that much of a living, though I think they're doing better with the war. And the James lads are worth thirty-one-and-six a week to them. It's nearly another wage coming in. See what you think, Alice. But we can't wait. Could you make it this weekend?'

She turned towards Elsbeth. 'Maybe you could go with her, my dear? Two pairs of eyes are better than one. The two of you out walking — you could just be passing. Thought you'd call in on the off chance. See how the lads are getting on, et cetera? Unless you can come up with something better. Checking on whether they're attending church or chapel, something like that? Can you manage tomorrow?'

She was looking at Elsbeth, her strongly marked eyebrows raised. Again, Elsbeth coloured, more noticeably, and there was just the slightest hesitation, and a faint hint of it in the tone when Elsbeth answered. 'Yes, that'll be fine.'

Alice picked up on it, and was a little piqued, as well as by the fact that Miss Laverton hadn't even bothered to ask Alice if she could manage it. It niggled, all the way through the afternoon, as the last lessons of the week dragged on. It was advanced dusk by the time they finished, and they swiftly tidied away in the deep gloom before going out into the cold afternoon.

'I'll meet you by the bridge. Half ten all right?' Alice said, while Algy fidgeted and sniffed at her side. Elsbeth nodded and Alice recalled her hesitancy. 'It is all right, isn't it? You haven't got anything on tomorrer?'

'No, no. Not really. It's just — Luke Denby's coming home tomorrow. A weekend leave. Mr and Mrs Denby want me to meet him.'

'Who's he when he's at home?' Alice's question came out a little more brusquely than she had intended. Or at least she thought it had.

'He's their son. He's in the Air Force. Stationed somewhere in the East Riding.'

'Ooh! A Brylcreem Boy, eh?' Alice said mockingly. 'Well, don't fret, love. You'll get your chance to meet the hero. I'm not planning to spend the weekend up at High Top! Unless they kidnap us and sell us off to the white slavers.' She could not help the note of disappointment which crept in. 'But look! If it's that much of a bother, forget it. I can go up there on my own. Just send a posse if I don't turn up on Monday.'

'No, no!' Elsbeth protested quickly. 'Not at all! Of course I'll come. If it's not raining, it'll be good. I love walking, you know I do! And *I* want to get to the bottom of this business, too. I am a teacher, after all. See you in the morning. Half ten!' Impetuously she leaned forward, and gave a quick, clumsy kiss to Alice's cheek, followed by a nervous little giggle as she turned and hurried off into the twilight.

'She's your girlfriend!' Algy cackled with hoarse laughter as he ran off ahead.

★ ★ ★

The yard was a puddled mess. The windowless openings of the long, low barn and the other outbuildings were boarded up with odd bits of old crates nailed across, with great dark gaps between them. The gate leaned lopsidedly and seemed to be propped permanently in its half-opened position. A frenetic, shrill barking made Alice and Elsbeth draw back in dismay as a furious black and white collie came hurtling through the dirt towards them, to be pulled up in snarling impotence by the long length of chain stretched to its fullest.

'Keep clear of 'im, Miss, or he'll have yer.'

Norman had appeared round the corner of the barn, and trailing behind him was young Frankie. Behind them came a small knot of the Symmonds children, who stared with curiosity at this alien intrusion. Even Alice was surprised at the dirty, unkempt appearance of all of the youngsters. Almost every inch of exposed skin — and there was far too much of it considering the coldness of the morning — was black, or close to it. Lips and eyes stood out palely from the grime, and noses glistened slimily.

Elsbeth had instinctively slipped behind Alice at the dog's vicious charge. She stared at the group in silent dismay. Alice checked that they were out of the snarling dog's reach and edged in through the gate. She addressed the children heartily. 'Just thought we'd pop in. We've been out for a walk. Come to see how you're getting on, Norman. And Frankie. Where's your Alfred?'

'Out,' Norman answered. His eyes narrowed, his face was closed and suspicious.

'He's helpin' me dad,' the oldest of the Symmonds girls offered. Her ragged, bare head jerked vaguely backwards.

'Is your mam in?' Alice gave her a beaming smile, which was not returned. The girl turned and ran to the doorway of the house. She called out, and eventually Mrs Symmonds appeared. Her dress and cleanliness were marginally superior to that of the children. She was wearing what looked like a man's shirt, and tied over an ankle-length black skirt was a piece of sacking, which served as pinafore. The tight bulge thrusting out both sacking and clothing advertised her state of advanced pregnancy. Alice did some rapid calculations. Four of the Symmonds's offspring were at the village school, and at least one that she knew of had already left school and worked with his father on the farm. There was a grubby toddler of two or three among the group of spectators.

'How do, Mrs Symmonds. Can we come in? We were just passing this way. We thought we'd pop in and see how the lads are getting on.'

'Why? Nowt wrong, is there? Shurrup, ye gormless lump!' This last remark was bellowed at the dog, whose fearsome snarls turned to a low growl, as it scuttled backwards, close to the stone wall and the stout post which held the chain.

'No, nothing wrong.' Alice maintained her cheerful tone. Elsbeth still hung back, a pace behind her as they advanced towards the back door of the farmhouse. 'Are you managing all right?' She nodded at the crowd of youngsters. 'Bet you've got your work cut out with all this lot. And another on the way.'

'We get by. Have to, I reckon. They're not in any bother, are they?' Mrs Symmonds shot a suspicious glance at the two James boys. 'Not been saying owt?'

About what? Alice wondered. She shook her head. 'No. But they've been playing up a bit lately. This is Miss Hobbs. She's Frankie's teacher. We just — '

'I know fine who she is! Don't worry, I'll have a word with me husband, Bob. He'll soon sort them. Tek his strap to them — '

'No, there's no need . . . ' Elsbeth spoke involuntarily, and blushed a deep red at her outburst.

'Look, you've got to teach 'em who's boss. You're nobbut a bairn yersel' by the look of yer.'

'Can we come in a minute, missus?' Again Alice nodded, more significantly, at the standing group of children.

'It's not convenient.' She turned back to the children and bawled, 'Clear off, you lot! Don't stand gawping. Away with yer!' They turned and ran off at once, disappearing round the corner of the building again. 'Now! Say what you've got to say and let me get on. We can't all take time to go strolling of a Saturday!'

Twin red patches stood out on Elsbeth's cheeks, and she blinked in dumb consternation at the woman's fierce rudeness. Alice was not so overcome.

'The lads don't seem very happy at school. Frankie's been throwing some right tantrums, and we've had tears.'

'You know what some of these vaccies are like. Spoilt rotten, they are. Don't seem to appreciate how lucky they are, coming out here — '

'And he's not very clean, either!' Alice said

bluntly. 'He smells! Doesn't look as if he's had a good wash in ages! When do they get baths?'

'You've got a bloody cheek, haven't you? Who the hell you think you are, you jumped-up townie? I'll be down to that school meself to see your boss. Saturday nights is bath night, for the lot of them! Hot water, the lot. Kids have to get mucky. A bit o' muck never hurt nobody! And what would the pair of you know about it? It's a good job our Bob isn't here, or he might have taken his belt to you two and all, yer cheeky baggages!'

Elsbeth had fallen back another pace, but Alice stood her ground against the angry woman. 'Just make sure they're clean when they come to school on Monday. They've got a clean change of clothes. If you've any problems just let the school know.' She turned to go. Ahead of her, Elsbeth almost ran towards the safety of the leaning gate, but Alice turned back towards the thick, glowering figure. 'And don't take it out on the kids, Mrs Symmonds. If you can't manage to look after them properly, we'll have to find somewhere else for them.'

There was no further response as they picked their way through the muddy expanse that led back onto the track.

'It looks pretty grim,' Elsbeth said tentatively. She glanced back at the grey buildings. The roofs of the outbuildings were little better than ruins, and there were slates missing from the main house.

Alice thought her friend had made a poor show of supporting her, but when she saw the anxious look on Elsbeth's face she softened. This privileged rich girl was out of her depth up here with this scruffy lot. She belonged to a different world: the world of the Big House, and those posh kids from that toffs' school that was quartered there. She felt a wave of sympathy for the slim figure trudging beside her, and for the effort she was making to take in this strange environment and to make a go of it. She smiled reassuringly and hooked her arm firmly in that of her companion. 'Aye. I'll try and get Alfie and Norman on their own, have a talk to them. You never know, they might open up a bit with me. It's like ould Lavvy says — I'm not a teacher, am I? Not one of you brainy lot!'

Elsbeth had smiled guiltily at the disrespectful nickname used by generations of pupils at Lister Road, and she responded warmly to Alice's tight grip and her comforting strength. 'You're doing just as good a job. Better, probably! The children love you. Miss Laverton's right. She's always saying it. We couldn't manage without you.'

Her cheeks were pink, and not just from the cold wind. Alice could see the ingenuous look of friendship and admiration in those wonderful blue eyes, and she felt an intense quaver of pleasure stir her inside. She squeezed the gloved hand harder, held it more firmly in her grasp. 'Come on. We'll cut down through Barker's field and down along the beck side. Get you back home in time for you to tart yourself up for your RAF boy!' She tried to inject the right heartiness into her teasing remark, and nobly ignored the tiny niggle of jealousy the thought gave her.

* * *

Alice felt both a measure of pride and shame at her skill as a sleuth, particularly as her own sister, Doreen, proved to be an important if innocent source of information concerning the James brothers. 'Alfie's keen on us,' Doreen confided, with a smirk that was altogether too worldly and aware of her charm for a girl not yet eleven. 'He treats me at Mrs Floyd's.' Mrs Floyd ran the village shop.

'Where does he get his pocket money from?'

'It's not pocket-money, it's wages!' Doreen

answered knowingly. 'That miserable old Symmonds pays him for helping out. He works on the farm, and goes off looking for the sheep. And he helps Gus out an' all.'

Gus! Alice didn't like the familiar way her sister referred to the Big Swede, nor did she approve of her burgeoning friendship with him, but at the moment she was more concerned with learning what she could of the situation up at High Top. She had already discovered that living conditions were hard: no piped water to the house, a pump in the yard, no gas or electricity, only the old kitchen range and oil lamps and candles. The lavatory was also outside, no more than a bucket beneath the wooden seat, which had to be emptied on the moor beyond the dry-stone walls every day. But these circumstances were by no means unique in Howbeck; indeed, there were houses in towns like Margrove (the James's residence being one) where facilities were little better. But it was still possible to keep reasonably clean, Alice knew; at least cleaner than the state the three James lads were in. She was certain that the declared Saturday 'bath night' was more a case of 'once in a blue moon', if then.

'Is Mr Symmonds all right with them?' Alice kept to her casual tone. 'Has Alfie or the others ever said owt?'

'Like what?' Doreen's elfin face took on a sharper, more curious expression.

'Yer know! Like — he doesn't knock them about, does he?'

'Naw, I don't think so. No more than usual. He gave Norman a clout, I think. Norm wanted to go with him and Alfie on to moor. Symmonds told him if he followed them he'd give him a good thrashing. But he belts his own kids far worse. You ask 'em!' Then Doreen's dainty features were set in a scowl. 'Hey! Don't you go saying owt to Alfie, our Al! Don't mek out I've been blabbing out of turn. He wouldn't like it.'

'Oh aye! Stop yer getting yer penny dabs and your treats, would it? Don't fret yourself. Listen!' She shot out an arm and seized Doreen's collar as she was about to make her escape. 'Don't you go taking treats from anybody, mind! And don't you be doing owt bad with that Alfie James — or anyone else, all right?'

'I don't know what you're on about!' Doreen answered indignantly, but her brown eyes did not quite meet Alice's gaze head on, and she squirmed away with a clear sense of relief.

Oh God! Summat else to maybe start worrying about, Alice thought grumpily. She thought back to her own eleventh birthday.

Eight long years ago. She'd be nineteen in just over a week's time. Had kids really changed all that much? Boys hadn't been buying treats for her, that was for sure. She'd have knocked them flat on their backs if they'd suggested anything of the sort. She did that anyway, just for fun. She'd enjoyed their company, but not for sparking or owt daft like that. She liked the games and the mischief they got up to: nicky-nicky-nine-doors and all the rest. It was the daft lasses she couldn't stand, with their crimped hair and clean socks and best frocks, and their whispering secrets, and their sniggering and simpering. Lasses like — Elsbeth Hobbs! she acknowledged, feeling a wry grin tugging at the corners of her mouth at the sudden thought.

She recalled a much more recent, vivid scene, of that morning, and the lovely face pink with embarrassment, the eyes wide with alarm; how Elsbeth had hovered at her elbow, nervous and totally out of her depth in those surroundings and with that glowering, bulging figure in the sackcloth pinny. Poor Elsbeth! And Alice felt once again that warm inner feeling of tenderness and protectiveness, remembered the linking of the arms, and that tight grip of her hand so trustingly returned.

She'd be getting out her posh frock tonight

all right, and her silk stockings and all her pretty frillies; combing and crimping that glorious golden hair, smelling divine for those toffs, and for that swanky young airman, with all his chat and his charm. Alice's jaw set, and her fists clenched as she thought what she'd like to do to the smarmy bugger and all like him. He'd better not try on his dirty tricks with her Elsbeth or he'd rue the day!

★ ★ ★

Alice would have been dismayed to know the reaction Luke Denby produced in Elsbeth's mind, and his effect on her senses during that first afternoon and evening up at Howe Manor. Of course, Elsbeth Hobbs was not entirely unaware of her looks; she had spent, for her, a considerable time making the most of them, in anticipation of the meeting. But shy by nature, and in the still social backwaters of Margrove, she was far from confident in, or even aware of, the power of her attractiveness. She had been well sheltered. She had seen only the fairly decorous beginnings of her charm, in a few, hasty, nervously snatched lip kisses at the tennis dances, and even fewer more daring neck-nuzzlings, from which she had shied away, more startled than shocked, for she was not worldly enough for real awareness.

Luke Denby was four years older than she was, but a whole hectic world wiser. He had been about to start his third year at Durham — he had no inclination or ambition for academia and had resisted his father's attempts to place him at Oxford or Cambridge — when war broke out. He had volunteered at once for the RAF. Commissioned and embarked on a fighter pilot training-course as the battle over Britain's summer skies had begun, he had failed to make the grade, but had managed to get himself transferred to bomber training, where he was presently learning to fly the twin-engined Stirling, the first of the RAF's heavy bombers, at an aerodrome in East Yorkshire.

Bitterly disappointed at his failure to join one of the fighter squadrons, who were in the process of making history in what would be seen by many as Britain's first victory, he nevertheless eagerly reaped the reward of the 'trailing clouds of glory' that came from the air force uniform and, in particular, the glamour of the wings over the left breast pocket.

He had grown used to adulation even in the last few short months, and to easy conquests. What he had not become used to, certainly not in the eventful year since September '39, was such unawareness of her own stunning looks in a girl like Elsbeth Hobbs, or such ingenuousness. She was shy — he preferred to see it as totally lacking in any 'side' — and coloured almost every time she spoke. But done so prettily, he thought, that it was simply another on the list of her exquisite charms.

He had paid only one fleeting visit home, back in the summer. No time, he had told his parents, in letters and infrequent telephone calls. They had journeyed down to meet him in York one weekend, and he had spent an evening dining with them in their hotel, feeling guilty for his duplicity. Now that he was well on in his flying training, there were regular off-duty spells when he could easily travel the sixty miles or so north-eastward to Howbeck. He had been very lax in filial duties, he chided himself, as he eased back her chair to allow Elsbeth to rise from the table, and managed to catch a whiff of her fragrance from her shining hair when he leaned over her. Things would be very different from now on, he promised himself.

7

Gus Rielke emerged from the side door of the Oddfellows as Alice was passing on Sunday morning. He was carrying a wooden crate of empties and, despite the December damp chill, his arms were bare, with shirt-sleeves rolled well above the elbows. The muscles bulged, and his forearms were liberally covered in fine, pale sandy curls. 'Hello there, miss. You been to de church like a good gal, hey? I hope you say one prayer for me, ya?' His laugh boomed, his breath a steamy cloud.

'You won't catch me inside there!' She jerked her head back up the hill, towards the dark, squat tower of the Anglican church of St John's. 'Nor t'other place neither!' This time she nodded down the hill, over the bridge, in the direction of the humbler building of the Methodist chapel, out of sight round the bend in the lane. She was about to hurry on, feeling uncomfortable with the notion that her disparaging remark about religion might somehow make him feel they shared some common ground. But then she remembered her chat with Doreen, and she stopped, waited as he dropped the crate on top of the others. There was a shivering little rattle from the dark bottles. 'As a matter of fact, I was just looking to see if the James lads had come down to the village. See if they'd be going to Sunday School.'

His smile broadened, his pale eyes moved mockingly over her wrapped up form. 'Isn't there something in English about you practise what you preach?'

'Your English is bloomin' good for a foreigner.'

'I speak it all the time back home. In summer we get many English visitors. I learn as a kid.'

'Oh aye? Where was that then?'

Again, the lips were pulled back over his even teeth in a sneering grin. 'You know Norway well, then?'

She shook her head lightly. 'I've never been further than the end of Margrove pier. This is the back of beyond to me. You haven't seen the James lads then? You know Alfie James, don't you?'

His sandy lashes flickered as his eyes narrowed. The sneer seemed moulded permanently to his features. 'What you want him for? He's been a naughty boy, has he, miss?' The last word was loaded heavily with sarcasm. There was a kind of veiled threat almost in the hissing sibilance of the final sound.

Again she shook her head, but said nothing in further explanation. He gave another guttural laugh. It jarred her nerves. 'I know. Bob Symmonds was in the bar last night. He said you been up his place, snooping, ya? You and that girlfriend of yours — the pretty blonde one.'

Alice could feel her face grow hot and she was angry with herself. 'We were just checking up on them. It's part of our job! We have — '

'You lucky Bob was out when you go snooping. You don't get on the bad side of *him*, girl. Take my advice. And you don't worry — them boys are fine up there.'

She tried to match the bold directness of his stare, and hoped the colour had faded a little from her face. Was he warning her off? And why? What on earth did it have to do with him?

'You want to learn from your little sister. Doreen's a good kid. She knows how to be friendly!'

His words stung Alice. She felt the anger flare hotly, so that she had a sudden urge to strike out at him. There was something sinisterly unpleasant about his words, and the tone that lay behind them. 'Good God! A little girl of ten! A bit young for you, I'd have thought!'

'You right there, Alice. I'm more interested in the big sister. When you gonna come for that drink with me? We can be real good friends, ya?'

He reached out and caught hold of her arm in the thick winter coat Elsbeth had given her, and she snatched away from him. 'No thanks! I've got better — '

'You should learn from that pretty little Goldilocks friend of yours. She might look like a fine little lady but she knows how to enjoy, ya? She was in the pub here last night with that young pilot feller up at the Big House. And they were in the hop together over at the hall. I bet she knows a thing or two she don't learn in school! Yessir! She don't need no hot-water bottle in the bed last night, I bet you!'

'You need plenty of soap and water, you do!'

'Oh ya? What that for, then?'

'To wash your mucky mouth out!'

His laugh followed her as she moved off. 'Sound like you maybe jealous, ya? Why you don't tell her to ask her friend to find nice airman for *you*, too? I bet you look just as good as her if you get out of them old trousers. Like that Jane girl in the paper!'

She forced herself not to look round as she strode off, following the incline down to the humped bridge over the beck. The water was rushing, loud and whitening in places as it swept over the larger stones. When they had first arrived the stream had been a lot narrower, scarcely knee-high, with pock-marked, muddy margins on either side. The volume of water had increased greatly with the recent wet weather. It sounded angry, anxious to be off and on its way, to escape. Like me! Alice thought.

Why had the Big Swede's words riled her so much? Why should she feel a sudden rush of hot temper and hurt at his words about Elsbeth? So she'd been in the pub last night? And the village dance, with this Air Force feller. So what? Women went to pubs on a Saturday, nothing wrong with that. Her mam used to go to the Black Horse of a Saturday, sometimes, with her dad — even if she *did* use to come home on her own and leave him to his guzzling! If that's what Elsbeth wanted to do then good luck to her.

Bit of fast work, though, the flighty little madam! She hadn't even met this Luke Denby lad yesterday morning — and she'd been out drinking and dancing with him by nightfall. Mind you, it was going on all the time these days. Eileen was always on about those land girls, the way they carried on. They went right into the spit and sawdust of the public bar, wearing their breeches and all, puffing their fags and supping ale, and playing darts with the locals. And that tart of a landlady, Vera Rhodes, never turned a hair, welcomed them with open arms.

And they weren't the only ones she welcomed with open arms. Alice's thoughts centred on Gus Rielke once more. The evil-minded bugger! The very idea of him entertaining such smutty conjectures about Elsbeth Hobbs made Alice's blood boil anew. But if Elsbeth had been that keen on going to the hop and being ogled by these clodhopping farmers, she could have asked *her*, couldn't she? Alice would have gone with her, just to look after her and make sure she was all right, even if it was all just a load of nonsense, and the last thing she would want would be a great sweaty farmhand breathing his beer breath all over her.

She realized that the Big Swede's disclosure had put her in a thoroughly bad mood, and she was even angrier with herself that it should have done so. She tried to reason herself out of it. What's it got to do with you what Elsbeth Hobbs gets up to? Of course fellers are going to want to take her out, a lovely-looking girl like that. Best around here for miles. Mebbes Gus Rielke was right. Mebbes you *are* jealous. But not the way he meant, she admitted, and shied away from the thought. She headed on up the slight incline towards Miss Ramsay's house, one of the last in the village, and made her way up the gravel path, the garden still neat even in its winter deadness. The grass was short, the edges of the black flower-beds sharply outlined, the rose bushes pruned to low stumps. She went through the side gate around to the rear door. She was surprised to see Miss Ramsay herself open the door that led through a small cloakroom to the spacious kitchen.

'I haven't been to church this morning,' the spinster explained, ushering her inside, with the caution to 'slip your boots off in here'. Alice complied, padding in her thick grey socks and open winter coat in the wake of the slim, immaculately groomed figure. 'I've got a bit of a chill. I was awake with a cough half the night. Doreen's been pampering me, haven't you, dear?'

Doreen appeared, grinning, and Alice was struck at her sister's dainty prettiness. She was wearing a heather jumper and grey pleated skirt — her 'Sunday best', and long grey stockings slightly bagged at the knees. On her feet was a pair of blue velvet slippers — a luxury item which had certainly not come from Maudsley Street.

'Have you been to the service?' Miss Ramsay asked, then took in the bulky dungaree trousers beneath Alice's smart coat. 'Oh, no. I suppose . . . are you chapel?'

'I don't go reg'lar,' Alice answered diplomatically. She knew Doreen had claimed nonconformity as an excuse for avoiding attendance at St John's, and had been disgruntled when Miss Ramsay had made her go to the Methodist Sunday School. 'You behaving yourself?' Alice asked Doreen, in order to divert the conversation away from matters spiritual.

'Of course she is. She's a treasure, aren't you?' Elizabeth Ramsay beamed at her and Alice felt relief, tinged with wry amusement at the youngster's ability to pull wool over older eyes. 'She's so good about the house. Tidies up around the place. She's just been laying the table for lunch. Mrs Addis leaves us something for Sundays, and Doreen takes care of everything for us.' There was a small but definite pause before she continued. 'Would you care to join us?' She gestured at the neatly laid places for two at the long wooden kitchen table. The pause and the tone of the invitation subtly but clearly indicated that it was not meant to be accepted, and Alice declined.

'No, I won't stop, Miss Ramsay, but it's

130

very kind of you to offer. They'll expect me up at Beck Side. We don't have Sunday dinner till two or after. Just thought I'd pop in as I was passing. Mek sure our Doreen is behaving herself still.' The delicate face assumed such a modestly virtuous, downcast pose that Alice felt an urge to burst into raucous laughter as Elizabeth Ramsay continued to wax eloquent in her young lodger's praise. 'You can have a walk up to Beck Side after dinner if you like. See our Algy.'

'I see him every day at school,' Doreen said quickly. She glanced across at Miss Ramsay, while Alice thought, You might catch sight of him of a dinner-time, you little minx, but you never exchange two words with him.

The spinster came to Doreen's rescue. She gave a glance through the leaded window, marred by the thick swathes of tape, which had been stuck there even before war had been declared, though through the length of the dale no one had heard the throb of enemy planes, and the gunfire from the coastal anti-aircraft defences was no more than the faintest rumble. 'It's a nasty damp day, don't you think? We were going to practise our embroidery after lunch. She's got a neat hand with a needle and it's very good for her. And it gets dark so quickly this time of the year, doesn't it?'

'Aye, right-oh.' Alice gave in with a good grace. 'But stop and have a chat with him tomorrer dinner time,' she told Doreen. 'Don't go racing off with your mates. He's only a little bairn, you know. He misses you. And Mam and Dad and Ethel and George.'

'Well, three more weeks and it will be Christmas,' Miss Ramsay said brightly. 'What's happening? Will you be going home or . . . what?' Her voice tapered off uncertainly. 'You haven't seen your parents, have you? I mean, they haven't been through . . . '

'No, they haven't. It's not easy. Dad works shifts, and Mam's got our Ethel to see to.' But that wasn't the reason, and if Miss Ramsay thought about it she might well figure it out. Hardly any of the kids had seen their folks in the last three months. Margrove might be only an hour and a half away by train, but fares were expensive. They had increased and at the same time the cheap day excursion fares had been abolished. It was rumoured that free rail warrants were supposed to be available, one every six weeks, but no one from Margrove had so far taken advantage of this, or else they had failed to deal with the bureaucracy involved in obtaining them.

There were still cheap fares in operation for Sundays, but scarcely any trains on the new timetables to make use of them. The whole policy concerning rail travel seemed to be to discourage the general public from travelling by train, and to free the network for essential goods and troop movements.

'I've told Doreen to let your parents know that if there's any emergency they can contact me by telephone.' Miss Ramsay sounded faintly defensive. The telephone was another rich folk's toy. There was probably no private house within a mile of Maudsley Street which would have such a luxury. Her folks would doubtless be terrified of using the public telephone kiosk round the corner in Lister Road, and who could blame them?

Even letter-writing was something foreign to her mam and dad. Alice had received only two, both from her mam, in the months they had been away, and both hardly more than four or five pencilled lines, no doubt laboured over long enough, with much rubbing out and tongue poking through her lips. Miss Laverton insisted that the children, all except the very youngest, like Algy, wrote a letter home every week. Although they were, in theory at least, encouraged to add to the copperplate sample on the blackboard they had to copy, very few did so, content with or resigned to letting the phrases *we are all well* and *Yours lovingly* express their thoughts.

Little had been said so far about the coming holiday, but Alice reckoned the silence on the subject was eloquent enough, and only those who could afford to pay for their offspring to travel back to Margrove would be reunited with them. She felt guilty at the thought that being away from home for Christmas did not seem so terrible to her. The prospect of parents and children being separated didn't seem to bother Miss Ramsay either.

'Well, never mind. We'll have a jolly time if you do have to stay here, Doreen.' From the grateful smile the little minx flashed at her, it obviously didn't worry Doreen. It was also obvious that the warmth of this promise did not include Alice in its radiance. Well, good luck to her, Alice decided. Doreen had done well to get her pretty, slippered feet under this affluent table. And Alice remembered the main if devious reason for her visit.

'Miss Ramsay,' she said diffidently, 'is Gus Rielke still working for you?'

'Well, there's not much to do in the garden through the winter. There's no grass to cut and he's tidied up the beds and the shrubbery. He brings logs, still, but that's about all. Why?'

Alice strove to make her tone casual. 'Oh, I just met him outside the pub. I was wondering. What do you make of him? Is he all right?' She was aware of Doreen's sudden attention, the fixity of her stare.

'What do you mean?' Elizabeth Ramsay was looking at her with sharpened curiosity.

'I was just wondering how he manages. He was saying he knew one of our lads — Alfie James. Him and his brothers are up at High Top. I think Gus goes up there sometimes.' She sensed Doreen's tension now.

Miss Ramsay's handsome features betrayed a small grimace of distaste. 'Oh yes. The Symmonds tribe. Not an ideal place to have those boys of yours staying, I'd have thought.'

Alice seized her opportunity. 'That's what I was thinking. They seem a bit rough up there. The James lads are looking scruffy. They seem to be running wild. And black as chimney-sweeps even when they come to school.'

Miss Ramsay gave a refined but eloquent little sniff. 'I'm not surprised. They let their own tribe run wild. Thank goodness they're well out of the village. Their father's not much better. Looks like he's half-Romany to me. From what I hear he spends far too much of his time in the Oddfellows. I don't know where he gets the money from. That ramshackle place of his can't bring in much of a living. I don't know why Mr Denby hasn't had him out of there long ago. Give it to a decent tenant who might make something of it.'

'See? What did I tell you?' Alice turned towards her sister with something of triumph in her tone. Colour flooded Doreen's face, and she looked deeply embarrassed.

Miss Ramsay noticed the exchange and again her face sharpened with curiosity. 'Why? What on earth has it got to do with Doreen?'

'Oh, it's just that she's been knocking about with Alfie James. Getting pally with him. Been treating you at Mrs Floyd's, hasn't he?'

Doreen flashed her a wounded glance. She twisted in mortification. 'No, I haven't!' she snapped. 'Just the once,' she muttered, through closed teeth, her head hanging.

'You don't have anything to do with any of that lot!' Miss Ramsay said, her neat form bristling. 'You keep away from them, you hear?'

Doreen's chin was practically on her chest, as she murmured abjectly, 'Yes, miss.'

'I just wondered,' Alice pursued, again attempting to make her tone casual, 'with Gus working up there sometimes. He was saying, Mr Symmonds has Alfie out in all weathers, helping an' all.'

But Elizabeth Ramsay was quick to spring to Gus Rielke's defence. 'Gus is too soft hearted sometimes. He'll give anybody a hand. I'm sure he won't get much back for his pains. But then some people do tend to put on him. To take advantage of his good nature. I think he's just so grateful to have found himself a safe haven, after all he's had to endure, the poor man. He's lucky to be alive. He's quite a hero, you know. And always so cheerful for a man who's lost everything. His home, his family, his friends.'

Aye, Alice thought sceptically. He certainly tells a good tale, any road. And he knows how to charm the ladies, from that blowzy landlady at the pub to this elegant, posh spinster — not to mention a sneaky little lass like our Doreen. Another one who could tell a good tale. She's certainly got herself well in here, that's for sure. Alice glanced round at the comfort of her surroundings, as she said her goodbyes and pulled on her boots in the cold porch, ready for the long climb up through the commencing misty drizzle, out to Beck Side.

Alice had no intention of letting the matter of the James lads rest. From the reception she and Elsbeth had received on their trip to

High Top, she was more and more certain that the Margrove boys should be removed from there. She'd try to get them together on the morrow, for one more chat, to see if she could learn anything fresh to add to her feeling of unease, but she was determined to make it known to Miss Laverton.

And Gus Rielke seemed somehow to be tied in with this feeling of hers. It was odd that their visit to the moor top farm should have aroused such concern that it led to talk in the bar of the Oddfellows. The Big Swede had practically warned her off, with his veiled threats about Bob Symmonds's temper. Something definitely fishy about the whole business, and she wasn't prepared to let it lie. Especially not after those things he had said about Elsbeth. Her fingers curled inside her woollen gloves as her anger was rekindled. How dare he talk of her friend like that? She tried hard as she toiled up the long hill through the increasing gloom and mist not to feel oddly betrayed by Elsbeth's actions of the previous evening, and her deep sense of hurt by her exclusion from them.

★ ★ ★

'Did you meet your RAF feller then?' Elsbeth coloured up at Alice's question, delivered in a light-hearted, teasing manner. 'What's he like?'

'He's very nice. He took me out for a spin in his car yesterday. We went into Whitby, but the weather was awful. We spent most of the afternoon drinking tea in the hotel up on the West Cliff. Couldn't see a thing for the fog.'

It was Monday morning, and they were setting out the classrooms while the children huddled about the steps outside the door, like sheep seeking the shelter of a wall. 'Is he nice? Good-looking, is he?'

Elsbeth's glance flickered away from Alice's smiling face, looked towards the wall clock. 'I wonder if we could let them in yet? It's so cold out there. He's all right, I suppose. I don't really know him.'

'What about Saturday? What did you get up to?'

Again the swift glance at her, which showed her awareness of the provocative phrase. Elsbeth's pinkness deepened. 'We popped down to the village — for a drink.'

'And a dance!'

'Oh — er, yes. We looked in here, the hop. Who told you?'

'Lots of little birds! Don't forget, kidder! You can't do owt round here without somebody knowing all about it. You've got to be careful if you don't want to get found out!'

Elsbeth gave her an uncertain, half-apologetic look. 'We didn't stay long. I think he just wanted some company. To get out of the house for a bit.'

'A bit of what?' Alice laughed coarsely, and Elsbeth continued to blush.

'I told you, we'd only just met. I thought — it's a dangerous job, you know, flying.'

'So long as you keep both your feet on the ground, eh?' She stared challengingly at the discomfited girl and winked salaciously. 'Are you seeing him again?'

Elsbeth shrugged, turned self-consciously away from the steady gaze. 'I dunno. I expect he'll be back home again some time.'

'He will now, lass, I'll bet money on it!' Elsbeth looked relieved as Edith Bowen came in and gestured for the children to follow her.

'Good weekend?' Edith asked, unpinning her limp, wide-brimmed hat.

'For some!' Alice replied, with another growling laugh, before she headed for the tiny, makeshift kitchen.

After the dinners had been served Alice was waiting to pounce, and she stopped Alfie James as he headed for the door. 'Just a sec, Alfie. Can I have a word?' Immediately his thin face assumed a shut-down, suspicious expression, his eyes slitted.

'Yeah? What about? Me mates are waiting.'

She followed him out into the small enclosure around the hall, which now served as schoolyard. 'We called up at High Top Saturday. Is everything all right for you up there?'

'I know. They told me. What you after? The boss weren't too pleased. He don't like folk nosing around.'

'The *boss*?' she echoed scornfully. 'Aye. I hear he keeps you busy. Not much fun working outside in this weather, I should think. What's he got you doing?'

'Oh, nowt much. Cleaning up. Looking out for the sheep. You have to be careful in winter. Get them in if weather turns.'

'Didn't know you were a shepherd, Alfie.' He made no acknowledgement of her grin.

'What you want?' he said bluntly.

'I want to know that you're all right. You *and* your brothers. You're looking right scruffy, the lot of you. And you could do with learning a few manners, all right?' He stared back at her, with such an open hostility that she felt a sudden urge to clout his untidy head for him. Then she saw how lean his frame was, and how raggedly clothed against the cold. 'What's old Symmonds so worried about folk coming out to the farm for? What's he up to?' She saw beneath the belligerent stare a flash of

141

genuine unease, and she responded to it.

'There's nowt. It's just an old farm, that's all. And we're fine up there, right? So just keep yer neb out, will yer?' And he turned and ran off, leaving her staring after him in some anger and greater concern.

She felt a little guilty about searching out the snotty-nosed young Frankie, and her coaxing efforts to extract information from the ingenuous six-year-old. She questioned him gently, and deviously, so as not to alert him, but even so he appeared cautious, and at first reluctant to offer anything. He began by asserting what she suspected might be a well-drilled lesson reinforced by his elder brothers, perhaps. 'Yeah, everything is all right, miss.' To him, Alice was grown up, she was in school, and therefore she was a 'miss'.

'You're not scared of Mr Symmonds, are you? I mean, does he wallop you sometimes? When you're naughty, I mean.'

'Naw.' He thought a little, his brown eyes grew slightly rounder. 'Only if we do owt bad.'

'Like what?'

He frowned, and paused a little. 'If we play round the shed, or that sheep pit thing. Usually he has one of the dogs up there. Says he'll set 'em on us if we go near.'

'What shed's that then?'

His tousled, dirty mop of hair shook fiercely. 'I don't go there, honest, Miss. It's way up, 'cross the field. And the pit. I've never seen owt, miss.'

He sounded genuinely scared now, and she strove to keep her own mounting concern from revealing itself in look or voice. 'I wonder what's inside it, do you think? And this pit. What's that all about?'

'Dunno. It smells. Stinks, like a garage. The shed's always locked, our Norman says. And the winders are all done up with wood and stuff. Nobody could see in, he says.' His head shook again firmly. 'I've never been, miss. Never tried to.'

'All right, Frankie, love. Don't you worry about it. And keep our chat a secret, eh? A game — like we were spies or summat, yeah? Let's promise we won't say owt, to nobody, right? Not even your lads. Our secret, right? Cross your heart?'

'Yes, miss.' He aped her gesture and sighed with relief when she smiled and rewarded him with one of Annie Hogan's home made scones.

8

'I think mebbes we should wait a bit, miss,' Alice said, when Miss Laverton asked her about the visit to High Top farm. 'Let me keep an eye on things, see how it turns out. I'm not that happy about it, but the lads seem content to stop there. It's a rough and ready sort of life, but I reckon it's not much different from what they're used to.'

Privately, she was more uncertain than she sounded about advocating a wait-and-see policy, as much from the cloudiness of her own motives as anything else. She was convinced things were not right up at the Symmondses' place, but she was intrigued by the mystery, and keen to get to the bottom of it. And the quickest way to do that, she felt, was to keep quiet about her suspicions and continue her own investigations. However, she acknowledged her own unease about leaving the James boys up there, especially when Elsbeth offered her opinion that the children should be moved forthwith.

'It's awful up there,' she contributed to the discussion. 'They — they're running about like a pack of savages. The whole place is filthy — and so . . . uninviting.'

'You haven't seen what they live like at home!' Alice countered strongly. 'You've no idea what goes on back in Margrove — what some folks live like!'

Elsbeth coloured, and fell silent. She looked squashed and a little hurt, as though Alice had accused her of something, as maybe she had without quite knowing what. At any rate her diffidence, along with Alice's apparent confidence in her own advice, helped to make up Miss Laverton's already overburdened mind. 'Very well. We'll leave it as it is for the moment. But keep an eye open, both of you. Watch out for young Frankie especially. We'll look at things again, perhaps in the holiday. I assume they'll be staying put?' She addressed her question to Alice rather than Elsbeth.

'I should think so, miss. I don't think they've heard sight nor sound from back home. Can't see the James stumping up to bring the lads home for Christmas. Don't see as how they can afford to.'

'I think that will be true of most of our parents. What about you, Alice?'

'I'll stop on here, miss. Our kids'll need an eye kept on them. I dare say I can make meself useful, try to see they have a good time. Me mam's hoping to get through some time over the Christmas to see us.' She gave a cynical little smile. 'And as for our Doreen, I think she'd be dead disappointed if she *had* to go back home. She's well pleased with Miss Ramsay.' Fairness made her add, 'I don't think our Algy will be that bothered, either, miss. He's settled in with the Aygarths. Gets on well with their kids. They treat him — and me — like one of the family. We've been lucky.'

Elsbeth's blue eyes were full of concern. 'Oh — but surely . . . I mean it must be awful for the children, *and* their parents, to be separated at Christmas. Now of all times. Isn't there something we can do — the government? — to get them home for the holidays?'

'I've been in touch with the education committee,' Miss Laverton said, a defensive note creeping into her voice, 'but they claim to be at full stretch as it is. If you can come up with any ideas I'd be most grateful. The Church Society say they can't afford to help, except maybe in one or two of the extreme cases. But then, they're all rather extreme, aren't they?'

But the next few days brought news which made them all reassess their misfortune in being away from Margrove and their families. For five nights in a row, at the beginning of

December's second week, the town and the area to its north around Teesside were themselves the target of bombing raids of a sustained intensity hitherto aimed at bigger and more distant targets. The air-raid siren sounded in the village, which was in itself a rare occurrence, for the drills which had taken place around the outbreak of hostilities had long been suspended. Alice and Algy woke to its piercing rise and fall for the first time for over three months and joined the bleary, night-garbed figures on the landing of the old farm cottage. Alice was glad of the dark-blue siren suit, the gift from Elsbeth, which the blonde girl had claimed was second hand but which looked, felt, and even smelt brand new. So far Alice had only worn it in the evening, or sometimes under the dungarees the Aygarths had given her and which had become her favourite gear for getting out and about at the weekends.

She helped Eileen settle the children in the outbuilding a few yards from the back kitchen door, where 'Big Malcolm' had transformed a thick-walled room into a kind of bunker, with sandbags lining the outside walls and others on the solid roof, along with a good layer of earth. Most of the floor was covered in straw-filled mattresses, which prickled in places and made a rustling noise at every movement. They had been so little used that the novelty of being bedded down on them made the four children highly excitable. This was a game of tremendous fun, once they had recovered from being hauled from warm beds and deep sleep. Becky Aygarth tried to assert her nine-year-old seniority over her sister, Maureen, and Algy. But two-year-old 'Little Malcolm' was totally immune to threats or persuasion. Eventually, he remained clinging like a monkey, arms round his mother's neck and legs about her waist, while the other three huddled under the communal blankets in sniggering, whispering democracy.

Alice and Eileen, wearing winter coats and wellington boots, joined Malcolm round the side of the house, on the cinder path that led to and bisected the long vegetable garden. They stared towards the north-east, where the low clouds were rosily lit on the underside, and slender fingers of pale light from searchlights criss-crossed the darkness. 'Looks like they're getting it Middlesbrough way,' he said. They could hear the bark of the AA-guns, muted by distance, and, only occasionally, a lower, deeper, more indistinct rumble, like thunder from a far-off storm. 'Margrove, too, I reckon. They'll be going for the steel works.'

'Malcolm!' His wife's sharp word was

accompanied by an ungentle blow to his shoulder.

'What? What the hell — oh, aye.' His voice sounded sheepish and awkward. 'Sorry, Alice. Didn't mean — '

'That's all right.' She spoke quickly. 'They'll all be in the shelter, I expect. It's just round the corner, near the school.' But she thought of that crowded, inadequate little cubby-hole under the stairs, and felt a hollow queasiness in her stomach. And her dad — she hoped he wasn't on the night-shift this week.

The sounds of war died, but the rose tint to the clouds remained, even when the all clear sounded a while before dawn. The three huddled shapes were all fast asleep, and the two-year-old Malcolm had dropped off in his mother's arms. 'I'll stay down here with this lot,' Alice volunteered. 'Shame to disturb them now. You two get off to bed with Little Malc. Be time to get up in a while.'

'You snuggle in with them and pinch a bit of their warmth,' Eileen said gratefully. Her round face had lost its fresh, youthful cast, and looked creased and doughy. ' 'Night and God bless.'

'What's left of it,' her husband grumbled. 'Howay, lass. Get up them stairs!'

The children were all wildly excited the

149

next day, and school was a noisy affair, with tired teachers' voices sharp with irritable threats. Miss Laverton spent a frustrating day trying to communicate with the town authorities back in Margrove. She decamped from the village school back to Howe Manor and availed herself of the services of the estates office. 'I'm trying to get them to check on our evacuees' families. To find out if there have been any casualties,' she told the sympathetic agent, Mr Barr.

There had been widespread damage, for the low cloud cover had meant that an already difficult task of hitting the targets had been made even harder. Yet the casualties on the ground had been surprisingly low, and, once again, most of them in what was known as 'old town', the area that hugged the coast close to the docks. Only a few strays had fallen further inland, and none in the close vicinity of Lister Road. The material damage had been considerable, though, again, more to private property than the intended goal of the steel works and railway, but people had learnt the lesson from that first comparatively minor raid, so long ago in the summer, and had taken to the shelters: Anderson, or communal. 'We've been lucky,' Miss Laverton told the staff soberly. 'Perhaps we shouldn't moan too much about the hardships of evacuation, eh?'

*   *   *

Friday, 13 December, was far from being unlucky for Margrove, for it was the first night since the previous Sunday that there was no air raid on the town. The Glass family, minus their senior member, Fred, who was on night shift, had endured the first attack in the claustrophobic familiarity of the cupboard under the stairs, though Maggie, for one, soon began to regret it, as it became clear that this was a raid of a severity they had not experienced so far. The droning engines of the bombers were louder, and did not fade quickly as the formations passed high above on their way to other destinations. They seemed to hover overhead, and get thunderously louder still. Several incendiary bombs, from the preliminary layer, which was dropped in order to help illuminate the target, fell in the vicinity of Maudsley Street. Whistle blasts, shouts, and running feet, and, eventually the sound of jangling bells and revving motor engines, added to the general atmosphere of alarm and dawning panic. George, who as a sixteen-year-old labourer was not required to work shifts, insisted on leaving the cubby-hole to investigate, in spite of his mother's vehement, tearful protest. He returned to inform them excitedly that there was a fire engine at the corner of the street and that a blaze had started in the yard at the back of Wilson's shop.

His sister, Ethel, was eager to follow his bold example and go to take a look for herself, but a vicious slap from her overwrought mother on her cold bare thigh made her smart, as well as reminding her that her shift and a woollen shawl were inadequate as well as indecent attire for public exposure on a cold December night. 'Get in and shut that bloody door!' Maggie moaned at her son.

'Lorra good that'll do!' he muttered. 'Think shutting the door'll keep a bomb out?' But he obeyed, and ungraciously cuffed Ethel about her head to assist her in removing herself from the easy-chair he had vacated. She was already rubbing at her stinging thigh, and felt herself badly done to, but she surrendered with a few sullen imprecations. With Fred out at work, and her other three siblings long removed, the narrow, sloping cupboard was no longer the sardine-tin it had resembled in former nights. But they soon felt trapped and increasingly frightened, when the pounding guns continued their clamour, and the faintly trembling detonations of heavy bombs were felt.

'Oh God! Where's your father?' Maggie wept, as though he were somehow responsible for the chaos.

'It'll be the works that's getting it,' George observed, and made her ashamed of her unreasoning anger at her husband's absence.

'I hope to God he's all right!' she said. This time her reference to the deity was more of a pious plea than a blasphemous imprecation.

He was, and so was the precious 'Works', thanks to the inaccuracy of night bombing. Fred Glass turned up with the late, fiery December dawn. His 'Thank God!' was piously intended, too, when he stood in his cycle-clips at the end of Maudsley Street and saw that every humble dwelling on both sides was intact. But then he felt a lurch of both anxiety and rage as he turned and saw the corner of the blackened wall at the side of the Black Horse, and the acrid, burnt remnants of the boxes and other detritus scattered and spilled out across the roadway from the brief but fierce conflagration in the pub's narrow yard. Relief set in once more as he made a swift, critical survey of the building and could detect nothing which should delay the opening of its doors to customers a few hours hence. A trip out back to the gents might be a bit messy, but then what could you expect from a trough inside a roofless bricked enclosure? And there were yards and yards of wall in the back street in a real emergency. There was a war on, after all!

Greatly comforted, he turned to the bosom of his family. Maggie had been dozing in his chair by the kitchen range, and she hurried to him while he was still propping his bike in the narrow passageway just inside the front door. 'Fred! Thank God you're all right!' She clung to him, ignoring the grime coating his face, clothes and hands, smudges of which transferred to her cheek and the bosom of the shabby coat she was wearing over her nightdress. 'What a night we've had! George and Ethel have just gone up, no more than an hour ago. I told her she needn't go in to school today.'

'It was a bit bloody lively down our end and all!' he said, in an aggrieved tone. 'It was us they were after all right!'

'Sit yerself down, pet. The pot's fresh. I'll pour you a cup before you have your wash.' She picked up the dark-brown teapot from its circular little stand on the hob, and poured the strong tea into his tin mug. She added the milk, fished out a stray, swirling tea-leaf, and reached for the tin where the collective sugar ration was stored. She noted the level, then, in a gesture of appeasement to the fates who had brought him safely home, ladled in two spoonfuls and stirred vigorously. 'There you go, pet.'

She sat down on the creaking, hard chair by the table, fought against the urge to have yet another cup herself, aware of her already uncomfortably full bladder and the coldness of the early morn. 'Eeh, I hope our Alice and Algy are all right.'

Fred supped noisily. 'They'll be fine, lass, don't you fret yourself!' His tone was bitter with his sense of injustice. 'They'll have had a good night's kip and not heard a thing, mark my words.'

'It's her birthday on Saturday, Fred. Nineteen, eh? I wish she could get through to see us. She's a young woman now. Real grown up. I really miss her, you know.'

'Aye. Young woman, is it? I wish to hell she'd start acting like one then! More like a lad than a lass, that one! Needs to smarten herself up a bit. Wake up her ideas. She'll never get a lad the way she carries on.'

'Aw, give her a chance! Could be a lot worse. Look at that Lamberts' lass. Dolls herself up like I dunno what. Different lad every night — some of them not *lads*, either, from what I hear. Older blokes who should know better!' She stood, reached for the pot again to top him up. 'I wish she could get back for Christmas. Could we not afford to bring the three of them home? Our Algy's little enough to pass for under five. We might only need Doreen's fare.'

'I thought we'd agreed. You were gonna travel down one day in the holidays. Spend the day with them. I'll have another word with Knapper Hayes. He's got his kids down there. He's always on about getting these travel permits. We're entitled, he says. We should get your fare paid for nowt.'

Her face was stamped with her worry. 'I don't know, Fred. You know what I'm like. Hopeless at things like this. How will I manage with the train and all that? Couldn't you come and all? Or better still, fix up for them to come home? Our Al's as bold as brass when it comes to owt like that. The travelling's nowt to her.'

'Good God, lass! All you've got to do is get yourself on a train, and get off at t'other end! What's hard about that? There's hundreds doing it every day.' He sighed noisily, tilted his mug and drained it, filtering the last of the liquid through his teeth against the log-jam of the leaves. 'Well, I'll get a wash and hit the hay. Wake me up for half eleven. I'll see if I can have a word with Knapper at dinner-time. He might be in the 'Oss.'

One thing's certain, *you* will! she thought, but then she remembered the fearful night, and how alone and frightened she'd felt, in spite of George and Ethel beside her. 'Aye, right-oh, pet.' She took a cloth and lifted the heavy pan from the top of the range and carried it out to the back kitchen, where towel, bowl and soap were laid out, along with the jar which held his shaving things.

★　★　★

Luke Denby eyed the small group of schoolgirls appreciatively. I should have been coming back to the old homestead a bit more often, he acknowledged, basking in their wide-eyed looks of adulation. He was glad of the mandatory wartime stipulation that officers on active service should travel in uniform instead of civvies. It certainly helped when shooting the line, for even these young fillies knew what the wings over his pocket meant. His discreetly private efforts to make them look not quite so conspicuously new, and the time expended on crushing up his cap, bending it to take on the battered shape of veteran headgear, brought its dividends, too. These senior girls, sixteen- and seventeen-year-olds he guessed, were like wasps round the proverbial jam pot, as their flashing eyes and animated faces, twitching, flicking hair and nervous, quick shoulder and limb movements betrayed their excitement.

To think they'd been under the ancestral roof since late summer! The chaps would be chomping at the bit when he told them about it — rather like this clutch of well-bred peaches were doing at this moment. He was suddenly very much aware how wrong he had been to write off the winter uniform of schools like St Anne's as lacking in any charm. This batch of nubile maidens certainly gave the lie to his former ill-considered judgement. For a start, this gear afforded an unencumbered view of the wearer's legs to a height on a par with that normally displayed by the chorus line of the more saucy theatrical reviews. The gym slips were abbreviated to positively indecent minuteness, so that the black-stockinged legs were revealed in all their splendour; so much so that what was in essence an undergarment was required to be brought coyly into view, to hide the altogether too decadent glimpse of pale, forbidden thigh above the stocking-top, and the suspender strap which held it. These garments, with elasticated legs, were in fact a kind of knicker, but were known technically as 'tights'. It amused him greatly to reflect that these bastions of privileged society should sanction such libidinous attire for the virgin daughters of the upper echelons to parade around in, when any humbler female attempting to venture out in public dressed thus would be immediately branded as immoral.

His musing and his focus of attention were abruptly terminated by the arrival of Elsbeth Hobbs, crunching up the wet gravel drive in the far more modest garb of long winter coat and woollen tam. The girls twittered both polite greeting and farewell and spun leggily away. As he watched the pink invade Elsbeth's features, Luke thought how much more worldly the fifth form pupils appeared than the young teacher. Wiry tendrils of yellow hair poked from beneath the tam, and her blue eyes gazed with that shy vulnerability that he found so enchanting — and exciting, he had to admit. She looked as she felt, tired by the disruptions of the previous night, and the long hours of unstinting toil in the classroom, dealing with six- and seven-year olds far from home and over-stimulated by the excitements of the air-raids.

He greeted her warmly. 'Hello again. I've got tonight and tomorrow morning off, so I thought I'd just pop home. Make sure the old pile is still standing. That's my excuse, anyway. The truth is I wanted to see you again. You don't mind, do you?'

'Of course not. It's — nice to see you,' she ended lamely. 'How are you?'

'Still here. In one piece,' he explained, and she blushed again. 'And feeling better every minute. Come in and have a noggin. Or is it a refreshing cuppa you're in need of?' She nodded. He reached for her arm and escorted her up the steps to the front entrance and porch, where the girls were gathered, waiting to go in for their tea. He knew all eyes were on the pair as he led Elsbeth inside.

'Come along, gels! Blackout up, if you please! Then we can have some light on the situation.' The teacher's penetrating tone rose above the hubbub.

Luke was steering her to the left, through to the family's quarters, and Elsbeth let him lead her. 'Where's your dragon?' Luke said. 'She trusts you to come straight home, does she?'

'Miss Laverton's no dragon. She'll be down at school still. It'll be an hour or more before she gets back. She works far too hard.'

'You poor things!' He ushered her into the lamplit warmth of the drawing-room, where the curtains were already drawn, and the fire burned brightly in the large fireplace. 'Mum! Is there any tea in the pot? Our poor little evacuee here is totally exhausted. Here we are, my dear. Sit down and warm your little tootsies.' He knelt at her feet and began to ease off her solid shoes. 'God! They're like ice.'

He gripped her stockinged foot, and pressed firmly, massaging her toes, and she reddened helplessly, very aware of his indecorous familiarity in the presence of both his parents. It felt nice, though, in a naughtily decadent sort of way, and she felt a little quiver of physical excitement stir her, in spite of her embarrassment, as she surrendered herself to his ministrations.

There were two small bathrooms set aside for the staff, where the teachers could bathe in solitary privacy, if not always in hot water. The next time Elsbeth and Luke Denby met, therefore, she was suitably refreshed and freshly groomed, wearing a sensibly warm evening frock, though the thick stockings had been replaced by artificial silk and dainty heeled shoes. She had been invited to join the family for drinks, and for 'a bite of supper afterwards', the invitation extended by Letitia Denby with easy charm, though prompted by her son.

The meal was a great deal more substantial than the word 'bite' had suggested, both in variety and volume. The deprivations of the war had had little visible effect on life in the

Big House, though Elsbeth had already noticed that country folk in general fared a lot better than the inhabitants of the town and city. 'Why not? We grow most of it, don't we?' Vera Rhodes, the landlady of the Oddfellows, had roundly declared during Elsbeth's early stay there.

The informality of the meal, served in the cosy warmth of the drawing-room instead of the chilly grandeur of the dining-room, could have been a little marred for Elsbeth by the polite but insistent probing into her family background conducted by Letitia Denby, unenthusiastically aided by her husband. But Luke soon rode in to the rescue, heading off each query with some light-hearted quip, until he swiftly decided that a more direct approach was required. 'Good God, Mother!' His laughing tone did nothing to disguise the edge in his protest. 'You sound like a Scotland Yard police detective! What do you think? The poor girl's some sort of Jerry spy?'

'I'm only interested in Elsbeth's family, Luke! I *do* apologize, my dear, if it sounds as if I'm quizzing you. I just want to know all about you. I want you to feel thoroughly at home with us.' She radiated her warmest smile at the blushing girl, who immediately protested that she was delighted with everyone and everything about her, and that she had never felt more welcome anywhere.

When Luke got their guest away, to show her the library and to check that the gramophone installed there still worked, Letitia's warm smile vanished. 'Tradesmen, Norman! That's what her folks are. Some jumped-up photographer, I expect. A snapper who's jumped on the war bandwagon and set himself up as a business tycoon!'

'Sounds quite a nice little concern. Hobbs Printers — I'll ask Patrick Barr. Might be able to arrange something.'

'It's amazing, isn't it?' his wife said cuttingly. 'Suddenly Luke seems to have all the time in the world to pop through here now, whenever he feels like it. We scarcely ever saw him before.'

'Well, he's got his wings now. It's combat training he's embarked on. They've got to build up a crew, as he says. The routine's different now. More regular.'

'She's a bit of a mouse, though, isn't she? Be honest, Norman. She can't pass the time of day without blushing. I hope to God Luke isn't smitten!'

'She's pretty enough,' Norman observed. 'Better a blushing violet than some of the dolled-up hussies you see knocking about these days.'

She eyed him levelly. 'You think so?' She

reached out to take a cigarette from the carved box which lay on the round gin table at her elbow. She flicked the ornate lighter, her carefully made-up eyes almost closing as she lit the thin tube. She sat back and smoothed the material of her dress over her jutting knee, and admired the still trim shape of her ankle. 'I'd say he's entitled to sow a few wild oats, poor boy. The sooner the better.' She gave a hard little laugh. 'I don't think Miss Hobbs comes under that category. More a cherished little hothouse plant for a provincial front parlour!'

9

'It's my birthday tomorrer. Eileen and Malcolm have insisted on doing a special tea. Just the family, and Jess Corbett's gonna look in. Will you come an' all?'

Elsbeth's face was stamped with her consternation. 'Oh, why didn't you say something earlier? Why didn't you tell me?'

'I thought you knew. And I didn't want anyone else to know.' She nodded towards the empty hall behind them. 'I don't want a load of fuss. I only let it slip up at Beck Side by accident, really.' Alice felt the keen stab of disappointment. It was obvious from Elsbeth's reaction that she wasn't going to be able to come. 'It's all right,' she went on gruffly, her dismay making her brusque. 'If you've got owt better to do, it's no matter.'

'Oh, it's not that!' Elsbeth cried penitently. 'I'd love to come, but it's just — I've made arrangements to go home. To stop overnight. You know — after the raids and everything. I promised Mummy.'

Alice shrugged, and even managed a grin. 'Oh well, never mind. You can come some other time. You haven't really met Eileen and

165

Malcolm, have you? They're smashing.' She saw the hesitation, the colour mounting in the pretty face, and she waited tensely.

'I'd — if I could I'd put it off — the visit home. I mean, I've spoken to them on the telephone — you know that. They're all right. It's just . . . ' she seemed to draw a deeper breath before she continued: 'I've got the chance of a lift through, by car. Luke Denby — he said he'd run me home. Mummy said he could stay the night. He'll bring me back on Sunday.'

'Oh, right.' Alice drew the words out significantly, nodded as though in affirmation of something unspoken. Red spots of colour heightened on her own cheeks now. 'God! He's never away from here these days! What's he done? Has he had the sack from the Air Force?'

'No, of course not! It's because he's finished the first part of his training. He's a fully qualified bomber pilot now. He's training with his crew, proper missions. They'll be joining a squadron, going on raids, in the spring.' She paused, and the silence hung between them, prickly with tension and unease. 'In fact — I've just thought . . . we could have given you a lift, too . . . so you could see your family . . . '

'Aye. And our Doreen and Algy an' all, eh?

Be like a charabanc trip!' She waited, saw the downturn of Elsbeth's mouth, the vulnerability of the great-eyed look she cast upon her, and felt the boil of frustration and rage inside. 'Pity you didn't speak up sooner, like! I can't say no to the Aygarths now — can't do the dirty on me friends, can I?'

The blue eyes filled with wounded reproach, and regret, and were luminous with tears. All at once the slender throat felt choked, and Elsbeth swallowed, murmured huskily, 'I'm sorry, Alice. Truly! I never thought — '

'No, you didn't!' The words came out like bullets, harsh with accusation, and Elsbeth flinched. 'But don't worry about it, kidder! You go off with your Brylcreem Boy and enjoy yerself. You'll have a much better time, I'm sure. And say hello to your mummy and daddy for me! Oh, sorry! I forgot! They won't know who the hell you're talking about, will they? 'Cos they've never heard of me, have they?' she yelled, her angry face thrust forward at Elsbeth, who looked even more upset.

'Of course they have! You know — I've told them — lots about you — about how good you are — how we . . . ' she swallowed back the tears, and suddenly reached out for Alice, tried to catch hold of her hands. 'Please, Al!

Don't be angry — I didn't mean — '

'Oh, bugger off back to Big House, and your fancy friends and your telephones and your motorcars! And leave me to my mates!'

She spun on her heel and strode away through the encroaching dark, her eyes blurred by her tears, which enraged her even more than the sudden, murderous urge she had had to give that pretty face a slap that would make its perfect little teeth rattle.

In her wake, Elsbeth stood gazing after her, her mouth open in a silent O of shame and hurt, as though the cheeks down which the tears trickled had indeed felt the sting of Alice's capable, hard hand. She felt doubly guilty now, for she had thought quite long and hard about inviting Alice to make the journey back to Margrove with them. But she could not shake off the feeling that it would prove awkward and downright embarrassing, not least for Alice, despite her cheerful, cocky approach to life. Though it made Elsbeth's toes curl inside her smart winter boots with distress, she could not prevent her acknowledgement of the social gulf between her and her friend — financial status, background, even speech — which would embarrass both of them in the presence of a third party, especially someone like Luke Denby.

She had become a lot more aware of the

demarcations between the various strata of society. Elsbeth was deeply conscious of the difference between herself and Luke, mostly in the presence of his parents. When she was alone with him, he was quick to put her at ease. It was one of his most attractive qualities, she thought, his ability to do that, and to make her feel relaxed and more confident with herself. He had that easy, friendly manner with most people, of all classes, she had noticed in the short time she had known him.

So why should she be so uneasy about Alice and him meeting up? It was complicated — she hadn't even got it clear in her own mind, but she just knew, somehow, that Alice wouldn't come over as warm and wonderful as she really was, wouldn't respond to his easy charm the way Elsbeth herself did. It sounded odd, but she believed that Alice — Al — would be resentful, and jealous of the special closeness she shared with Elsbeth, as if this was threatened by Luke's entry on to the scene. And she wouldn't be urbane enough to hide it, nor be appeased by Luke's efforts to coax her out of it. In fact, that would only make matters worse, cause Alice to be even more prickly and rude. Better to try to make sure the twain should never meet.

Such subtleties and lack of them were

highlighted for Elsbeth that very Friday evening, when Luke arrived from his aerodrome and Elsbeth was once more a guest at another informal drawing-room supper. Without straying in the slightest from her smiling and impeccable good manners, Luke's mother, Letitia, made the sensitive girl all too aware that she considered Luke's accompanying Elsbeth to Margrove and spending the following night at her home to be an extraordinary and slightly dubious occurrence, given the brevity of their acquaintance.

'I *do* hope your mother won't mind your turning up on the doorstep with a perfect stranger to spend the night under your roof.' The low murmured laugh that went with it gave the remark the delicacy of an expert stiletto thrust.

'Same roof, different beds — unfortunately!' Luke's laugh was open, music-hall bawdy, and Elsbeth was glad of it, even though she turned as red as the beetroot which was part of their fare.

'I told her — she knows . . . on the phone,' Elsbeth fumbled, before Luke stepped in once more.

'Really, Mum! Haven't you heard there's a war on? The age of calling cards and maiden-aunt chaperons has gone. Two weeks is an age these days! We're the best of chums, know all about each other! Let's face it. We've got over a hundred nubile maidens living under our roof. You can't blame me for paying court to the fairest of them all.'

Though the heat rushed all too visibly to Elsbeth's face yet again, there was a distinct element of pleasure along with the toe squirming that went on inside the flimsy evening slippers.

★ ★ ★

By the time Alice had toiled up the hillside in the early dark, clouds of condensation rising like a fully stoked Puffing Billy around her head, she was beginning to experience the twinges of a remorse which would increase to definite pangs of conscience as the night in the warm cottage kitchen wore on. She had no right to have a go at Elsbeth the way she had. How could the poor lass have known that a celebration would take place the following day, when Alice hadn't even told her of the birthday until its very eve? You think everybody's just waiting on you? she chided herself. Waiting to arrange their lives round things that matter to you? Of course Elsbeth couldn't turn down the opportunity of a trip home, after the events of the past week in Margrove. Alice herself would have jumped at the chance, had waited every day, her guts churning with anxiety. But as Miss Laverton had kept saying, no news is good news in this case.

But Alice wasn't the only one who kept secrets! Why hadn't Elsbeth mentioned her weekend ride home? She hadn't said a dicky-bird! And wouldn't have told her at all, she'd have just gone off tomorrow with her pilot! Would she even have told her when she got back after the weekend? Mebbes not!

Conscience struck in again. And why the hell should she, only to have you going at her like a British bulldog with jaws snapping? You silly jealous little cow! The thought was too painful to contemplate; it touched on the facet of her personality she had always shied away from, refused to explore, sealing it off from the rest of what went to make up Al Glass.

The Saturday afternoon was a great success. The Aygarths, or at least Eileen, had really made an effort. The fire was lit in the front parlour, the dining-table was covered with good things to eat, which scarcely acknowledged 'there's a war on', including a cake, complete with candle in the centre, a decorated paper frill, and a figure 19, cut out of paper and coloured, the result of painstaking effort, and several fierce arguments, by Becky and Maureen Aygarth — wisely, Algy said nothing, content to be ruled over by his two benevolent female despots.

There were even presents — a bottle of scent from the children, including Algy (courtesy of Eileen, Alice was sure, generously surrendered from the small store she had in her top dressing-table drawer). There was a very neatly wrapped tablet of perfumed soap from Doreen, who had walked up from the village with Jess Corbett. Doreen also brought a box of three dainty, embroidered handkerchiefs, a gift from Miss Ramsay. But most impressive, and touching, of all, was a bulky parcel, clumsily wrapped, which was marked simply: *From your new family.*

When she had torn aside the double layers of wrapping-paper, she let out a gasp of genuine surprise. There was a pair of pale breeches, in fine corduroy, and reinforced on the inner thighs and knees with soft, creamy buckskin. There was a belt of beautiful, polished leather, with a heavy, circular metal buckle, and a pair of thick, ribbed, high knee socks in olive green. She stared at the spilling bundle on her lap, struck dumb for long seconds. 'You shouldn't of,' she said at last, in a husky whisper. She was deeply touched, and couldn't look at them for embarrassment.

'Aw, come on, lass! That's your birthday and Christmas present rolled into one, so anything else round the tree will have to come from Santa!' Eileen went on quickly, 'I think they're the right size. Same as your slacks. I did a bit of sneaking around.'

'We'll have you riding t'oss yet!' Malcolm said heartily. 'You'll be out with the hunt at New Year's.'

Alice felt the prickle of tears behind her eyes, and her face was hot with more than the heat from the fire. 'I don't know what to say. Thank you. They're lovely.'

'Well, we know you can't be doing with skirts and frocks and all that. You'll look right smart in that lot. And I've got a right good pair of boots to go with them, and all. I've hardly worn them — they're too good for knocking about the farm. I've given them a good dubbin-up and polish. They've come up lovely. I'm only a half-size bigger'n you, and with thick socks like them you'll never know difference!'

Alice stared at her wordlessly, and Eileen dispersed the awkwardness by striding over with a beaming grin and holding out her arms. 'Come here and give us a kiss, and let's get on with the party!'

Alice responded, hugged her tightly, and blinked back the tears which were threatening to spill over.

'Hey, don't forget me! I reckon I can snatch the chance of a kiss, eh? Any excuse! I've been waiting days for this!'

She embraced Malcolm, felt the strength of his arms as he clasped her to him, and let his lips brush swiftly against her cheek and ear, before she hooked her chin over his shoulder. His father and brother stood in line to embrace her, too. 'You'll look like one o' them land-girls!' David, the brother, quipped, as he gave an embarrassed peck at her cheek.

'A damn sight better-looking than them flibbertigibbets!' Mr Aygarth senior declared, as his sinewy arms reached to encircle her. 'You can treat us to a fashion parade later on. Now, when are we gonna get stuck into this grub? My belly thinks my throat's been cut!'

The gathering was a great success, and seemed to set the tone for the Christmas festivities which were now less than two weeks away. Eileen was inspired after the guests had all left as darkness was closing in to send Malcolm scrabbling in the loft space above the bedrooms of the old cottage, to haul out the box of decorations, and she and Alice and the three children spent a large part of the evening, after Little Malc had been settled in his cot, spreading them around the parlour — 'We're not going to waste this fire,' Eileen insisted — and carrying out renovations. Alice organized nine-year-old Becky, assisted and impeded by her younger sister, Maureen, and Algy, in the making of new paper-chains.

It wasn't until she was lying beside the snuffling, restless Algy in the heaped warmth of their bed much later that Alice's thoughts were diverted from the warm glow of gratitude for the day to more sombre reflections. A card had come from home yesterday: *Love and best wishes for happy birthday* had been inscribed in her mother's laboured script, with its trailing row of Xs. There was a postal order for five shillings enclosed with it. Alice felt guilty as she thought of the effort which must have been exerted either by Maggie or another member of the family, involving the trip down to the post office in Whitby Street and no doubt the waiting — there seemed to be no aspect of daily existence in Margrove which did not involve queuing for far too long. Yet another hardship which people in the countryside scarcely suffered from. She thought of how much more difficult it would have been for her mother to lay on a spread such as Eileen had provided so readily this afternoon. Here in Howbeck there were still fresh eggs in comparative plenty for baking, as there were rashers of bacon and joints of good meat. Milk, dairy produce, so much which to Margrove folk, except, maybe, for an affluent few, was available only in the meagre quantities permitted by the ration book, was still so easily obtainable that Alice felt ashamed at the comparative luxury of her present life. She knew of course that most of the country people saw it almost as their right, and made no bones about it. 'We're the ones feeding the whole bloody country, working all hours, turning every bit of land over to foodstuffs.' She'd heard it lots of times already. The term 'black market' didn't apply here, they righteously asserted.

But this past week her incipient feelings of guilt had mushroomed with the bombing-raids on her home town and on other coastal areas in the region. She had come close to a few explosions of her own when she had heard people like Annie Hogan moaning on about their two nights of slumber disturbed at the beginning of the week by the wail of the sirens, and even the distant rumbles and thuds of bombs and guns. She felt a sudden recurring urge to weep as she lay in the peaceful dark and thought of her mam, probably weary from lack of sleep, nerves stretched tight — she knew how frightened her mam got when that awful wailing rose and fell — making the effort in all that uncertainty and fear to get a card, to persuade Ethel or George (she would never ask Fred, Alice guessed) to go to the post office for the money order. Who knows? Maybe she even ventured so far afield herself, struggling into her corset and forcing her feet, broadened by years of soft, sloppy slippers, into the painful constriction of her best shoes, to leave the comfort of familiar, soot grimed streets and face the larger environs of the war-damaged town.

Alice vowed that she really would make a great effort to get home somehow during the coming holidays, and take Doreen and Algy with her. She didn't even say her prayers any more. Except when things were truly desperate, she recalled with shame, remembering her muttered pleas to God during these past nights when the bombs had been dropping on or around her loved ones. She tried painfully to imagine how she would feel if the disastrous news came of their loss. She would be responsible for Doreen, and the snuffling little five-year-old lying so trustingly beside her. It was a scary thought.

In her mood of critical self-examination, her thoughts returned to her shameful aggression towards Elsbeth. She vowed she would make a point of seeking her out next day and begging her forgiveness, but then remembered that Elsbeth had said she was staying at home overnight. She might not be back till late tomorrow, and in any case this fellow, Luke, would most likely still be around. The last thing she wanted was to meet up with him. The squire's son! He'd think her a right rough diamond, *he* would! And why not, when that was exactly what she was? Why on earth a lovely girl like Elsbeth even bothered with her was a mystery. An educated, well-spoken lass like Elsbeth — what the hell could she see in someone like me? Alice couldn't answer her own question. Maybe now she wouldn't want anything more to do with her. And that's nobody's fault but mine! Alice confessed to herself, as she lay miserably in the darkness. No, she'd better not go sniffing round Big House tomorrow. She'd probably only make matters ten times worse, make a fool of herself and embarrass poor Elsbeth into the bargain. She'd have to wait till Monday. But first thing, before school started, Alice promised herself, she'd go straight to her and apologize, tell her what a bloody fool she'd been, and plead to be forgiven.

Alice was delighted with her new breeches, the neat fasteners round the calf hidden snugly beneath the thick green stockings. The boots Eileen had given her were beautifully burnished, and were only slightly roomy. 'You look a right country lass now,' Grandad Aygarth said approvingly, when she walked with the children up to the main farmhouse after their late breakfast. 'You'll have a few wolf whistles when you go down village.'

'Oh, I don't think I'll bother going down the hill today,' Alice answered, trying to disguise her unease. 'I've got enough things to do up here to keep me busy.' She was worried that if she did venture down into the village, as she usually did, she might bump into Elsbeth with her Brylcreem Boy.

The ceremonial Sunday dinner, and the washing up which followed, took up the afternoon until the early dark had set in, and the curtains were drawn and the lamps lit. They all settled down in front of the blazing parlour fire, lit for the second time in two days during this momentous week. 'Reckon old Adolf heard it was your birthday.' Malcolm grinned. 'That's why he's packed in his bombing raids.'

'Blooming good job, too!' Eileen glanced

up from the Sunday paper. 'Will your friend see your family at all? Make sure everything's all right?'

'I don't think so. She doesn't live anywhere near us.' She hesitated only fractionally before she carried on. 'They live up near the park. Lovely big houses up there. She's well off, you know. Talks real posh — I mean, nice. She's nowt like me.' She pulled a deprecating face. 'She's a real bonny lass.'

'She'd have to be to beat you!' Malcolm said, and Becky sniggered.

Eileen poked her tongue out at him. 'Watch yourself, Casanova! I'll have to keep an eye on you, me lad.'

'It's all right, Eileen,' Alice quickly interjected. 'He's only being sarky.'

In the midst of his protests, one of the dogs began a furious barking. Geordie leapt up from the fireside and raced for the window, joining in deafeningly. Malcolm bawled him down, and the collie growled, his fur rising. The girls had run to the window, and swept aside the thick curtains and the blackout drapes behind them, though nothing but blackness showed beyond the misty, icy panes.

'There's someone out there!' Becky called excitedly. 'Look! There's a torch waving.' They heard a faint, wavering cry.

'Stay inside!' Malcolm commanded. He was slipping his feet into the rubber boots which stood inside the porch, and dragging on the heavy coat from the pile of clothing hung on the hooks above. They all crowded in the open doorway. The light spilled on to the path, which stretched towards the dimly seen stone wall, and the narrow gate.

They could see a thin, wavering light flickering from some low lying source hidden on the other side of the wall, then they heard a high, thin voice calling out, catching on a sob. 'I'm suh — sorry! I couldn't see — I've fallen.'

'Elsbeth? Is that you?' Alice was scrabbling now, frantically pulling on her old boots, which were among the pile of footwear in the porch.

'Hey up, love! Never mind. Come on, let's have you out of there. You're soaked. Here. Put your arms round my neck. I've got you, you're all right now.'

By the time Alice had rushed down the path to the gate, Malcolm was holding the sodden, weeping bundle that was Elsbeth Hobbs in his arms. 'I'm so sorry!' Elsbeth blubbered as he bore her into the dim light and twisted to ease her through the doorway. 'It's so dark. I had no idea I'd — I just stumbled, fell. Into that ditch. I feel such a fool.'

It wasn't until Malcolm got her inside that they saw just how badly Elsbeth had fared. She was truly soaking, her clothing heavy with the muddy water which had lain several inches deep in the shallow ditch to the side of the gate, on the other side of the boundary wall. 'Get them wet things off her!' Eileen commanded, taking charge now that they were all once more safely inside, on her territory. 'What on earth's happened to you?'

Elsbeth's head was bare — she had lost her woollen hat when she fell into the ditch — and even her yellow hair was limp and sullied with mud. Alice added her own interrogation, her agitation making her words sound harsh. 'What the devil were you doing stumbling about out there in the dark?'

The sharpness of her tone brought the tears again, and Elsbeth shook her head helplessly, fighting against the onslaught of her grief. 'I just wanted — I didn't know it would be so dark. I got lost — I couldn't see the path any more. And the torch was useless.' It was one of the wartime regulation appliances, which cast a feeble pencil beam, meant to be aimed directly at your feet.

'Come on, then. You're all right. Let's have a look at you.' With Eileen's help, Alice got the heavy coat and scarf off, and the mud-encrusted boots. It was then that they saw the gaping tear in the black stocking, at her right knee, and the blood which showed on the exposed muddy flesh.

They eased her down on to the sofa. 'You're soaked right through!' Eileen exclaimed, feeling the tweed skirt and jumper. 'You'll have to change. But let's have a look at that leg.' She lifted the skirt, to reveal the pale thigh above the top of the stocking and the suspender-strap, which she quickly undid and carefully rolled the wet material down. Elsbeth gave a soft gasp, and then whimpered as the stocking was eased down over the knee, to the ankle, and the short, grey socks, dark with the muddy water. Eileen slipped the stocking and sock off over the narrow foot. 'Your feet are frozen, love. We'll soon have you warm. Alice, bring a basin of hot water, and the kit from the kitchen.'

Eileen cleaned the wound. The cut just above the knee was about two inches long, but quite shallow. The blood oozed a little, then ceased to flow. 'It's all right. Not as bad as it looked. We'd best make sure, clean it up, though. This'll sting a bit.'

Elsbeth gave a little yelp, and her leg jerked when Eileen dabbed the iodine on the cut, and the bedraggled figure apologized. 'I'm sorry. I'm an awful baby when it comes to anything like this.' Her tearful eyes turned to seek out Alice's, in an instinctive need for comfort, and what she saw there clearly reassured her. 'I was coming to see you — to see if you'd had a nice day yesterday. To let you know I hadn't forgotten.'

She glanced down at her leather bag beside her. 'There's a card. And just a little gift.' She fumbled, drew out the envelope and a small, slim parcel in bright red paper.

'Keep still, love,' Eileen said. She had smeared some ointment on a small square of gauze, which she pressed firmly over the wound, then wrapped a bandage tightly about the limb. 'It's awkward, being over the knee, like. But that'll do. You'll have to make sure you keep it clean.'

Meanwhile, Alice had opened the card, read the printed verse of good wishes, and the neat inscription beneath in Elsbeth's own hand: *To my dearest friend, Al, with love, wishing her a very very happy birthday.*

Alice tore the red paper from the little cardboard box. Inside, on a pad of red velvet, lay a fine silver chain bracelet of fragile beauty. Alice's eyes misted at the thought of such a gift. Again, the words jumped immediately into her head — I can't take this! She didn't say them, didn't say anything, feeling the colour steal up into her face. She was glad of the diversion which Eileen's bustling organization was causing, as everybody jumped to her orders. 'You've got to get out of these wet things! You're soaked right through. You lot, out into the kitchen. Malcolm, make sure everyone stays out — including *you*! Alice, get some more hot water so your friend can get herself cleaned up.' She swept aside Elsbeth's protests. 'Nay, lass, you're not moving from this fire till you've had a wash and change. Alice — bring that siren suit of yours. You'll have to get out of them wet things before you catch your death! And you can't walk all the way back to Big House, not with that leg of yours. You might break your neck next time! We can send Malcolm along to the Wrights — they're just down the road, at yon end of Beck Side. They've got a telephone line. They can let Big House know you're stopping here the night. You'll have to get in with Alice here, but that'll be no hardship, eh? I bet you'll be awake all night nattering, the pair of you! All right?'

Elsbeth glanced up at Alice, and wiped at the smudge of dirt on her tear-stained cheek. The blue eyes looked in mute enquiry, then she gave a helpless, grateful nod.

10

Elsbeth was already in bed when Alice came back into the room. 'Algy's settled down at last. They were all a bit excited, him being in with the girls. But they're all fast asleep now.'

Alice had waited, making sure Elsbeth would have ample time to get into her borrowed night attire before she made her re-entrance. The blonde girl lifted her arms above the eiderdown and smiled shyly, as she pushed the pink sleeves up off her wrists. 'I'll probably be far too warm in this.' The nightdress was a thick winter one, borrowed from Eileen. One of her best, Alice knew, though she did not say anything to Elsbeth. Alice could feel her heart beating a little more quickly. She was shocked at her own nervous shyness. Why should she feel like this? It wasn't as if she wasn't used to sharing her bed. In fact, she couldn't recall a night when she had slept alone.

It was her partner for whom this was a novelty. She had already laughingly confessed. 'This is the first time since I was a little girl that I've slept with someone else.'

Alice slipped off the cardigan she had

pulled round her shoulders. She was wearing her own blue cotton nightie, in honour of this unexpected occasion, instead of the shift she normally wore. She put out the lamp, and climbed into bed. She lay stiffly unmoving, at the edge of the bed, aware of the coldness of the sheets, and of the space she was carefully keeping between her and her partner. But then the bed creaked softly, and she felt the blankets move as Elsbeth turned, and a cold foot brushed against her own, and a tentative hand came groping towards her arm.

'I'm sorry for making such an idiot of myself tonight,' Elsbeth whispered, glad of the darkness which made this intimate confessional so much easier. 'You must all think I'm an awful fool. But I felt so bad about not being here yesterday for your birthday. Don't be angry with me, will you? I was thinking about you all day yesterday, wishing I could be with you.'

'Don't be daft! It was *my* fault, having a go at you like that. I should have said earlier. I know you couldn't change all your arrangements. I'm a right selfish bitch. I couldn't believe it when we found you outside. Coming all the way up here in the pitch black. You might have killed yourself, broken your neck. And just for me.' There was a pause, and Alice's voice was husky with emotion. 'Listen. That bracelet. It's beautiful. You shouldn't, you know. It's far too good — '

'Shut up! I wanted you to have it. I wanted you to know — you really *are* my friend, Al. Truly. The best, closest friend I've got. I mean it.' She moved closer, their legs touched, then their arms were holding each other, their warming bodies close, touching, their breath mixed as they sought out mouths, kissed each other. Elsbeth turned, away from Alice, but her back curved, her buttocks nestled against Alice's belly and thighs, and she drew Alice's hands round her, placing them against the warm softness of her breasts covered in the pink flannelette. She tilted her head back against Alice's face, so that Alice felt the soft hair tickling her lips.

Alice could feel the beat of her heart in her own breast, so strong that she wondered if Elsbeth would feel it, too. Her mouth brushed the girl's ear, as she whispered, 'What about this Luke feller? Your new friend. How do you stand with him then?'

'Don't be daft!' Elsbeth breathed, in a fair imitation of her friend's broad accent. 'I hardly know him. He's just — you know! A boy!' She pressed Alice's hand tighter against her breast.

'No, I wouldn't know,' Alice answered drily.

'So tell me. He hasn't got *this* far with you, has he?'

She felt Elsbeth squirm against her, and the hand slap against her wrist before clasping her to her bosom once more. 'Certainly not, and not likely to, either!'

'I bet he'd like to, though, eh?' And suddenly Alice felt her heart thudding yet again, and her throat constricting, as she acknowledged that shameful yet poignantly sweet ache stirring so deeply within her. Her body suddenly felt so hot that she was convinced Elsbeth must feel it burning against her. Her mind spun off, lost in physical sensation now, so rousing, so shocking, and so wonderful, that her muscles were tight as an overwound spring; she wanted to fling the bedclothes away, to leap up from the bed, or . . . With a great effort that shook her like a sob she pulled her arms free of the warm contact and wriggled back from Elsbeth's form.

She let out a long, theatrical yawn. 'We'd better get some shut-eye. I might have to carry you down the hill with that gammy leg of yours temorrer. Old Lavvy would have a fit if she'd seen you rolling about in that ditch! Wait till she sees the state of you in the morning! Probably think you and that Brylcreem Boy have had your wicked way with one another, I shouldn't wonder.'

Miss Laverton's thoughts did not stray as far along the path of unseemliness as Alice had fancifully supposed, but the head did find time for a quiet, confidential 'chat' during the following day, which marked the first of the last working week before the holiday. 'It was very silly of you to go wandering all the way up to Howbeck Side in the dark like that. We were all very worried when the telephone call came. Mr Denby was thinking of sending the car up to fetch you.'

Elsbeth gazed with pink contriteness at the older woman. 'I was fine, honestly. Just a bit — shaken, that's all. Mr and Mrs Aygarth were very kind. They looked after me just fine. I'm just sorry I caused so much fuss for everyone.' It soon became clear, however, that the accident was not the prime reason for the 'chat', to Elsbeth's even greater embarrassment. 'You and Luke Denby. You've become very pally, all of a sudden. I think his folks were a little surprised, you going off for the weekend with him like that. With so little warning.'

Elsbeth could feel the colour sweeping up into visibility, but could do nothing to stop it. 'Well — it was just, you know . . . after the air

191

raids . . . he offered to give me a run home. It was very good of him. My parents were glad to put him up for the night. They thought he was very . . . nice.' The blue eyes looked embarrassed, but carried a hint of injured reproach. 'It wasn't . . . they didn't think anything improper . . . '

'No, of course not. But you're still a very young girl, my dear. Eighteen. Just finished school, still. And these days, with this wretched war . . . the squire and his wife — particularly Mrs Denby, I think — were just a little concerned. Their son's quite a bit older — '

'Twenty-two!' Elsbeth interrupted. The redness of her cheeks was confined to two circles; her voice was unsteady with her agitation. 'I hope they're not thinking there's been . . . anything wrong. I can assure you — '

'No. I think they're probably more concerned for you, Elsbeth. Four years older might not seem that much, but I think you'll admit — he's seen a lot more of life, especially over the past year or so. I'm sure he's a perfectly decent young man, but the life they have to lead, these young chaps nowadays. And there are some girls who haven't had the advantages you've had, my dear. A good, comfortable home, a decent education and a Christian upbringing. Things are so fluid now, people of all kinds, all backgrounds, mixing. So much danger, people living on their nerves.'

'What is it I've done that's wrong, Miss Laverton? Have I behaved badly in some way?'

'No, I am sure you haven't. This is really just a kind of friendly warning, for you to be on your guard. Don't let your feelings — the feelings that are prevalent in the times we're going through — lead you to be too hasty in your friendship, that's all. I am responsible for you, Elsbeth, just as I'm responsible for the children — and for the other members of staff — like your chum, Alice Glass, for instance.'

'Are you telling me I shouldn't be friendly with Luke? Don't his folks want us to go out together? I suppose they don't think I'm good enough — I mean the right class — for him. But all we've done is go for a drink in the village, and look in at the village hop. And I've explained about this weekend, the trip home. It was his idea — he was just being very kind.' Her voice had been growing more and more unsteady, and now quivered on the edge of tears.

'You really shouldn't let yourself get upset like this, my dear. A note of caution, as I said.

That's all. And take care of that leg. I'll have a look at it tonight for you. Make sure you have a clean dressing. And no blundering about in the dark, my girl, all right?'

Elsbeth was still brooding over the interview when Alice seized the opportunity to question her about it at the end of afternoon school. 'You sit and see if you can make another sheep for the manger,' Alice instructed Algy. 'I just want to have a word with Miss Hobbs.' She saw him settled in front of the nativity scene, before she moved across to her friend. 'Well? What did Lavvy have to say? Tick you off for stopping out all night?'

Elsbeth shook her head. 'No. More like ticking me off for going away at the weekend.' Alice stared at her, eyebrows lifted, waiting for her to go on. The pretty face was screwed into an expression of discontent. 'She was sort of suggesting that I shouldn't have gone with Luke — that I shouldn't be so friendly with him.'

Her conscience pricked by her jealousy, Alice indignantly sided with her friend. 'What's it got to do with her? You should tell her — '

'Oh, I know what started it off. It's not really Miss Laverton. The Denbys have been talking to her. Mrs Denby's been making it pretty plain ever since Luke met me that she's not happy about it. About us going out together. It's only been twice — when we went to the dance . . . and then this weekend. I know she thinks I'm not good enough. You know — not the right sort of background. Not in their class.'

'Bloody nonsense!' Alice burst out, with typically robust loyalty. 'More like t'other way round!' she couldn't help adding, which made Elsbeth's mouth twitch in a smile.

'It's not as though . . . I mean, we're not, you know . . . like I say, we hardly know one another . . . '

'She thinks you're after him?' The directness of Alice's question brought the flood of pink to Elsbeth's face. She shrugged uncomfortably.

'Maybe she's worried I might be.'

'You're not, are you?'

The blue eyes widened, she stared at Alice in hurt surprise. 'No! Of course not! But . . . I suppose . . . maybe I shouldn't have accepted his offer to drive me home. And putting him up for the night. P'raps it was wrong after all. I never thought of it like that. I thought . . . it was just a nice thing for him to do, that's all. And I was worried about things, like we all were last week.'

She cast a troubled look at Alice. She looked so young, and so vulnerably beautiful that Alice felt her heart give that little flick. 'Mebbes it's because she thinks he's after *you*. His mam, I mean.' The blush came again, and Elsbeth looked even more distressed. 'Is he?' she pressed, and watched Elsbeth's shoulders lift, and turn slightly, like a child caught in embarrassment.

'No!' she answered quickly — a shade *too* quickly, Alice noted, for comfort.

'Are you sure? Has he — you know — tried it on?'

'No! Well . . . you know . . . he just . . . he tried to kiss me. It wasn't anything — '

'Did you let him?'

'Not the first time. Not after the dance! But then yesterday . . . after we got back here . . . '

Alice was torn between a sudden spark of anger and compassion for the girl's discomfiture. 'Well of course he would! A young bloke like him, and a lass as pretty as you! Any lad would try it on!'

Elsbeth was looking even more forlorn. 'It was just kissing. And I stopped him after . . . a minute or two. It was just . . . he'd been so good. Taking me all that way. And he was so nice, friendly to Mummy and Daddy.'

'I'll bet!' Alice couldn't keep the bitterness

196

from creeping into her voice. 'I bet he thought he was well in.' Her tone was hard once more, edged with aggression. 'Have you ever had a boyfriend? Been out with a lad — proper like?' Even her speech sounded coarser, as though that was part of her antagonism.

'No!' The denial came quickly, then an embarrassed qualification. 'Not really. Just — I've been to dances. You know — the tennis club, that kind of thing. And to the pictures, once or twice. You know how it is.'

'No I don't! And I don't bloody want to, neither!'

Elsbeth was staring at her. Those wide blue eyes, that look of dismay, her lips parted. 'Now *you're* angry with me again!' she cried. 'What's wrong? What have I done?'

Alice felt that swirling mix of emotion rising to swamp her again, a murderous anger and frustration, the urge to grab the slender frame and shake her furiously, or hug her crushingly against her, kiss those lips. All at once, she recalled the fierce joy and the sweet torment of holding the girl in her arms last night, lying so intimately with her in the dark, inhaling her fragrance, and miserably the solid wall of her own abnormality rose in front of her, with no way round it. 'Don't mind me,' she said bleakly. Knowing that the crude forthrightness of her lie would only hurt the sensitive girl further, she nevertheless said brusquely, 'Time of the month coming. Makes me as bad-tempered as an ould biddy. Come on, our Algy! Clear up. You can finish it temorrer. We'd best be off.'

Elsbeth's leg was stiff, and throbbing a little by the time she had completed the walk out of the village and up the southern slope of the dale as far as the twin stone pillars marking the entrance to Howe Manor. The pulsing discomfort was painfully in tune with the pangs of conscience which were troubling her yet again, ever since Alice's probing words. Elsbeth had not been completely truthful — she shied away from the word 'lied' — about her latest encounter with Luke Denby and its nature. His determined efforts to place their relationship on a more intimate footing the previous day, after their return to Howbeck, had gone way beyond any youthful amateur passion she had experienced at the Margrove tennis club dance.

She had not been kissed like that before. She had been excited by his kisses, by *their* kisses, she was forced to admit, for she had responded, unknowing and ignorant as she was. But then the excitement had gone beyond her limited experience, had slipped into a wildness which had frightened her, which she had recognized as being something new, and uncontained. His teeth, nuzzling and biting into her neck, his tongue in her surrendered mouth, and his hand, like a claw clasping at the softness of her breast through the layers of her clothing; then worse, and the thing that had brought her gasping and struggling from what had seemed to be her helpless compliance: his hand had clutched at her knee, thrust up brutally, under her skirt, and her coat, climbing up her silk-clad leg, until she was fighting, and jerking and trying to pull away, trapped in the tight bucket of the car seat, and she was half sobbing, and pleading, and truly alarmed now, before he finally desisted, and left her shivering and close to tears, feeling sullied and ashamed, and somehow strangely sharing a complicit guilt.

The words of apology he fired at her were as full of passion as his previous actions, and though they followed the conventional form of asking for forgiveness, they sounded angry at the same time, and accusing. 'I'm sorry, Beth.' He had begun calling her Beth, saying it was so much prettier than her full name, so much more like her. 'But you're so damned attractive — so good-looking! A chap can't help it! A chap like me, anyway! With someone as pretty as you — I felt it from the first time I set eyes on you. I've been wanting to kiss you like this ever since.'

Had she made herself too attractive? Doing her hair like that, combing it out, curling it into that wave, painting and prettying herself? A dab of powder, and lipstick — it wasn't fair, making her feel like some sort of Jezebel simply because she had prettied herself up a bit, just to look . . . nice.

When he left in the afternoon, she had let him know, or think, he was forgiven, and had even let him kiss her again, in a snatched moment alone before he put his bags into the back of the little Morris Eight, then walked towards the steps of the front entrance to bid farewell to his parents. 'Bye, Mummy. Bye, Dad. Don't know if I'll get off next weekend. Might pop through one night in the week, if poss.' He had slipped his arm casually about Elsbeth's waist as he stood there; a kind of declaration of intent, Elsbeth thought, intensely embarrassed, and one very much intended for his mother's smiling eye.

Elsbeth was embarrassed, too, at the element of flamboyant theatricality about the whole scene; the deliberate underplaying of emotion, when these casual farewells might be the last ever enacted between them. For even though he was not flying combat missions yet, he had let it be known, always with that careless touch of light-hearted gallows humour, of course, that the casualty rate, even on training, was significant. 'It's not the crews they're bothered about,' he laughed. 'It's bending their precious kites that really upsets them!'

In some way, Elsbeth reflected with almost tearful resentment, he made her feel that she was behaving both ungenerously and unpatriotically, that she was failing to 'do her bit' by not letting him have his way, and preventing him from pursuing that way beyond her stocking-top and the suspender to which it was attached.

* * *

Elsbeth's sense of propriety would have been further offended if she had been aware of the animated conversation which had taken place among some of the pupils that Monday lunch time. Becky Aygarth relished the chance to snatch her moment of glory in front of the girls of Standard Four, a year senior to hers, who included Doreen. Alice's sister was more than a little peeved that she had not been part of the excitement. 'She were soaked right through to the skin!' Becky told her eager audience. 'Covered in muck! She had to strip off and Al and me mam had to scrub her down!' She sniggered. 'They even had her vest and panties drying out in front of the kitchen range. I saw them — pretty pink, they were, with bits of lace round the legs! She slept with your Al,' she said, nodding importantly at Doreen. 'Me dad had to go along to Wrights' and telephone to t'Big 'Ouse, to let them know where she was.'

'I'd heard summat from our Al this morning,' Doreen lied casually. 'She didn't have time to tell us all about it. I'll find out from her later on.'

'Ask her about her fancy drawers!' a classmate cackled, and there was a burst of laughter. But Doreen's snub nose was still a little out of joint at Becky Aygarth having snatched the limelight like that, especially when Doreen should have been at the centre of events. After all, it was *her* sister who was the star player. It had all happened because that drippy Elsbeth Hobbs had gone wandering off in the dark to visit Al. She must be crackers. Her and her fancy knickers! Well, she wasn't the only one who could flash her drawers around! Doreen gave a guilty little smirk as she recalled the threepenny-bit she'd earned for her bit of bold daftness with Gus Rielke yesterday. It wasn't the first time, but it was the first time he'd paid her for it.

She hadn't cottoned on the first time he'd

talked about it — about how if you wanted to be a dancer, or good at sports and that, you had to learn to do gym. And exercise properly. 'Bet you don't know how to do de hand stand, ya?' he had said scathingly. 'Up against de wall; dere. Go on! You try. I dare you!'

She was scared to kick both her legs up, way over her head. 'Try it!' he urged, encouraging her now. 'Take off your coat and that hat. Look, I hold you. I won't let you fall.' And he had caught her, by the ankles of her boots, and held her feet up over her head, resting them against the wall, and the world was topsy-turvy, his big red face grinning down at her from between her feet, and her spread legs in the wrinkled grey stockings. It wasn't until she'd practised quite a few times, outside in the school yard with a classmate to assist her, that she was able to kick her legs up and bring herself to rest, feet uppermost against the wall. She showed off her newfound skill to Alfie James. 'It makes yer dizzy!' She grinned, her face red from her efforts when she swung her feet down. He was staring at her with a funny expression on his face.

'I can see everything. Your drawers and everything!' When she squealed in outrage, his thin face twisted in a sneer. 'I'm not daft!

That's what yer did it for, isn't it? Showing off what you've got!'

She pretended to disgust, and even anger. She had to, to save her face a little, but she could see he was right. And she knew damned well that was why the Big Swede had egged her on. It made her feel strange: hot and ashamed, but kind of excited, with a fluttery, weakening stirring in her belly. A little bit like feeling sick, but sort of nice, too, even though it shouldn't be.

Yesterday, after Miss Ramsay had gone off to church and Doreen sneaked back from her supposed visit to chapel, Gus had been there, stacking some new logs in Miss Ramsay's little shed. Doreen was in her Sunday best, with beret, scarf and gloves, and the long brown stockings Miss Ramsay had bought for her — and the clean new knickers of navy-blue. 'Go on! Let's see if you do it on your own!' Gus said, and she'd made excuses, but keeping up her air of innocence.

'I've got me best clothes on. It's Sunday. I can't.'

'Can't 'cos you are a scaredy cat! That's what they say, ya? You afraid, ain't you? Go on. I bet you.'

'No,' she said. Suddenly, she didn't feel she was pretending any more, she really did feel shy.

'I bet you. I bet you threepence you afraid.'

She took off her woollen beret, unwrapped her scarf, and slipped off her coat. Her heart was beating fast. 'Right. Threepence!' she said. She spread her palms, felt the cold bite of the gravel, then kicked off, swung her legs up over her head, felt the collision and scrape against the bricks of the wall. She saw the short, thick, winter skirt bunched about her waist, hanging down towards her, felt the cold on her thin legs, extended in a long Y against the bricks, the little gap of white flesh between the gartered tops of her stockings and the elastic legs of her pants. There was a long, endless interval of silence, while the blood rushed into her face, and she felt the merciless stare of his eyes absorbing her. She swung her feet down, toppled over, and the world lurched dizzily as she sprang to her feet. 'That's threepence you owe me!' she said breathlessly, appalled to feel herself close to crying, and unable to look at his grinning face as he dug in to a pocket and produced the dull, octagonal-sided coin.

⋆　⋆　⋆

The memory of those skinny child's legs splayed out against the wall in the baggy brown stockings returned to Gus Rielke now, and made him smile as he gazed at the pale, fleshy limb exposed before him. He could see the tracery of blue veins showing faintly through the whiteness of the skin, like some ancient map. But the skin was smooth and soft, and fragrant with soap, and with powder dusted on after the bath. In contrast with the leg, the foot was narrow and delicate, high-arched, girlish almost in its daintiness. The heel was resting in Gus's trousered lap, very close to the tumescing flesh of his sex, and he enjoyed the sweetly teasing titillation, took a keen pleasure in delaying the satiety which would surely follow. He held the foot lightly, his fingers around the instep, while with his other hand he lightly drew the matchbox back and forth over the nails, filing them to a smooth roundness.

He let his gaze drift up, like a caress, over the rounded knee to the spread plumpness of the thigh, and the frank exposure of the flesh, all the way to the furrow of the vulva, and the brown curls, soft now and silky, that adorned the mound at the base of the belly.

The landlady of the Oddfellows sighed, and shivered, and he observed her bare flesh, where the dressing-gown had fallen open on either side. 'Ooh, I love you doing my feet! It always makes me shiver when someone plays with my feet. Gets me going.' She stirred, and he watched with rising pleasure the way her flesh moved, beckoningly, as she withdrew her leg, then offered the other in its place.

'Did your Philip used to do this for you?'

Her grey eyes met his, narrowed and crinkled a little around their mascaraed edges in warmth and excited recognition. He knew she liked him to refer to her POW husband, knew it added powerfully to her pleasure in the adulterous sex she enjoyed with Gus. It worked for him, too, he acknowledged, and sighed with contentment at his good fortune. He got to work with the matchbox once more. 'I bring you a nice leg of pork. Be good for the Christmas, ya? With the goose.'

'Oh, Gus!' Her voice was husky, warm with promise, but tinged with disappointment. 'You don't have to go out again tonight, do you? That's twice this week. Why don't you give it a rest? It's dangerous, you know. You shouldn't risk it.'

He laughed. 'No risk. But the van it comes tonight. It was difficult, with the air-raids. This one come from Middlesbrough. Plenty meat. Lot of money. I make you rich, Vera, my honey.'

She pouted, her mouth turned down. 'I don't like you leaving me alone. I thought, tonight.' She arched her foot, stretched her leg and let the sole of the foot prod and press unmistakably against the swollen thrust of his flesh through the cloth.

He looked at the clock and grinned. 'I don't go till midnight. And is only half past ten. What we do for one hour and a half?'

She rose to meet him as he leaned forward, and swept the open dressing gown from her shoulders as the pale body moved fiercely into his embrace.

11

The last week of term for the Lister Road contingent in Howbeck was as hectic as it had ever been on their home ground. Although the more senior standards, Three, Four and Five, combined with the village children for most of their lessons, in the school proper, the rest had remained a cohesive unit, in their own territory — at least from morning until approximately 4 p.m. during weekdays — of the village hall, led by Edith Bowen, and her eager subordinate, Elsbeth, assisted more and more as the term wore on, in various unofficial but important ways, by Alice. A maternal, close scrutiny was kept on this little sub-division by their overall commander-in-the-field, Miss Laverton. She it was who encouraged, and largely organized, the Nativity play, which Lister Road Infants was to offer as an added contribution to the festivities to mark the second Christmas of the war. Though the events of the last week were meant to emphasize good will, and to reflect, in their small way, the spirit of co-operation between the splendidly loyal Empire and the mother country in its beleaguered isle, an element of competition began to arise, as the day of the joint performances drew near.

Edith Bowen came up with the idea of stealing a march on the other production, by the juniors of Howbeck C of E school and Lister Road combined, through the incorporation of live animals into the manger scene. 'Can't you get Mr Aygarth to lend us a sheep, or maybe two? And a calf? He doesn't have any donkeys up there, does he?' she asked a dubious Alice.

She was gently but firmly dissuaded by Miss Laverton, who pointed out that the hall was required the very evening of the show for some seasonal adult entertainment. 'Cleaning up after real livestock might add somewhat to our problems.'

'I don't fancy shovelling up sheep — and cow-shit to round off the proceedings,' Alice said, more forthrightly, to a giggling Elsbeth.

An extra item, which Miss Laverton proposed, was a party, to take place on Monday, the 23rd, though term officially ended on the previous Friday. Only nine out of the fifty-plus total of evacuees were returning to Margrove for the holiday. The very recent spate of air-raids in the town had doubtless helped to swell the numbers who would not be returning home, though not by much, many of the adults privately thought. 'We've got to make sure we give our children the best possible Christmas we can manage. An early visit from Father Christmas, as good a beano as we can provide, and some rip-roaring games are the order of the day, I think. Alice! What's the position as far as you're concerned — and Algy and Doreen, of course? Will you be staying?'

'Yes, miss. Me mam's hoping to get up for a day some time before New Year.'

'And Elsbeth? Any chance of you being able to hang on to help out? You could still get away by teatime, I'd say. Not sure about the trains, though. I shall be leaving Christmas Eve — I've got a lift. I dare say we could squeeze you in.' She added quickly, with an air of apology, 'I'll be back again after three or four days. Certainly before New Year's Eve.'

As usual Elsbeth was pink. Alice noted it, and wondered if it was just her normal reaction to being addressed publicly, even in this select gathering, or whether she was suffering from the incipient feelings of guilt, which seemed to infect all those who were getting away from Howbeck. 'Oh — er, yes, Miss Laverton. I'll be here. I'm not sure . . . I may go later. Or next day. But I'll manage, thank you.'

Now, another reason altogether suggested itself for her blushes, in Alice's mind. Does this mean Brylcreem Boy rides again? she speculated cynically. So your blushes are really for me? Well, don't bother on my account, sweetheart! Because I'm not. She tried very hard to convince herself that that was the truth.

'Listen,' she said to Elsbeth, when Miss Laverton had departed. 'You don't have to hang on here till Monday, if it's gonna mess up your arrangements. There'll be loads of us to manage. More than enough, likely. We'll be getting under each other's feet. Half the village'll be turning up to help out.'

'No, honestly! I *want* to be here for it. It'll be all right, I'm sure. I can still get a lift on Christmas Eve.' She saw the beginnings of something in Alice's eyes and added swiftly, 'My father's coming through — if he can't make it himself he'll send a driver to pick me up. In fact I've been meaning to say. I'm sure there'll be room for you and Doreen and Algy, if you want a lift home. I can let him know in advance. He won't mind at all.'

Alice beamed a grateful smile, then her face screwed up in a look of resignation. 'Thanks a lot, love, but I'd best leave things the way they are. To be honest, Doreen would far rather stay in Howbeck. She's got so well in here. Miss Ramsay spoils her rotten. From the looks of it we're not gonna see much of her up at Beck Side on Christmas Day, the little madam! They're having their own do at Northend Cottage.' Alice put on her caricature of a toff's accent. 'Dinner will be at night, don't you know! Lizzy's having a few of her friends round, wants our Doreen to be there for it. She makes such a fuss of her. It's 'Auntie Elizabeth' now, you know. Jess Corbett reckons Doreen's taken the place of her little pet dog she used to have. Treat it like a child she did, Jess reckoned. She was broken-hearted, apparently, when it died. Went into mourning for months! So our Doreen's come in useful. Ready house trained and all! And she can do tricks all right, the crafty little bitch!'

Elsbeth smiled. Alice continued. 'To be truthful, our Algy's happy as laddy here, too. He'll have a far better time with the Aygarth kids than he would at home.' Her light-hearted veneer faded, and that expression of realistic acceptance returned. 'Christmas has always been a bit of a disappointment in our house. Father Christmas never brought a lot. And me dad was usually sleeping off the skinful from the night before, then working his way through the next lot all day. If the pubs weren't shut, we'd never have seen him.'

She frowned, and nodded with half-jocular resignation. 'Been a damn sight better off if they *had* been open.'

Elsbeth was gazing with mute sympathy, and Alice's face split in a wide, sudden grin. 'Hark at me! Right little ray of sunshine, eh? Enough to put anybody off. We'll have a great time with the Aygarths. In any case, with all these raids going on, we're better off where we are. It'll be me worrying sick about you till you get back safe and sound. Don't forget your gas-mask. I don't even know where mine is any more! I never think about it.'

'I'm not going to be away long. Just a few days. I'll be back before New Year.'

'Well, you take care, you hear?' Then Alice said in her brusque manner, 'I'll miss you.'

'Me too. See you in the morning.'

Alice quickly thrust her face forward, aiming a kiss to land lightly on Elsbeth's cheek, but the blonde girl turned her face a little, intercepted it, and their lips touched.

★   ★   ★

It was Becky Aygarth who started the clock of suspicion ticking in Alice's mind a couple of nights later. Malcolm had been out and had cut down the young fir tree earlier that afternoon, and the four children chattered excitedly as they hovered and fussed, and generally got under the adults' feet as they began the task of decorating it. Several wrapped parcels lay to hand ready to place at its foot, which had been anchored in a milking-pail disguised with cloths and a layer of crêpe paper.

'Your Doreen's got some presents of her own!' Becky sniggered, her dark eyes glinting with less than innocent mischief. She had lowered her voice, and glanced round to make sure no one else was within hearing. 'That Alfie James has given her all sorts! One of them real scenty bars of soap. Lux. Like the fillum stars use. Some squirty scent — and some glittery hair-slides, like diamonds! Ever so posh!' She giggled, with just a hint of nervousness, as though she was not quite sure she was not doing wrong in her betrayal of these secrets. 'He must really fancy her! Like a boyfriend. Mary Briggs says he must have pinched 'em. They must have cost a fortune!'

Alice knew the child was watching her, to see her reaction, and for an instant felt a blaze of anger that made her palm itch. She set her face in an expression of careless disregard. 'Probably somebody telling daft tales. I know how soppy you lasses can be.'

'No, it's right. She was showing them off to

215

Mary, and one or two more. And Mary said he bought the soap at the shop — Mrs Floyd's.' She was still awaiting some further reaction. Evidently, Alice's calm did not completely reassure her, for she added warily, 'You won't say owt, will you?'

It was Alice's turn to give way, for a second or two, to her own malice. 'You'd better hope not, eh? Our Doreen can be a vicious little devil sometimes. She made a lass twice her size pee her pants with fright once!' The look of anxiety which transformed Becky's features made her repent her own mean triumph, and she said, 'Don't worry. I won't let on. But it doesn't always do to go telling tales out of school. Remember that!'

Alice made a point of walking up the hill to the village school at playtime next morning, and seeking out Doreen, leading her away from a close-knit bunch of girls from her class. 'Regular little star attraction, you are!' she said sarcastically. 'Must be that new soap you're using!' The tide of red which crept into the delicate face was testament to her guilt. 'Shouldn't go blabbin' your secrets round and showing off to your mates if you don't want to get found out. You can give them things back Alfie James has been giving you. I don't know where he gets his money from, with his arse hanging out of his breeches, but he's up to no good. And you're just as bad taking them from him! And what do you have to do for *him* in return, eh?'

'Nowt! I can't help it if he likes me, can I? Just 'cos *you've* never had a boyfriend in your life . . . ' she paused, glared at Alice with a show of defiance, but her lips quivered, and there was an edge of alarm in the brown eyes.

Alice's mouth curved in contempt. '*Boyfriend?* You're ten years old, not twenty! Stick to your skippy ropes and your Raggety Pegs! Don't you take owt else from him, you hear? And don't go encouraging him. Don't you have owt to do with him, or maybe you'd like your *boyfriend* and all your mates to see me tek your drawers down and give your behind a good leathering, eh?' The scowl was still there on Doreen's face, but there was a wariness, too, and a tension in the thin figure that indicated she believed her sister's threat might well be more than an idle one. Alice glanced round, scanned the groups of children quickly. 'Anyway, where is the gorgeous Alfie? Time I had another word with him, I reckon. Tell him he can stop playing Father Christmas, as far as *you're* concerned, any road.'

'No, don't! I'll tell him, honest. I won't take owt else from him, I promise. He doesn't mean any harm by it, but I'll tell him to stop it. He's been doing extra up at the farm, for Symmonds. Been busy for Christmas.'

'Sounds a very generous sort of feller, ould Symmonds. Didn't know he was so well-off.'

'Alfie's been working real hard. All hours. Up half the night sometimes. Trails all over the moors.'

Once again, Alice's curiosity and suspicion were aroused. She was reminded of her former doubts about the set-up at High Top Farm, and the connection with Gus Rielke. It was definitely a matter for further investigation — and for discretion. She decided she had done enough with Doreen for the time being, and eased off on the sternness of her manner, so that they parted amicably enough, after a final, much more big-sisterly warning.

Doreen heaved a sigh of relief as she watched Alice striding off down the road again. She was blowed if she was going to give any of those things back to Alfie James, but she'd better have a friendly word with him, to warn him that Alice was off on the warpath. She felt another twinge of guilt as she thought of her real feelings for the scruffy lad who had taken such a shine to her. He was dirty, and as rough as a lad could be, and his slouching figure and generally scowling face was anything but attractive. He reminded her powerfully of some of the sullen, cowed and crafty mongrels that roamed the streets round Maudsley Street: the so-called pets of households where they were kicked and cuffed and turfed out to fend for themselves from dawn till dark. But for all his bullying and his bluster, he was as clumsy, ignorant and innocent of boy-and-girl things as any lad of his age. All she had to do was be a little nice and smile at him, pretend to be a bit interested in his bragging talk, and he brought presents to her like one of those dogs fetching a stick. Alice making such a fuss over it was daft. A smile twitched at the corners of Doreen's pretty mouth as she thought of what her big sister would say if she knew what Doreen had to do to earn the threepenny-bits that Gus handed out. Now that really *would* get her going! But even that was really nothing to get all worked up about. He was only looking, when all said and done, and what harm was there in that?

★   ★   ★

Everyone agreed that Gus Rielke would make an ideal Father Christmas for the party organized by Miss Laverton for the day before Christmas Eve. His big, powerful frame, his open red face, even when hidden under a bush of cotton-wool beard, was just right for the part. On top of that his exotic accent would give added authenticity to the deep tones and hearty ho-ho-hoes. 'And he volunteered for the job,' Miss Laverton enthused to the staff, as the end of the hectic last week approached. 'Said he's an evacuee just like the children, so it was right that he should take part.'

Alice wisely kept her thoughts to herself, for they were not in tune with the general feeling at the Big Swede's generous spirit. Ould Lavvy had changed her tune from her early assessment, when she had seen at close hand the easy familiarity of his relationship with Vera Rhodes. 'Living under the same roof' had carried a connotation, when pronounced in the head's precise tones, that indicated a distinct lack of approval. But, as with most others in the village, familiarity in Miss Laverton's eyes had not bred contempt but rather an altogether too easy acceptance of the big foreigner's presence in their midst.

Alice was well aware that her own instincts placed her in the minority — of one, she sometimes felt. Even Elsbeth, the only one with whom she could share her suspicion and distrust, was inclined to adopt, at best, a position firmly on the fence as far as he was concerned. She looked at her dubiously when Alice held forth on the subject. 'I'm gonna find out more about him and that Bob Symmonds. Everybody you talk to says Symmonds has always been scratting about to make a living out of High Top. Hasn't got two ha'pennies to scratch his arse with. Sorry!' She grinned repentantly at the automatic wince from Elsbeth at her indelicate phraseology. 'But he's had Alfie James working all hours lately — the kid's been coming to school half dead. And I told you about our Doreen, all the things he's been buying her.' As Elsbeth began to speak, Alice held up her hand. 'All right. I know they're just daft bairns, and he's just been showing off in front of the lasses, but the little bugger's flashing more money round than I've got, from what I hear.'

'But Alice — '

'Al!' Alice corrected automatically.

'Sorry. Al.' Elsbeth coloured, and the slight rush of breathlessness in her voice marked her embarrassment. 'Listen. I'll try to remember — I *do* try to call you Al. You can pinch me every time I forget — but will you do something for *me*? Will you call me Beth? I've always hated Elsbeth. Sounds like some old spinster. Beth's much more . . . well, it's just nicer, I think.'

Alice laughed, adopted a broad imitation of a Hollywood accent. 'OK, it's a deal. Al and

Beth, that's us, from now on! Sounds like a good team.' But Elsbeth's enthusiastic accord faded at Alice's next words. 'And you can help me, kidder. This Saturday, we're gonna take another walk up on High Top. I've been putting it off, what with one thing and another. But I want to take a look round. See if we can find this shed little Frankie was on about. And what else was it? Summat about a pit of some sort, for animals. Remember? He was on about a funny smell coming from there. But they weren't allowed to go anywhere near it. Time we did a bit of snooping, eh, Beth?' Elsbeth's lack of eagerness was evident. 'Come on! We'll keep away from the farmhouse, and I promise I won't do owt daft if we see anybody. Just out for a hike, that's all. You can come back to Beck Side for tea — Eileen'll be baking something nice. Howay!' She caught hold of Elsbeth's arm with both hands and squeezed it encouragingly, but suddenly she let it go, and her face darkened with fresh suspicion. 'Hang on! Got summat else lined up, have you? Brylcreem Boy putting in an appearance again? Time to be off with the toffs again, is it?'

'No!' Elsbeth's voice was full of indignation. 'I've no idea if Luke's coming home this weekend.' She had a fair idea that he wasn't, for he would have let her know if he was. 'And even if he is . . . ' She paused, looked at Alice with gentle reproach. 'I'd just as soon be with you.' She savoured the flash of contrition — and pleasure — on the volatile face, and reached out for the hands which had just released her arm. 'I'm not a toff, you know. Not one of them. I'm just an ordinary girl.'

'Don't be daft! That's one thing you're definitely not! There's not a thing that's ordinary about *you!*' She grabbed her and gave her a hearty squeeze before she thrust her from her, with a forced laugh. 'If I was a lad I'd never let you out of my sight!'

Elsbeth giggled. 'If you were a lad I wouldn't dare walk down the street with you. All right, I'll go for a hike with you. But, please, *please!* Promise you won't do anything stupid, to get us into trouble. It was bad enough last time. I was petrified of that fierce old hag.'

'Don't worry, princess! I'll protect you, sweetheart. I wouldn't let anyone harm a hair of your head — Beth!'

She guyed the passionate tone of a lover, and pulled her in close, their well-wrapped bodies pressing against each other. Alice continued the pose of ardent lover, and with rough playfulness captured Elsbeth's face and planted a smacking kiss on the mouth. They were both laughing, but then they held the kiss; their lips moved, and searched, and kept contact until Alice thrust Elsbeth away roughly, and turned with savage laughter to put distance between them. 'Shame I'm *not* a lad, eh? We'd make a lovely pair!'

★   ★   ★

The dog set up a fierce, shrill barking that rose piercingly in the dead winter air while the girls were still many yards from the low, dilapidated building. 'Bugger!' Alice declared feelingly.

Elsbeth remained dumb, but her expression spoke eloquently of her nervousness. The pretty face looked small and pinched, muffled in the thick scarf and the pixie hood which made it even more childlike. Her complexion was pale, apart from the shiny pink of the tip of her nose, and her even shinier, darker lips. They were parted, with breathlessness from her bodily exertions and from her rapidly increasing apprehension. Clouds of steam puffed from them and hung in the cold paleness. Overhead, the sky was one dull grey-white, pressing down on them with its weight of unshed snow. Its heaviness seemed to muffle every sound, except for that jangling, hysterical yapping which set Elsbeth's nerves on edge.

She glanced back up the steep slope of the field and the ragged line of black hedge. She knew that not far away, far too near in fact, the neglected outbuildings of High Top, and the shabby house itself, lay in wait. 'They're bound to hear!' she panted. Her blue eyes fixed on Alice's ruddier face showed her anxiety. 'Look! There it is, see? Is it tied up?'

'Yeah, of course it is. Come on. We're all right. Let's get a bit nearer. Don't let it see you're scared.' She tried a reassuring smile. 'They can smell fear, you know.'

'No wonder it's going mad then. I must stink of it!'

Alice giggled, and linked her arm firmly through Elsbeth's, almost as though she were preventing her from escaping. 'Come on! You're getting as bad as me, you little devil!'

There was only a thin layer of snow, a crust that did not cover the tall, dry tufts of uneven grass, where the low, encroaching heather crunched blackly underfoot, in spite of the rough, tumbledown fencing Symmonds had erected to bound the enclosure. The Aygarths had warned Alice not to stray far from the moor road. 'There's a bellyful of snow in them clouds,' Malcolm had said. 'If it starts coming down and the wind starts to pick up, you get yourselves back home quick, you hear?' Elsbeth, too, had tried to put her off, using the weather as an excuse. But now Alice's eagerness was such that even the furious snarling and bared teeth of the collie at the end of its rope failed to deter her. She kept talking to it, in an even, pleasant tone as they approached, and its yapping did decrease in volume a little. Her bravery did not extend however to moving within range and trying to make physical contact. She already had enough experience of these farm dogs to know that they were quite likely to snack at the hand that fed them if it was a strange one. When they got close to the small building it became obvious that, although old, it was kept in a far better state of repair than any of the others at High Top. The thick stone walls had only two high window openings, glassless but stoutly and comprehensively boarded up to allow no possibility of seeing inside, even if anyone curious enough to try could reach them.

'I could mebbes bunk you up on me shoulders,' Alice murmured dubiously, and Elsbeth's eyes widened in alarm. 'But they look nailed up solid. I doubt we could break in.'

'For goodness' sake!' Elsbeth exclaimed, with much more feeling than the form of the mild oath suggested.

There was a wide door, also very solid, painted green and also stoutly unassailable. The keyhole of the old-fashioned lock looked freshly painted, and beside it a sturdy padlock and chain were attached to another iron hasp driven deep into the stone beside the frame. 'By God! They don't mean for anyone to get in, do they?'

Round the angle of the wall, the dog's pitch of fury had risen once again. 'Come on! Let's go! Please!' The frantic quality of Elsbeth's pleading had risen, too.

Alice turned away in frustration, but she glanced from the door to the white-patched ground. 'Look at this!' she said excitedly. She ran forward, her gaze fixed on the earth ahead of her. 'Look at these tracks. What the hell's been going on?' There was a distinct track worn through the tussocks of grass. Even under the light snowfall and the wetness of the ground, it was clear that a heavy vehicle had passed back and forth several times from the front of the shed. Its wheels had worn quite deep channels.

'It's just a farm tractor or something.' Elsbeth's voice was still high with tension. 'They're always — '

'Ould Symmonds doesn't have a hoss, let alone a tractor.'

'Maybe he borrowed one. They lend them out to each other. Come on, let's get out of here before — '

'What the hell would he need a tractor for, up here?' She was bending down, peering closely at her feet. 'Anyways, there's different tracks. Look here, see? Them's not tractor-marks, not all of them. There's been a lorry up here.' She stood up, stared away up the field. 'God knows how they got up here from the road. And why.'

But now it was Elsbeth who was tugging at Alice's arm. 'Al! Please! Let's go, before someone comes. There'll be someone here any minute. I'm scared!'

'God, you scaredy-cat, Beth!' She grinned at the frantic girl, but began to move away. They kept hold of each other as they headed for the low fence and the moor beyond. 'Now, where's that pit thing?'

Once they had climbed through the fence they trudged up towards the brow of the ridge, and the cluster of farm buildings came into sight, comfortingly distant. Elsbeth was still nervous, though. 'We're not going to find anything up here, are we? I think we should head back to the road.'

The fair-haired girl was proved wrong within the next few minutes, as she stumbled along complainingly in the wake of the shorter, sturdier figure. They were almost on the old sheep-dip before they discovered it. This time there was no dog to bark out its warning, and the concreted dip was well camouflaged among an outcrop of old feeding troughs and rusting farm implements. 'Looks like summat from the Great War.' Alice carefully picked her way through the debris of metal, and the barbed-wire entanglements. There was a mound of turf at one end, then a layer of corrugated-iron sheets, like those used to make the Anderson shelters. Their newness indicated that this might well have been their intended purpose. In fact, Alice at first thought that this was a cunningly constructed air-raid shelter, except that its location made no sense of such a use. But then she saw how clever was its concealment, for at the end opposite the mound of earth, where the concrete began, the sheets of iron were not as securely fastened as the others, and, lying flat on the wet grass, she could peer into the dark cavern beneath. 'Look at this!'

But Elsbeth, her feet inside her wellington boots frozen and her body, despite the warm layers of clothing, chilled, was a little more fastidious about sprawling in the muck. 'What is it?'

'There's great big drums. Four of them. You know — them big oil drums. And they stink! Can't you smell it? Here! Get your head down here, and have a whiff. What you reckon?'

Elsbeth squatted down, gingerly dipped her head and sniffed. 'Petrol.'

Alice nodded. 'Aye, lass. And a bloody lot of it an' all! What's it doing up here?'

'Well, farmers get an allowance. Extra ration. There's plenty at the Big House. Mr Denby let Luke have some for the Morris. There's always a bit spare.'

'That's all right for the squire and such like. They've got loads of land.' She stood, and wiped at the mud that clung to her breeches and coat. 'But like I said. Symmonds doesn't have a car — or a tractor. What's this lot doing up here miles from anywhere?'

'It might not be his.' Elsbeth glanced around, back towards the distant buildings. Her face was still pinched with her unease. 'This might not be his land even.'

Alice waved away her arguments dismissively. She had moved a few yards, was again peering at the ground around her. 'Look!' She pointed excitedly. 'Them tracks again!' She looked up triumphantly. 'Summat very funny going on up here,

Beth. And we're gonna find out what!'

Elsbeth stared back helplessly. She felt her cramped stomach tighten once more. She loved her friend to bits, but she did not at all like the sound of that 'we'.

PART II

THE SPY GLASS

12

'Would you like to come inside and get warm? You look wet through. Fancy a cuppa tea? Just made a fresh pot.'

Davy Brown stared at the grinning, curly-haired girl in the too-large sweater over the baggy brown dungarees. He was startled at her hearty friendliness. She had come down the steps from the village hall and was leaning over the stone wall at the edge of the yard. He had been working on the small, enclosed patch of land that lay beyond it, between the hall and Wynn's garage, and the lane that led to the station. The trees had already been felled, but the ground around the stumps was still a tangle of wild bushes: brambles and briars, and tall dead weeds among the long grass.

The girl was right. He was certainly wet, his clothes damply uncomfortable despite the heat he had built up through the violence of his efforts with the sickle. And with precious little visible evidence to show for it, he conceded. His blistered hands were throbbing painfully; he could hardly straighten his fingers from the claws they had formed. Hers was the only kind voice he had heard since his arrival in Howbeck three days ago, on the sixth day of this new year. 1941. Like most folk, he guessed, he tried not to look ahead too far to anticipate what might lie there. Still, as far as he was concerned, it could hardly be worse than the last.

'That's very good of you, miss. If it's not too much trouble.' He saw the girl's cheerful smile alter slightly, the eyebrows raising in surprise, occasioned, he intuited, by his non-regional speech, his 'posh talk', as he had heard it described so many uncomplimentary times in the recent past. He climbed over the low wall, and followed her through the door into the small kitchen at the rear of the hall. He could hear the collective tones of the children on the other side of the thin partition wall, and over them the clear, high tones of their mistress, scarcely less childlike.

'I'm Alice Glass, by the way,' the girl said, still beaming. She wiped her hand on her overall before extending it to him in formal greeting. He glanced at his own. It was much dirtier, and he, too, wiped it on his coat before he allowed it to make contact. He tried not to wince, but she noticed at once. 'Ooh, they look sore. You should get them covered. You shouldn't be working outside this weather any road.' She turned to the stove and picked up a large enamel teapot, holding the handle with a dish-towel. 'You must be the new feller that's come to Big House, yeah? Mr Barr said he'd be sending somebody across to clear out back. Didn't think it'd be on a day like this, though. School only started Monday.'

'I only arrived myself then. Thank you.' He took the proffered mug of tea, already pale with the added milk.

She gave a conspiratorial grin, and glanced around with mock furtiveness. 'You can have a spoon of sugar.' She held out the patterned tin. 'Nobody'll miss it.'

For just an instant he was tempted, but he shook his head. 'No, thanks. You're very kind, but I've got used to it without now.'

She gave a mock shiver. 'Brrr! You're very good. I couldn't stand it without. What's your name then?'

He blushed a little. 'Oh, I'm so sorry! I'm David Brown. Davy, my friends call me.' What friends? he asked himself in bitter irony.

'Pleased to meet you, Davy. *I* like people to call me Al, but not many do. Alice is such a soppy name, I think.'

He havered politely in the ritual of disagreeing. 'I'll try to remember.' His gallantry sounded awkward. He felt it, too. He realized how unused he was nowadays to making casual conversation, especially with a personable young girl. At that moment the door opened, and two women entered, in headscarves and shabby overcoats, underneath which they wore overalls similar to Alice's. She introduced them quickly. 'This is Jess Corbett, and Annie Hogan. We're the ones that feed the hungry hordes next door. This is Davy Brown. The new lad up at Big House.'

Jess muttered an embarrassed reply to his polite greeting. Annie gave an emphatic sniff, and glanced eloquently at his wet boots and the linoed floor. 'Made yerself at home, I see. And left yer mucky prints all ower the floor.'

'Hey! I invited him in!' Alice answered, red-faced with anger and embarrassment on his behalf. But he was already gulping hastily at the mug and replacing it on the table.

'Yes, well . . . I shouldn't be in here. You're quite right. I'd better be off. Sorry about the boots. And thanks.' He was blushing as he nodded quickly at Alice then made his escape.

'What the hell's the matter with you?' Alice said aggressively. 'Poor bloke didn't know where to put himself! That was bloody rude!'

'You want to watch who you chat to!' Annie Hogan replied, matching Alice's tone. 'I for one don't want the likes of him setting foot in here. Or anywhere else if I had my way! You know who he is, don't you?' Her dark eyes glared in fierce challenge.

'Aye, of course. I told you! He's the new feller up at Big House. I just — '

'Aye! Didn't tell yer who he *really* is, though, did he? Young bugger's only a conchy, eh? Got out of army and everything. The' reckon he's even done time in gaol an' all. Should have kept him there and thrown away the bloody key!'

Alice's irascibility was swamped by her surprise. She glanced involuntarily towards the door. 'What? *Him*? Poor lad looks as though he wouldn't say boo to a goose.'

'Aye, well! Reckon you're right there! Just shows, don't it?'

Alice smothered the critical retort that came swiftly to her mind, and Annie Hogan turned away, mollified by the sensation her news had caused. Alice was meanwhile struggling with her own sense of guilt at the sympathy she could not help feeling for the shy, rather under-nourished looking young man. After all, Annie had called him a conchy. Conscientious objector. Someone who refused to fight for his king and country. And gone to gaol for it! her own conscience reminded her. But he wasn't in gaol now, was he? And now more than ever we needed lads willing to join up and do their bit. Doesn't matter if they're willing or not, they still have to go into the forces, so what's he doing safe and sound here in sleepy old Howbeck, with nowt more dangerous than blisters on his hands from a bit of hard graft? They're even gonna bring in law to make lasses sign up any day now, and as far as she was concerned she couldn't wait for it to happen!

At least, she thought she couldn't. She hadn't even thought about it at all for a long time now. It had been the chance to get away from Margrove and 'Little Hitler' at the Co-op stores rather than a desire to lay down her life for King George and Queen Elizabeth that had been her motivation. And she'd managed that all right with taking on this job with the school and looking after the bairns. She was really enjoying it, and doing something worthwhile and all. She wouldn't be so keen to give it up now. She'd really taken to the country life, she reckoned. For the first time in her life she felt she fitted in somewhere and was part of something good, a team. That poor lad. Davy Brown. He must really be a loner, poor bugger. He'd never be able to live down his past. In fact, it had got ahead of him, it seemed, so he didn't stand a chance. Not with long nosed, vicious cows like Annie Hogan to spread it round.

At that second, rising clearly through the thin wall, Alice heard the strained, high-pitched tone of Elsbeth, slightly wobbly as usual when she was under pressure. 'Now come along, children! Settle down! Be quiet, please! Billy, leave that alone and sit down!' It reminded Alice of another, even more powerful reason she would be reluctant to leave Howbeck, and brought a touch of heightened colour to her cheeks which could not be blamed entirely on the steaming pan of potatoes she closed in on determinedly.

★　★　★

It was nearly dark even though it was just 4 p.m. A drizzle had started again, and with it came a mist like feeble smoke, just beginning to hang about the trees across the neat furrows of turned earth that marked the extended vegetable garden and the remaining stretch of lawn. Davy was putting the tools back in the old potting-shed next to the long greenhouse. The aching cold seemed to strike through his wet clothing to his very bones, and his hands were throbbing abominably, but at least another weary working day was almost over. Apart from the 'firewatching' duties he had been assigned to, from eight to midnight. He suspected that this was a routine which had not been observed very thoroughly before his arrival, and probably wouldn't fall on any other shoulders but his. When he had asked who would relieve him, Pearson, the aged gardening 'gaffer', had chuckled wheezily. 'Don't tha' worry about that, lad. Just mek sure yer sign in t'book in stables at finish of yer stint. Mr Barr, or maybe squire hisself, 'll be round like as not some time to keep their eye on yer.'

Davy's thoughts dwelt on the luxury of stretching out in a hot bath, in decadent solitude, with soft, clean towels awaiting him at the end of it. The memory was very recent, for he had spent a brief interlude at his parents' home in a village outside York before coming here just a few days ago. It had been an unaccustomed extravagance, after the months of hardship and brutality he had endured. He forced his mind away from dwelling on ablutions at the vivid recall of the horrors inflicted in the bleak prison bathroom. He would be lucky to find any hot water in the staff washroom here, and maybe not even much privacy, but at least his heart need not pound with fear every time he entered.

As he was backing out of the gloom of the shed and pulling the door to, he heard a scurry of footsteps and an accompanying skirl of shrill voices and subdued laughter. All at once he remembered that today was the day when the pupils of St Anne's, the school which had been billeted here, were due to return. He found himself confronted by a gaggle of uniformed girls, mostly in their mid-teens, and disconcertingly mature in their abbreviated gym slips, despite the ties and sashes, and the dark winter hats. He realized suddenly that, instead of walking past, along the uneven pavement of the stable block, they had formed up in a double row, facing him, the white blurs of their faces fixed on him in a concentration that sent his nerves racing with apprehension. He felt helpless, felt their united gaze pinning him immobile against the closed door of the shed. He was trapped. He had the sensation of being a prisoner tied to the post, facing his execution squad: an image from his father's war. But there was no blindfold, no last cigarette. He couldn't look away from the impersonal mercilessness of those virginal eyes.

Somebody quickly counted, 'One, two, three,' and they all began to sing, their voices true and pure, in innocent treble, to the tune of 'Daisy, Daisy':

Conchy, Conchy,
Give me your answer do,

How will we stop old Adolf
If we all run away like you?

You're a funny little fellow
And your favourite colour's yellow,
But you'll look cute in an army suit
Or in Navy- or Air-Force blue.

There was a flutter of high-pitched giggling, louder this time, and they turned and ran off, in a jostling, scuffling flurry of black legs and pale, nudging elbows.

He stood motionless, staring after them, and hearing their excited, laughing voices fading into the wet mist. For several seconds he still felt helpless, pinned by that invisible force to the door behind him, and the ground at his leaden feet. He was shaking. Shivering, as though he had an ague. His heart was beating fast, and his chest was tight, and aching as he drew his breath in a deep sob. Oh God! His eyes, which had been fixed in a wide stare all the while, facing them, and then staring after them, stung and filled with tears. He blinked them away, raised his dirty hands and, in a childish gesture, knuckled them away. Helplessly, hopelessly, his mind spun away, out of his control, to span the long reach of time that had led to this shameful, shaming moment, when a bunch of schoolgirls could reduce him to trembling weeping.

The first great irony was that his pacifism might well have been anticipated: an inherited trait, from his parents, as natural as his brown eyes and dark hair, his lean frame, for both his father and his mother were Quakers, a term which had long lost its derisory meaning to denote the members of the Society of Friends, founded by George Fox in the seventeenth century. And maybe his rejection of violence was just such a belief, absorbed unconsciously, perhaps, from his constant exposure during his childhood to their religious principles. If so, it was, indeed, ironic, for he had absorbed nothing else of their theology, which he had rebelled against as soon as he was able to think for himself, or at least to act on what he thought. He had left the Quaker boarding-school in nearby York as early as he could, and under a considerable cloud, and with no noteworthy achievements, academic or otherwise. Still his parents had continued to support him, in spite of the undoubted pain his rejection of their religion and their values caused them. He left home and moved to London, and was angry with them for the money they continued to send, modest though it was, and even angrier with himself for needing it to survive. He tried to make up for his dependence on it by squandering much of it on alcohol, and trying to live a kind of Bohemian existence on the ragged fringes of the so-called intellectual young ne'er-do-wells who liked to class themselves as existentialists. Most of them weren't at all sure what it meant, and cared little anyway. Though it had thrived in the first decade of the post-war to end all wars, it was more than frayed round the edges as the thirties advanced. Political commitment, to one extreme or the other, took its place, and Davy threw in his lot with the left-wing, anti-fascist brigade. Fired with romantic enthusiasm, fuelled by alcohol, he enlisted in one of the international cohorts being formed to support the Republicans, and reached Spain, after an inadequate training period, in time to help defend Madrid against the Nationalists, successfully. But this was followed by almost an entire year of defeats and retreats as General Franco's forces relentlessly spread northward until they reached the Mediterranean, cutting the country in two.

Davy was lucky to get out, a few days after his nineteenth birthday, sleeping on the deck of a coaster which landed him in France. He had seen more than enough of violence and killing, witnessed horrors like the deadly air attacks by the German dive-bombers fighting for Franco, and rehearsing for the much greater terror they would unleash two years later. And he had seen horrors committed, too, by the side he had been supporting. The glamour and the excitement had all gone, along with the conviction of right and wrong. Pacifism seeped into his soul inevitably during his bone-weary sleep on the dirty, throbbing deck of the steamer taking him away from Spain. But the conviction that followed, that gave him the moral courage to resist the seemingly worldwide obsession with violence and to stand up and be counted, was not born then. That came only after he had met and known Lou.

Louisa Varron, or 'Lou' as she was to her friends, among whom he was deeply grateful to count himself, was a young woman two years older than he was, whom he had met within a day or two of arriving in Paris. As soon as Davy had made contact with his family, just to let them know he was safely out of Spain and done with its civil war, his father had arranged for money to be transferred to him in the French capital, along with an urgent request that he should get himself back to England as soon as possible. *The situation could deteriorate rapidly in Europe,* his father wrote. *The Germans are going to move into Austria any day. We'll have to stand up to them. You could be caught up in a far worse conflagration.*

But Davy's loss of appetite for violence had not impinged on his restless desire for adventure, and to find something to do with his life. He was grateful for his father's money, and moved by the loving, and forgiving, generosity of spirit which made it available to him, even though he had proved to be, in so many ways, a deep disappointment to all his folks' hopes for him. But he was not yet ready to return to the familial fold, and the smothering effect of that relentless goodness on his still searching, unquiet nature.

He was doubly glad, therefore, when he was able to find a menial job in a cheap student hostel, which would provide a roof and a shabby dormitory bed and a small wage — enough to hold out the hope at least that he would not remain entirely dependent on his father's financial support. It also brought him into contact once again with the young, student-based society similar to that he had known in London before he had enlisted in one of the International Brigades. It was at the hostel that he first became friendly with Lou.

He worked in the café and bar which operated in the basement of the building, and when he was not working he soon began to spend most of his free evenings there as well. She was tall and thin, as tall as he was, and striking. Only later did he begin to think of her as beautiful, and only later still, when he had 'lost' her, could he identify more objectively with the truism about 'the eye of the beholder'. She was in any case splendidly careless about her looks. She didn't wear make-up; her hair, a deep, bronzy gold, cut short in a practical style that meant it required little attention other than a comb or brush tugged through it to keep it tidy-looking. Her clothes, too, were unfussy: good quality but plain and functional rather than flattering. She wore skirts down to mid-calf, her stockings were thick against the spring chill, her shoes sensibly solid, with low heels.

Yet she attracted people of her own age to her. There was something about her — Davy felt and recognized it almost immediately, a quality he couldn't quite explain fully — that drew people to her, female as well as male. Within a few weeks he was falling in love with her. It shocked him. He couldn't get her out of his mind, or stop wanting to be with her, to know more and more about her. He waited with growing, and then almost frantic, impatience, for her to come into the bar, or to meet her and her friends at one of the pavement cafés on the 'Boule Miche', as the Boulevard Saint Michel was known.

The trouble was, he could never get to see her alone. Always there were at least half a dozen boys and girls surrounding her, part of the crowd to which he himself now belonged. Politics was, naturally, the eternally consuming topic. Hitler had moved into Austria in March, and within two days Austria had ceased to exist as a separate entity, but was part of the Third Reich. As spring advanced it was clear that he was turning his attention to Czechoslovakia. 'We have to stop him!' Time and time the phrase was repeated, with the same violence and determination. But nobody seemed to know, or to agree on, how. 'It must be ourselves and your country,' his friends told him, and he agreed. But hovering, like a ghost at his elbow, were the bitter memories still recent, and his own sense of repugnance at the thought of being personally involved in such things again. All his companions, like himself, were left-wing in their view, many were registered communists or their sympathizers. But few, if any, were pacifist, and those few did not proclaim their belief.

Meanwhile, personal matters were pressing even more urgently on Davy's mind.

Desperately, he confronted her, keeping his voice low, trying to make it clear to those around them that he wished to speak privately to Lou. 'Can I see you? Alone?'

The brown eyes widened, in genuine surprise, then swift concern. '*Pourquoi?* For what? Something is wrong, *oui?*'

'No, no! It's just — I'd like to see you. To talk. On our own. You know.'

She continued to look puzzled for a second, then light dawned, and he saw a faint pink spread over her face. She nodded. 'Ah, yes. Of course. I understand.' To his dismay, her expression became serious, even doubtful. She frowned, but then she nodded rapidly. '*Demain, oui? Tu es* — you are free? At one o' clock? I come to hostel?'

'I want us to be alone.'

His voice was tense, his face as solemn as hers. She nodded again. 'We walk. Alone. I promise.'

He seized both her hands, squeezed them. She darted her head forward and kissed him lightly on both cheeks, her usual greeting and parting.

She came on time the following day, and they did walk, through the now wonderful Parisian springtime, resting for long intervals in the parks and squares, and at the pavement-side cafés. She seemed to sense already that he needed her, that he was at some kind of crisis in his young life. She let him take her arm, and then her hand, and they walked like lovers through the fresh sunshine. She even returned his kiss on the mouth, and his heart beat fast with anticipation and hope. But when they climbed the hill and the long stretch of the steps leading to Sacré Coeur, and were seated among the artists and strollers under the dappled light through the chestnuts, opposite La Mère Catherine, and he took her in his arms, to try to show and tell her how he felt for her, the pressure of her hands upon his chest was gentle but implacable as she held him off. 'There is another. At home. I am not Parisienne. We have known since we are children.'

He was devastated — at first. Then hopeful again. She liked him — loved him, she said. She even kissed, let her lips touch his, and Davy told himself her feelings for him were strong — stronger than she herself would admit to, and that he would win her from this unknown childhood sweetheart, for whom he could find no compassion. He didn't even want to know his name. Others in their immediate group acknowledged the special relationship between Lou and the young Englishman; some were jealous of it. It helped to fan the flame of his hope.

Yet her attitude to him gave no real encouragement. She remained steadfast, a firm and special friend, but when, helpless against his feelings, he tried strenuously to express his need and love in physical passion, she fought hard against him, literally, when he caught hold of her. She was at the point of tears, he could see them sparkle in her eyes, and they made him desist. He felt cold and weak suddenly. 'I want you. I want to make love to you. Go to bed with you.'

'*Je suis vièrge*,' she murmured, almost as wretched as he was.

All at once he wanted desperately to be able to answer, '*Moi aussi*.' But he couldn't, because he couldn't lie to her. He had lost his own virginity, clumsily and half drunk, with a promiscuous woman in London, who laughed mockingly when it was swiftly over. Then, in Spain, he had sex with a girl who was a comrade-in-arms, less clumsily and more satisfactorily, but to her it meant little more than the kisses which had preceded it. Now, he wished he could be pure for Lou. But he realized that she was not to be his, however much he loved her.

That was when they really began to talk, when he really began to know her, not as some misty, mythical beloved, an object of worship, but as a very real and special person. In fact, he was ashamed as he discovered how little he had known about the person who had come to mean more to him than any other. He had not, for instance, realized how deep-seated, and unusual, was her religious conviction. She believed, she told him, in something called Baha'ism, of which he had never heard. It had originated in Persia, less than a hundred years ago — the son of its founder had visited Paris just before the Great War. Her father had met him, listened to his public speeches and been converted. Her parents were part of a small number of devotees of the religion in France. Thinking of his own background, and its effect on his childhood, he was prepared to be cynical — a mystic eastern sect, bearded prophets with flowing beards — she had shown him a portrait of 'Abdu'l-Baha, the charismatic figure who had visited Paris in 1912. But as she confided more and more about her faith the less esoteric and outlandish it sounded, coming as it did from one who meant so much to him. 'We believe you have to search for yourself — find out the truth. There are the Baha'is in England.'

As 1938 advanced, and crisis loomed, and British envoys shuttled back and forth in desperate appeasement and accepted the

254

sacrifice of Czechoslovakia, she urged him more and more to return home. 'I'm not going to be caught up in this madness,' he told her. 'I'm not going to be a part of it. I don't care what they say — what happens.'

Her brown eyes were solemn, and sad. She put both her hands on his wrist. They felt cool, despite the warm day. 'I know. And you know how much I am with you in this. But please — your parents. They worry so much for you. And they love you.'

'Why don't you come with me?' It was a desperate plea. The sadness was still there as she shook her head.

'I cannot. But you are very — dear to me, *oui?* You will not forget me.'

'I could never forget you. And I'm coming back, soon.'

He hadn't come back, and he hadn't forgotten.

13

At first, it was largely her sheer cussedness which made Alice befriend the lonely newcomer up at the Big House. She was damned if she was going to let a vindictive busybody like Annie Hogan dictate who she should or should not behave civilly to. Though, to be honest, Annie was far from being alone in her condemnatory attitude towards him. In fact, apart from herself, Alice doubted if there were anyone in the village who was prepared to show him any friendliness. She even exchanged heated words with Elsbeth on the subject.

'Don't you think you're being a bit too pally with that chap?' Elsbeth offered one day. He had been left to struggle on alone against the miniature patch of wildness on the other side of the stone wall — Mr Barr was glad to have him out of sight and out of mind up behind the village hall. The other farm workers, including the two volunteers of the Women's Land Army, were unwilling to work alongside him, and Mr Barr didn't mind if it took Brown the whole of the new year to clear the patch — even if the school *were* waiting enthusiastically to take it over as an extension of their 'dig for victory' vegetable garden.

Alice had more sense than to invite Davy a second time into the kitchen. Why expose him to a further dose of Annie's rudeness? But she made a point of taking a mug of tea out to him at mid-morning and, at dinnertime, some of the food they were serving to the children. She brushed aside his protests. 'Don't be daft! We've enough to feed an army.' She noted his glance across to the building.

'Don't get yourself into any trouble on *my* account.'

She had tried to reassure him, but it quickly became evident that Annie Hogan's attitude was the normal reaction he had come across in his contacts with the inhabitants of Howbeck. She was hurt to find Elsbeth lining up with the others in general condemnation of the young man. It prompted her to reply snappishly to Elsbeth's criticism of her friendly overtures towards him. 'What do you reckon, then? He shouldn't be allowed to eat and drink? We should just starve him to death? Might as well hang a bell round his neck like they used to do to them what's-its in the olden days. Lepers, wasn't it?'

'No, of course not! But you seem to be

going out of your way to be nice to him. Don't forget. He did refuse the call-up. If everyone did that, Hitler would be over here right now. I'm sure there was something he could have done. He needn't necessarily fight. There's all sorts of branches in the forces. Medical, that sort of thing. Or the AFS or something.'

'Well, isn't that what he's doing here? Working for the Denby Estate? He's helping on the land — just like them two lasses, them Land Girls.'

'That's not the same. That kind of work is what girls can do.'

Alice gave a sarcastic laugh. 'It's enough to keep most of the men round here out of uniform. You see precious few uniforms round here, except for the Home Guard! We can't all be Brylcreem Boy heroes, yer know!' Her last remark brought the quick flow of red to Elsbeth's reproachful face.

'I know that! But the men here — that's their job. They're all farmers. It's their life. Do you tell your Mr Aygarth he should leave his wife and children and go off to join up?'

'*I* don't tell anybody what they should and shouldn't be doing! Not like some — '

'But I bet if he *was* called up to the forces, he'd go, same as all the other men — *and* women, if it comes to that,' Elsbeth pursued vigorously. 'He wouldn't skulk at home, shirking his duty.'

Her words stung, not least because they reflected what Alice's natural response was to the young newcomer's belief. She realized more and more just how cloudy and uncertain her feelings were about Davy Brown. But her sympathy and her compassion for his clear loneliness and suffering in such a hostile environment were always uppermost. They made her a little overenthusiastic in her displays of friendliness towards him, but, in spite of his shy reserve, she could sense his warming to her in his desperate need for some contact, some hint of acceptability. Elsbeth's untypical disapproval, in addition to Annie Hogan's sarcastic contempt for her overtures towards Davy Brown, only made Alice more determined, and her talks over the wall grew lengthier, extending to most of the limited free time which remained after the pupils had been served their dinners. For her own peace of mind, she wanted to know more about him, what motivated him in his unusual stand, and eventually she plucked up courage to act upon her desire.

'Do you get Sundays off?' she asked him abruptly, on the Friday of his second week of working on the adjacent patch of reclaimed land.

'So far.' He eyed her cautiously.

'I was wondering if you fancied going for a walk? A bit of a hike. Over the tops — unless the weather's too bad.'

His face showed first plain astonishment, then lit up with pleasure. 'Yes. That would be great.' His expression changed yet again to his more accustomed wariness as he glanced past her at the low building of the hall. 'That's . . . if you're sure?'

She grinned. 'Don't get the wrong idea. I'm not in the habit of asking lads out. But it makes a change, somebody new to talk to. I'll bring a bit of bait — sandwiches or summat. And a flask of tea. I'll meet you outside Oddfellows at half nine, Sunday morning. Might be early enough to miss the churchgoers!'

Alice felt a little uncomfortable about not mentioning the proposed excursion to Elsbeth, never mind not offering her the opportunity to join them, but she eased her conscience with the thought that her friend would almost certainly have refused. In the unlikely event of her accepting such an invitation, the presence of a third party, especially one as distractingly pretty as Elsbeth, would rob Alice of the chance to really get to know something about Davy Brown, and his undoubtedly interesting and chequered past. She wanted to know what made this apparently unassuming and likeable man take on the label of conchy and all the rejection and hate that went with it.

She was feeling more than a little uneasy about it when Sunday morning came, with its sharp frost, which made a white picture-postcard beauty of trees and hedgerows and tufts of wayside grass, and the brilliant bright blueness of the winter-sunshine morning. She set out down the long hillside in her shining brown boots, and thick woollen knee-socks over her still new breeches, her shape hidden under a thick man's shirt (one of Malcolm's cut down and altered by Eileen), a thick sweater and scarf, a grey Balaclava and matching mittens (more contributions from Eileen and her swift and skilful knitting needles), and over all that an old brown padded waterproof which had withstood several keen Howbeck Side winters.

'I feel like one of them barrage balloons!' she laughed as she approached the waiting Davy, and held her arms out stiffly from her sides. 'Are you sure you'll be warm enough?'

Compared with her, he seemed to be much more lightly dressed, but he had on a pair of good, serviceable boots and trousers tucked into festively red football socks. He wore a cap with hanging earmuffs and woollen gloves, and a well cut, herringbone-patterned overcoat. 'What you can't see is even snugger! My unmentionables in the underwear department are of the stoutest winter variety. A present from my folks when they knew I was headed this way.'

'Winter draws on, eh?' she laughed. 'Let's go then. Along by the beck, then we'll head up by the farm there.' She took hold of his arm, linking him firmly as they headed off along the narrow path already thawing out into muddy puddles.

Two hours later, in spite of their still smoky breath, they were sweating inside their winter garb, and ready to find a spot on the outcrop of weathered rocks at the crest of High Top where they could rest and look out over the gently rolling slope of the brown heather and bracken, and see the ribbon of road that led from Howe Dale join the distant main coastal road heading south to Whitby. It was about at this dividing line that the moor surrendered to the segmented farming land, dark with ploughed furrows, interspersed with patches of bright green despite the winter, where fields had been left to grass. And beyond them the faint silver shimmer that was the sea, lining the horizon beneath the greatest sweep of all, the piercing blue of a cloudless sky.

There was a small square of oilcloth packed in the canvas rucksack that Alice had brought, and which Davy had insisted on taking from her to slip on his shoulder as soon as they had met. An almost flat, lichen-crusted rock served as seat, on which they spread the oilcloth. Davy had removed his cap. His brown hair was ruffled as he stood staring across towards the line of sea. He drew in a deep breath before he turned and joined her, his hip brushing companionably against hers through the thick layers of clothing as he settled at her side. 'It's so good up here! So much space. You feel as though you can breathe.' He put his hand on her arm, and she could feel the pressure of his grip. 'Thank you for asking me to come along. You're a real brick! Very kind!'

His gesture, and the force with which he spoke, surprised her. He had always seemed so withdrawn and guarded in the brief time she had known him. She felt herself blushing, and there was an instant of awkward silence, while the sudden uncomfortable thought occurred to her that he might have misinterpreted her friendly approaches to him. 'Nay, I'm glad of the company. A new face to talk to.' She busied herself picking out the paper-wrapped parcel of the sandwiches, and the flask of tea. She hesitated, her face growing even warmer as she took the plunge. ' 'Specially as I know how a lot of folk haven't made you feel very welcome round here.'

He gave a bitter little laugh. 'Oh, I'm becoming quite used to that, believe me!'

There was another pause, long enough to make her feel the need to speak again. 'Look, you don't have to say anything. I mean talk about it, if you don't feel like it. I just wanted you to . . . '

'It means such a lot to me coming out with you like this. And your kindness at the school. Everything. I want you to know how much I appreciate it. You're the only one who doesn't treat me like some sort of outcast.'

'If you don't mind me asking, why did you, you know, refuse to join up? Don't think I'm being nosy or owt, but I'd really like to know.'

'Why I'm a conchy, eh?' There was a bitter harshness about the way he emphasized the ugly word, but the laugh which accompanied it was sad rather than bitter, and the embarrassment between them fell away as he began to speak. Once started, it was almost as if he had been waiting for the chance to explain, to someone who was prepared to listen sympathetically, and he kept very little back. He began by explaining his family background and his upbringing, the religious code he had been brought up by.

'My father was an objector, too, in the Great War. But he volunteered to join the Medical Corps, as a stretcher-bearer. He was only called up for the last year of the war, and was sent over to France in 1918, for the last six months. He was just nineteen.'

'Couldn't you do something like that? Go in the Medical Corps, or something?'

'I could. It was offered, but I refused. I even argued with my father about it. To my mind, even doing something like that means you condone the war. You're part of the machine, the war effort. The only way to stop war is for all of us to refuse to have anything to do with it — with any part of it.' He flung an arm out towards the countryside which lay so peacefully before them. 'Even growing food — or what I'm doing now at Howe Manor — is part of the war. If everybody just said no, to hell with it! I want nothing to do with any of it! What could the governments do? Even Hitler and his Nazis? They couldn't put every single one of us, men and women, in gaol. Could they?'

'But . . . you're here now, aren't you? Working on the estate. Part of it, you said.'

He looked at her, and she saw the pain and the sadness in his gaze, on his face, before his eyes moved away from hers and he nodded. He stared down at his clenched hand on the blue cloth they sat on. The veins were raised, stood out darkly over the prominent bone structure. His voice was no more than a thick whisper. 'Yes. They sent me to prison. I was only in three months. When they let me out — I couldn't take any more. This was a way out for me. An easy way. I didn't have the guts to hold out. I gave in.'

She felt close to tears, and furious with herself for her insensitivity, and her selfish curiosity. She put her hand over his on the cloth, held her fingers over his. 'I'm sorry. I shouldn't have — I'm far too nosy for my own good. Let's forget it, just — '

'No, no! You've been so kind. I don't mind — telling you. I want to. I'm glad you're here — Al!' His face came close, his hand was still in hers. His lips touched her mouth, stayed there, in a long and gentle kiss, and she felt odd and dizzy, her heart thumping, and she was unable to withdraw, waiting for him to release her. She pulled away noticeably when he did so, and he started to apologize. She held up her hand to stop him.

'It's all right. It's just — I don't want you to think that's why I asked you out — for sparking — the lad lass kind of thing. It isn't. I've never bothered with all that. I don't want it. I just want to be friends, like. All right?'

'All right. But you can't blame me for trying. You're very pretty, as well as being the nicest girl I've met — '

'I've told you! Don't start any of that daft talk! It gets me mad when lads — '

Now it was his turn to hold up his hands, in a gesture of mock surrender. 'Right-oh, right-oh! Whatever you say! We're friends, yes? Good mates, eh? Let's shake hands on it.'

She did so, her face still warm with embarrassment and lingering suspicion, but she placed her hand in his, gripped it firmly in comradeship. And after they had eaten their sandwiches and shared the same tin cup for their scalding tea, he began to talk again about his own history, and the principles which had caused him to take such a drastic stand against the war. He told her something of Spain, and the horrors he had witnessed there.

'I'm sure there's far worse things happening now, and will happen. And in the past, too. My father probably saw far worse in the last war. Not that he's ever talked about it to me. Or to anyone, I guess. Funny, isn't it? All of them who were in the war never say much about it. They'll only talk to each other, like members of some exclusive club. As though all the rest of us must be kept in the dark about what went on.'

'Well, at least no one can accuse you of being a coward. Have you let them all know round here, about you being in the Spanish war? Wait till I tell that sharp-tongued Annie Hogan!' Her face split into the familiar beaming grin. 'You won't have to worry about folks not knowing then! She's such a busybody — she can't keep anything to herself. The whole village'll know in a day or two!'

He gave a quiet chuckle in return. 'Don't go making out I'm some sort of hero. I was as frightened as hell most of the time!' He shook his head, the smile fading. 'But it was enough for me, what went on out there, to put me off fighting for life.' He glanced at her, then looked away again, down at his hands, loosely folded in his lap. His voice was even quieter. 'Then something else happened, when I got to France. I met this girl.'

Alice was about to make some flippant, dismissive remark, but the sad reflectiveness of his tone, and his attitude, stopped her. She waited, instinctively aware that he was truly revealing himself to her, and feeling all at once very close to him indeed.

'Her name was Lou. She was . . . different, from any other girl I've ever met.' His eyes sought Alice's once more, and she waited silently, feeling that special intimacy between them. He told her about the French girl, about her strange faith, that all religions were essentially one, worshipping the same God, and that all the major figures of the various faiths throughout the ages were all messengers of that one God. 'They really believe in the unity of mankind, these Baha'is. I mean *really*! Everyone the same, equal under God. All races, men and women, all the same.'

'Are you one of them? One of these what-you-may-call-its?'

'Baha'i? No.' He shook his head, almost in a dazed way. 'But I want to find out more. There are some in England. I want to try and get in touch.' He stopped abruptly. A hard, bitter expression reasserted itself on his features. 'I haven't done anything about it yet. Haven't had much chance, what with the draft board, and the courts — and prison.'

She sensed his reluctance to give any detail about his time in gaol. 'And was it because of this lass, Lou — that you became a conchy?' At least her blunt use of the indelicate word put a smile, albeit a twisted one, back on his face.

'Partly. Or it confirmed what I was already feeling. It's not just . . . well, not religion in any specific way. It's something I feel, deeply, in here.' He put his hand to his heart, glanced up at her almost sheepishly. 'Are *you* religious, Al?'

'What? Our lot? Nay, we're all heathens! I won't even go to the village chapel! They've got me marked down as a bad lot!'

'I'm not a churchgoer either. I'm not even sure if I believe in God any more. They tell us He's all-powerful, cares about the sparrow's fall and all that sort of thing. Then you see all the wickedness going on in our world, the terrible things we do to one another. Lou used to go on about His testing our faith — tests and difficulties, she called them. And the mystery of God, how we must never hope to understand Him, not in this world.' He shrugged his shoulders. 'But I just feel it's up to us. We make our world the way it is. It's only us that can change it. And we've got to change ourselves. That's why I've done what I have. Become a conscientious objector. A conchy! That's the word most people prefer to use.'

She realized how shocked she was by his words. She had blithely condemned herself and her kin as heathens, but her belief in a God had always been deep-rooted, funda-mental, something she had never thought to challenge. Davy's ideas, and his doubt, made her deeply uncomfortable. To get the conversation back on a more even keel, she asked, 'What happened to this lass? Lou? Where is she?' She saw the sadness back in his eyes.

He shrugged again. 'I don't know. She might still be in Paris. Or back at her home. I've tried to get in touch, through the Red Cross. You know — the way they're helping with the men who were taken prisoner in France. But I haven't heard anything yet.'

'Does she know what you've done? I mean being a — going to gaol and all that?'

He shook his head. 'Not unless the Red Cross have been able to get my letters through to her.'

'You're sweet on her, yeah?' she asked bluntly, and he nodded.

'I asked her to come over to England with me. She said no. She said there was someone else. Back in her home town.'

There was a longer pause, while she struggled for something to say. The dazzling sunshine suddenly seemed cold and heartless, its brilliance uncaring. She felt an unreasoning rise of anger within herself at all the tugs and complications of loving, and the havoc they played. Desperately she searched for something to lift his mood, thought about the touch of his lips on hers, and thought she might fling herself at him and kiss him on the mouth again. But then the lovely face of

Elsbeth intervened in her mind.

'Hey!' The violence of her exclamation surprised him. 'What would you do if you came across a Jerry spy now? Right here.' She flung an arm out to take in the wide landscape. 'What would you do? Leave him to get on with it? Say it's got nowt to do with you?'

He was staring at her as though she had taken leave of her senses. She had certainly succeeded in diverting his gloomy thoughts for the moment. 'Because I think there is one in the village. There's summat funny going on, any road. The Big Swede. You know him?'

He shook his head, totally intrigued now, and she began to tell him of Gus Rielke, and all her suspicions. She nodded over her right shoulder. 'Just over there, on the other side, there's a shed — and a kind of concrete pit thing, in the side of the hill. All covered up. Everything's locked up — they've even got one of the dogs chained up to keep guard.' She told him about the Symmonds at High Top Farm, and the vehicle tracks through the winter mud. 'Tractors and lorries — loads of them. What they doing up here, off the road? The shed's all boarded up, you can't see in anywhere. Doors all padlocked.'

'Well, it must be a store place. Farm equipment, something like that. I mean they must have checked on this fellow, the foreign one. You say he's well known around the village? Got away from the Germans?'

She shook her head stubbornly. 'He's full of himself! Trying to be in with everybody. He's staying at the pub with the landlady. Bold as brass, and her husband a POW! Even me little sister thinks the sun shines out of — he's got 'em all fooled. Not me, though. I wouldn't trust the dirty sod as far as I could throw him, and he's a big bugger an' all! Whoops!' She grinned and clapped a hand to her mouth. 'Pardon my French!'

To her relief, he laughed aloud, and caught hold of her arm, dragging her upright. 'Come on then. Let's go do a bit of spy-catching! Come and show me this secret enemy den! We might even catch him at it, trying to send a signal off to Adolf! They might even give us a medal. Off to Buckingham Palace to see the king!'

He laughed even louder as she made a hefty swipe at him, and poked out her tongue. 'Just you wait! I'll teach you to make mock of me. You're as bad as my mate Elsbeth, you are!'

Ten minutes later, Davy was crouched at the edge of the old sheep-dip, staring at the carefully constructed roof formed by the corrugated-iron sheets, which had been securely nailed together. Only at the far end, the shallow entrance to the dip, could they peer between the supporting slats of wood and the edge of the sheets to make out the dim shape of the oil drums in the deep gloom. Davy was lying almost flat, his face pressed against the narrow aperture. 'It certainly smells like fuel. Petrol, I'd say.'

'It's rationed, though, isn't it? The Aygarths, where I'm staying, are always going on about it.'

Davy straightened up, brushed the dirt from his knees. 'I suppose farmers get a fairly generous supply,' he said doubtfully. 'But if those drums are all full, there must be a heck of a lot in there.' He glanced around. 'And why out here, so far from the farm? You'd think they'd want it nearer the house.'

'I don't think Bob Symmonds has even got a tractor. They've only got sheep — and a few cows. Farm's dropping to bits.' She nodded at the dip. 'Not this, though. Them sheets are new. And it's even more boarded up than before, when me and Elsbeth came up here.'

They could hear the persistent barking of a dog, muted by distance but carrying through the crisp air. 'That'll be the guard dog up by the shed,' Alice said. 'Want to take a look?' She turned towards the sharp upward slope of the moorland in the direction of the outbuilding and the farm. 'Oh bugger!'

The low shape of the black and white collie came streaking over the brow, its yelps suddenly fiercely loud, and then the dark silhouettes of two human shapes appeared against the skyline. 'Stand still!' Davy counselled. 'Don't run.' They both stood motionless, looking and feeling absurdly guilty, as the two figures approached, breaking into a lumbering run. The dog raced up to Alice and Davy, circling and yapping piercingly, its eyes wild, its sharp little teeth much in evidence as it snarled. It crouched very low, almost on its belly, and darted in, snacking at the heel of Alice's boot, nipping at it. Alice flinched and kicked out a little, stepping back.

'Keep still, ye daft bugger!' Bob Symmonds shouted, then roared at the dog. 'Jess! Heel, ye bastard, heel!'

Alice had already recognized the other, taller, burlier man, even before his booming laugh rang out. 'So! Liddle Missy Alice, eh? Long way from home, ya? And who's de boyfriend? A new face, ya? What you doing up on the Tops?'

'What's it look like? Out for a walk, fine day like this. Same as yourself, eh?' She had not failed to notice the shotgun, its barrel thankfully broken, pointing down across his right forearm.

'You up here again?' Bob Symmonds's scowl was almost a caricature, except that she didn't find it at all amusing just now. 'You always snooping round, you and that blonde lass from t'school. Got rid of her today, have yer?' His brown teeth showed as he nodded towards Davy. His leer was worse than the scowl.

'Always a favourite spot of ours, up here, Mr Symmonds.' Alice's tone was a lot chirpier than her mood. 'Lovely, isn't it?'

'Coming down to the farm, were yer? Spyin' on us again?'

'Spying? Us? What for? Like I said, we're just out for a walk, me and my friend here. This is Mr Brown. We — '

'Mr Brown! I know fine well who he is! Bloody conchy over to Squire Denby's! Both of yer! Keep off my land, you hear? This is part of farm.'

'Oh, sorry! I heard it was a public way, across the moor here. No notice up about trespassers. Seems plenty of people get up here, regular like.' Her heart was thumping, but she nodded at the ground. 'Come up here in their cars an' all, by the look of it.'

'You mind yer own bloody business! And keep yer conchy friend off here! We don't want your sort round here.'

'Whoa there, Bob!' Gus Rielke stepped forward, that big, easy grin spreading over his open features. 'No harm done, is there? It's good to see young folk out enjoying the good weather, out in the air. Good, ya?' He stepped forward, held out his great red hand, and, after a fractional hesitation, Davy took it. His arm was pumped vigorously. 'I am not against a man who stand up for what he believes, ya? I not meet you yet, but I hear about you. Welcome, Mr Brown. You come in Oddfellows, have drink with me. I tell you — you always welcome by me when I am in the bar, and dat's de truth!'

14

At the same time that the then largely unknown German General Rommel arrived in Tripoli, in February, the snow arrived in Howe Dale and over large parts of the surrounding dales and moors. It was a heavy fall, followed by a prolonged spell of arctic weather. This was an old and respected enemy, and the majority of the dales' folk had their minds and bodies fully occupied with fighting it. They were under siege, with roads impassable, high with drifts, which were dug out only for the cruel winds to sift the snow remorselessly back again, to block the briefly won freedom. The feeling of isolation, of being cut off from the rest of the world, exerted its influence mentally, as well as physically. British and Commonwealth troops might have achieved a great success in taking Benghazi, the war might be costing the British government eleven million pounds a day, but it was of little account to the dales farmers, who struggled to find and feed their flocks, and their herds, and to get their milk down to Howbeck station, the only lifeline that remained sporadically open for their produce to reach Teesside, or the nearer Whitby and Scarborough.

Not every inhabitant of the dale felt that way, though. Even the severe weather could not divert Alice from her determination to investigate the suspicious behaviour of the Big Swede and Bob Symmonds. Though her encounter with the dubious pair had given her a scare, especially when she had first caught sight of the shotgun resting over Rielke's brawny arm, it had unexpectedly provided her with an opportunity she was quick to seize on. 'We've got to make the most of the chance he's given us.' Her grey eyes shone as she discussed it with Davy Brown. 'You'll have to take him up on his offer. Call in the Oddfellows, call his bluff. Go for that drink with him. He'll soon be blabbing to you the way he never would to me. I know what blokes are like over a few pints. Me da's a prime example!'

Davy was far less sure, or enthusiastic. 'Apart from yourself, he's the only chap that hasn't treated me like some sort of pariah.'

Alice screwed up her face in comic bafflement. 'We used to have one of them but the wheels fell off!'

'You know what I mean!' he insisted. 'And he's only one man. A foreigner here himself. You can imagine what the atmosphere would be like if I *did* go into the bar. I'd probably be kicked out — literally! Or lynched!'

'Not if *I* was with you! Why don't you take me in with you? Next Sat'day's the village hop. There's one the start of every month. We can call in for a drink, then go on to the dance. There's loads of lasses go in the pub now of a weekend. Even that mate of mine, the blonde lass. Elsbeth. And she's a right toff!' she added, feeling a twinge of disloyalty to her closest friend.

'We'd be asking for trouble.' He gazed at her doubtfully, then smiled. 'I told you, I'm a devout coward, as well as being opposed to violence.'

'Listen, come Saturday, folks round here'll be thinking you're a cross between Robin Hood and that black boxer. Joe Louis. I'm gonna start spreading the word, how you took on General Franco and his gang practically single handed! And I'll tell them you're only stopping out of this lot because you made a vow to your French sweetheart that you would never fight again.'

She thought from his sudden sharp glance at her, and the way the smile faded from his face, that she had gone too far in mentioning the girl he had told her of, but then the smile, or a sad little ghost of it, came back. 'There's no need to perjure yourself on my account.

I'll be glad to take you to your dance, if you're prepared to risk being seen out with me in public. I'll even take you to the pub first, though I don't know if it's quite the thing for a young lady like yourself to be doing, even in these troubled times.'

She laughed heartily, partly with relief at his generous forgiving of her clumsiness. 'Hey! You're getting me mixed up with me mate. Elsbeth Hobbs. Mind, that's not likely, is it? You've seen her, haven't you? She's a real beauty, is Beth. You must have seen her up at Big House?'

He shook his head. 'We don't exactly mix up there. They keep me well away from the other inhabitants. I reckon they'd have me in the kennels if they could!'

For the first minute after they entered the Oddfellows together the following Saturday evening, Alice was afraid that Davy's drastic forecast of what the reaction would be would prove all too accurate. The animated conversations died magically; the darts hovered in mid-air, and the dominoes ceased to chink. In the resounding silence, Davy advanced across the sanded wooden floor to the bar counter, Alice a pace behind him but sticking close. He had to clear his throat audibly before he could speak. 'A half of draught and a sweet sherry, please.'

'We don't serve conchies here!' The loud voice came not from behind the bar but from one of the customers to their left. But Vera Rhodes, diamante jewellery sparkling, her yellow hair piled high on her head and generous bosom swelling, seemed to be entirely in sympathy with the expressed sentiment as she stared hostilely from her glowing layers of make-up.

No one else spoke, or moved, as frozen as in a still photograph, until, with a superb sense of timing as dramatic as the scene which confronted him, the cheery, beery, red, beaming figure of the Big Swede appeared in the doorway which led through to the private quarters. 'Well, well! Now dere's de surprise, ya? Mr Brown, dat's right? And my beautiful young friend, Alice! This is sure a hell of a nice surprise. What you have, both of you? First drink is on me, I insist!'

'What the hell you playin' at, Gus? You know who he is, don't you?' The voice again came from one of the customers. Vera was still dumb, struggling to replace her look of astonishment with one of the 'dagger' variety at her handyman.

'Mr Brown — Davy, ya? — is here invited by me to take a drink. And any friend of his is also friend of mine.' He turned his beaming face towards Alice and winked. 'If anyone got the problem with that, they speak up, now.' There was a sudden eruption of shuffles and coughs and murmurs, but no one took up his challenge directly. 'We better clear this problem now, I think. I know he's the conchy, ya, and I know what that mean. I know he stand up for what he believe, he go to de gaol for it. You think that's easy? You got the guts to do that, ya?' He looked round the crowded, smoky room, challenging the silent figures. 'You all so brave to go fight for your king, ya? I don't see one uniform in here now. Except for the girls there.' He grinned at the two Land Girls, who sniggered self-consciously.

'I tell you another thing also. I talk only about the young ones here. There is only two of us here who fight in a war — a real war. One is me.' He struck himself a hard, open-handed blow on the chest. 'When I escape the Germans in my own country. The other one is Mr Brown here, who fight in Spain. For one whole year. You think he afraid to fight? You wrong!' He made a hawking noise of disgust in his throat, and turned authoritatively to Vera, as though he was in his rightful place, and role. 'Vera, you get these people drinks, ya? I pay.'

As a speech, brief and to the point as it was, it caused quite a sensation in Howbeck. Those who did not actually witness it soon heard about it, as they heard about the 'young conchy' turning up 'bold as brass' with the 'young vaccy lass' on his arm at the hop later that memorable night. Reluctant as she was to acknowledge it, Alice had to admit that Gus Rielke's inflammatory outspokenness in defence of Davy had an outstanding effect on the attitude of the villagers towards the latest arrival. It didn't transform Davy into a hero, but it did cause many to reassess their antagonism towards him and to make for some kind of acceptance of his standpoint. Fierce, downright hostility was watered down to grudging or wary acceptance. There were cautious nods and even some muttered greetings from passers-by. He pressed home his advantage by calling in to the Oddfellows regularly for two halves of an evening, though he was careful not to get drawn into the noisy affability of the habitual drinkers who stood at the bar, among the sawdust and spittoons, presided over by the ever jovial Gus. True to his word, the Big Swede made him welcome, beckoned him into their midst on his entrance, and pressed him unsuccessfully to stay on beyond the two halves of bitter he allowed himself at each visit.

Alice was concerned, not at the success of their joint plan for this infiltration but at yet another example of how Rielke seemed so easily to dazzle and pull the wool over people's eyes, as Davy began to express doubt about her unshakable faith in the foreigner's devious wickedness. 'He's a bit of a loudmouth, I grant you, but he's not such a bad bloke. I think you might be wrong about him.'

She was full of voluble scorn for Davy's weakness. 'See? He's even got you fooled now, has he? You're as bad as me da. A few pints and everybody's his best mate. You just wait. And remember — keep your eyes and ears open. Don't forget why we're doing this, all right?'

'*We?*' He chuckled. 'This was all your scheme, if I remember rightly. The only spy round here is me, I reckon. One thing I'm sure of, the fellow's no Jerry agent.'

His grin broadened. 'Anyway, if anyone can worm his guilty secrets out of him, it's you, Miss Glass! He's really sweet on you, you know. He's always on about me getting you down to the pub again. His face drops a mile every time I walk in alone.'

She gave an exaggerated shudder, but she was only half-joking. 'I don't even want to think about it.' She felt him looking at her appraisingly, and was angry at the blush she could feel beginning around her neck. 'What about t'other one? Bob Symmonds? The pair of them are up to summat, I know it.'

'Ah! Now there you might have a point. He's a sly customer all right, I grant you. But he doesn't come in very often. He's not very popular with the other locals, and no wonder. Hardly says a word to anyone. I've seen him go off out the back with Gus, though. I don't think Mrs Rhodes is keen on him, either. I wouldn't say he was one of her favourite customers.'

★ ★ ★

The snow put a halt to many activities around Howbeck, nefarious or otherwise, but not those which took place behind the securely blacked-out and curtained windows of bedrooms, including those of the village pub, when the last of the few determined customers had been persuaded out into the bleak winter and the doors shut firmly behind him. Back upstairs, Vera Rhodes could not help feeling more than a little grateful for this severe spell, even though it meant fewer customers, and worries about getting fresh supplies, already limited enough through the exigencies of the war, from the brewery. At least it kept Gus by her side, both in the bar below and in the sturdy, creaking marital bed up here.

She shivered as she stared at her reflection in the smoky triple mirrors of the dressing-table, and not only from the undoubted chilliness of the air. In fact, she slipped her dressing-gown off, and left her nightdress draped over the back of the chair, while she contemplated her naked, generous body. Putting on a bit of weight, perhaps. But then she had always been a well-built girl, and men appreciated it; always had, from the time she had first started to develop, before she had left school. She examined the heavy breasts. They were full, ripe, despite the fact that they had never suckled a babby, and never likely to now. God forbid! She had soon been cured of any desire to bear children, after her marriage to Phil Rhodes. And she had made sure there should be no danger of her doing so, taking care of the two slip-ups that had occurred during the fifteen years of wedded 'bliss' she had shared with Phil, before he had gone off into the army and France, nearly two years ago.

He had never been any the wiser. She had gone through to Middlesbrough, supposed to be staying with her sister, and come back a day or two later, pale and wan and forced to take to her bed. 'Women's troubles'. Phil had been all sympathy, even slept in one of the spare rooms. If he'd had a tail, it would have been wagging furiously when she finally graciously summoned him back to the marital sheets here. 'I'm not bothered about kids, Vera, love. You're enough for me. I don't want to share you with anybody!'

The trouble was, he meant it. He was a good man. Certainly good, anyway. She loved him, in her own strange way, she thought. Even if he did drive her mad at times, until she was ready to scream, or turn viciously on him with her shrewish tongue, as she had countless times. And he just stood there and took it, red-faced, hangdog, looking as though he would burst out blubbing any second. Sometimes she wondered why on earth he endured it so meek and mild, why he didn't just clock her one, give her a good hiding and leave the bruises to show for it. But he never did, never even stood up to her. And maybe that was the trouble. Good but no man. Not enough for her.

She had encouraged him in his enthusiasm to go off to play soldiers, going for his weekly drills into Whitby or Scarborough, stopping overnight with a mate. And his weekends away, further afield, and the two weeks' summer camp off down south somewhere. The Terriers gave him a new lease on life. Maybe that was the manly outlet he needed. She was glad for him. She had her needs, too, and he could never satisfy them.

She had known that she was 'passionate' — that was how she liked to put it — from her earliest teenage days, long before she had ever met or known Phil. 'Randy', a bloke had called her, the bloke she had yielded her virginity to, far too easily, she realized, from the way he had treated her. It scared her, and she was careful after that. It was one of the reasons that helped her make up her mind so quickly to hang on to Phil when he came courting her. Respectability, a good husband who thought the sun shone from her, with good prospects to provide for her: everything she had had dinned into her as the recipe for success. It would solve everything. White wedding — even God would forgive her for her deceptions — and living happily ever after. But it hadn't, and they hadn't.

Maybe Phil enjoyed in some weird way being so viciously henpecked. After all, he was always a mamma's boy, terrified of his old lady. And Vera was careful to allow the façade to stay in place — like his joining the TA and going off to play at soldiers. Maybe he even knew in his heart why she did it; maybe he suspected her real reason for generously permitting this indulgence. It added to the excitement and pleasure she derived from her adulterous liaisons while he was away. Liaisons she needed, couldn't do without, she told herself, for the sexual fulfilment Phil could never provide.

Could she ever have been faithful to one man? Any man? Occasionally, she examined this painful question, and tried to assure herself the answer might be in the affirmative, if ever she found the 'right' one. There were several among her 'travelling gentlemen' who might be — she was no slut, no one-night-onlies like a tart with an anonymous client. That wasn't her way at all. But she could not deny the thrill it gave her to know that she was Mrs Rhodes, and that Phil was somewhere else, her lawfully wedded husband, and that she was in bed with another man — a man who wanted her body as badly as she wanted his.

There were even times — all the more shockingly exciting for her and her temporary partners — when those illicit attachments had taken place with Phil under the same roof, safely and drunkenly asleep on account of the unaccustomed amount of spirits he had imbibed, encouraged by Vera and the jovial travelling guest to whose room she would creep while Phil snored in happy ignorance.

But now things had changed so drastically, with the advent of the big foreigner she could hear now, preparing with noisy cheerfulness to mount the stairs and satisfy her to a degree she swore she had never known with any of her former lovers. She stood watching herself, stroking her nipples, which were painfully hard and swollen, ready for his caresses, the rougher the better. If ever there was a candidate for that 'one man' she had speculated on, this ruddy, hairy Scandinavian was he. And yet — she still needed that edge, that extra thrill of awareness that what she did was wrong, morally and legally. The photograph of Phil, awkward in his khaki uniform, stood in its frame on the dresser, smiling with shy pride. She had not turned him to the wall, or laid him face down in the drawer, among her underclothes. She wanted, needed, him to be there, smiling out on her infidelity.

A long while later, sated and sore, and lying under the blankets curled against his lightly damp bulk, she tried to reassert some measure of her independence. 'Why you getting so pally with that young conchy bugger? There's a lot of people still don't like it — me included. He's such a toffee-nosed sod an' all! Dunno what you see in him, I really don't.' She felt the deep rumble of his laugh against her.

'There's a lot you don't see, my little blondie. He is not a bad bloke, even if he talk like the bloody wireless!' His arm moved from her waist as he raised his hand and tapped a finger against the side of his nose, with a knowing grin that irritated her. 'He might come in useful to us one day.'

She noted the 'us', and guessed that it did not really include her. More than likely he was referring to that scruffy gyppo, Bob Symmonds and the like. Their illegal activities had burgeoned to a worrying degree in the weeks before Christmas. She didn't mind a reasonable amount of the AUC stuff, or the black market as folks had started calling it. The Christmas meat and poultry had turned out to be very popular, and highly profitable, too, she had no doubt, though she had no real idea to what extent. And she did well enough from the booze which he and his mates had organized for the pub, as well as for other private recipients. But, truth to tell, she was relieved at this spell of hard weather, which had put an end to so much of his going out on night expeditions. And not just because it kept him right here in the bar and in her sheets. She was worried that he was getting a bit too involved in the business of these illegal supplies. Not that she could put a stop to him — he was no Phil, to be told what to do, or not to do. He had already proved that — she had had the bruises to show for it, and hadn't been able to sit down without wincing for several days afterwards.

'We getting more and more customers now,' he told her, holding her to him. 'Gotta start getting around more. Into the towns. Middlesbrough. There's some big boys out there. That Davy — he smart, ya? He been in the prison, you know. He don't want nothing with this war, he's a bright boy, maybe good for us.'

'You don't want to be so daft, man! I wouldn't trust him. Summat wrong with him — folk don't become conchies and go to gaol for fun.' She turned and struggled up on her elbow, her face near to his, her voice low and urgent. 'Don't you have owt to do with him, you hear? I mean it! He's not to be trusted. It's bad enough you having to be so well in with that dirty bloody Symmonds, the filthy little tyke!'

Again there came the deep rumble of his laughter. His great hands slid over her, she felt them cup the soft globes of her buttocks, heft them playfully. 'You telling me what to do, missus? You think you my boss again, ya? You want me teach you another lesson, lady?'

'I'm only telling you for your own good.' She pouted, nuzzled up to him, her lips making soft, audible contact with the fine fuzz of curls around the base of his neck. Her own hands dropped between their closely aligned bellies, searching for him. 'You're no good to me in gaol, are you?' She shivered, acknowledging that his threat, playful as it was, was as rousing to her as the stirring flesh she could feel between her caressive fingers.

★　★　★

Alice was both disappointed and then increasingly angry at Elsbeth's continued disapproval of her friendship with Davy Brown. 'You can't tell me you approve of what he's done?' Elsbeth protested, after Alice's glowing account of their first visit to the Oddfellows and the Big Swede's vigorous defence of the newcomer. 'How can you defend anyone who would rather stand by and do nothing while Hitler and his thugs rampage over all Europe? Anyway,' she added, rather meanly, Alice thought, 'you've changed your tune, haven't you? I thought you said this Swedish fellow was up to all sorts of wickedness? That he was a German agent!'

'He's not a Swede, he's Norwegian!' Alice snapped impatiently, ignoring the illogicality behind her correction. 'And I'm still sure he is doing something wrong.' She toned down her anger, her voice becoming far less certain.

'But I've got to admit, he really stood up for Davy and put all those sods in their place, good and proper!'

'Like me, you mean? People who don't see him as some sort of hero for refusing to go and do his duty when his country needs him! He certainly seems to have used his charms on you all right! You'll be joining him, will you? Signing up as a CO when you get your call-up? Seems he's turned your head right around.'

'Don't talk daft! I'm not a conchy and never will be! But I don't think I'd be so quick to throw a bloke in gaol just for what his beliefs are. I thought that was what we're supposed to be fighting against, that kind of thing. But pardon me, eh? What the hell would I know, a stupid little lass like me? Fresh from the Co-op and only good for cooking and cleaning up after the bairns!'

'No! Stop it! That's not fair! I've never — you know you're far more than that here. Nobody thinks that — '

'I couldn't give a damn, kidder, what they think! But I must admit. I thought *you'd* be a bit more sympathetic. I'm right disappointed in you, and that's a fact.'

Her words hit home, and Elsbeth began to make an effort to readjust her opinion of the young man. She even agreed to meet him one

Saturday afternoon, and joined Davy and Alice, along with scores of children and the younger adults, on the long slope of meadow below Howbeck Side, which had become a popular rendezvous for sledging and snow-balling and even, in one or two cases, for skiing, all the way down to the black hedgerow marking the edge of the half-frozen Beck.

Only a few of the older children called out, 'Conchy!' and, to Elsbeth's relief, he swiftly diverted Alice from her bristling intention to race after them in retribution.

'Suffer the little children,' Davy quoted philosophically. 'Sticks and stones may break my bones — especially if they're hidden inside a snowball!'

The snow, and red, runny noses, and chapped hands and chilblains, and wet clothing, and the smell of gently steaming garments hanging about school and homes, seemed to have been with them for ever, but the rapid thaw came with the advent of March. The beck flooded its banks and briefly threatened one or two cottages in the bottom of the dale, and the Oddfellows. Previously filled sandbags were deployed against the old adversary and even the cellar was kept dry. Part of the village hall yard was under several inches, but the flood stopped short of the building itself. The piles of snow at the sides of the lanes, blackened by the chimney soot and weeks of splashing vehicles, diminished, and the tired green and dark brown of the earth beneath appeared, and spread ever wider. Another week and all signs of snow had gone, except for a few thin lines and patches lying on north-facing slopes, in the lee of stone walls or hedges.

Luke Denby had been posted to Scotland for the final phase of his training. 'He won't be back until Easter,' Elsbeth said.

'Well, that's the end of March, isn't it? That's only four weeks away.'

'Hey, listen you! I've told you! I'm not bothered. There's nothing going on between me and Luke. All right? Not like you and Davy!' she couldn't help adding, and saw the blush rising in Alice's face.

'And don't you start *that*, either! I've told you, too. We're just mates, that's all.'

'Oh yes?' Elsbeth smiled quizzically. 'Just like you and me then?'

'Yes. Spot on, kidder.' Alice felt a strange little quiver of denial inside her, a quickening which she refused to acknowledge, or recognize. 'Listen,' she went on hastily. 'Will you do me a big favour, and come to the hop on Saturday? Davy wants me to go and you know what I'm like. I've got two left feet when it comes to dancing. I really can't be doing with all that daft carry-on. If you come, he'll at least have someone to dance with. Please? I'm begging you.' She was still a little unsure of how she really felt when Elsbeth finally agreed to her proposal.

She was even more mixed up in the decorated hall, as she watched her two friends embracing each other as they moved and turned competently around the floor to the gramophone records of Ambrose and his orchestra. They looked good together, Elsbeth moved so deftly, seemed to fit so well into his arms. Well, that was what she had wanted, wasn't it? He must feel dazzled, to have such a lovely girl so close. And he was nice looking himself. Far better than that cocky Luke, in spite of his flashy uniform. That one thought far too much of himself, she judged, ignoring the fact that she had only seen him once or twice, and had never even spoken to him.

What the hell was she feeling so riled up and on edge about then? And just who the hell was she jealous of? Elsbeth — or Davy? The dilemma hit her hard. She had a sudden powerful inclination to turn on her heel and leave. Sneak away before they came back to her, and the chair on which Elsbeth had left her pretty little evening bag. Don't be so bloody soft! she scolded herself sharply.

Later on, not long before the last waltz would signal the end of the night's official festivities, one of the two Land Girls, Evelyn, the prettier one, came over bold as brass and asked Davy for a dance. Alice bit back the sarky retort that sprang immediately to mind. When the couple had spun away from them, she leaned in close to Elsbeth's fragrant ear and murmured, 'That's a turn-up for the books, eh? She's changed her tune! Wouldn't give him the time of day a couple of months ago. Wonders'll never cease!'

Elsbeth turned to her, and put her hand lightly on Alice's shoulder. 'It's a slow one. Everyone's up on the floor. Come and have a dance with me. *Please!*'

It was quite common for girls to dance together. There were never enough men to go round, especially until the Oddfellows called the notional 'last orders', which signalled the departure of most of the younger customers for the hop, and the settling down of the hard core of regulars for the long session of the lock-in. In any case, few of the males had the skill or the enthusiasm to get up for every dance.

Alice's reluctance was as genuine as any of the farmhands around her, but Elsbeth's plea, in her voice and in her wide blue eyes, was too strong to resist, and she rose, reluctantly, though more from her acknowledgement of her own ineptitude than an unwillingness to accompany her partner.

'You lead,' Elsbeth ordered, moving decorously into Alice's hold, and trying as inconspicuously as possible to pull her forward in the steps intended for the male to perform. 'Oh, never mind! I'll be the man!' Elsbeth giggled in her ear, and propelled her round in the opposite direction.

'See? I told you you were a bossy-boots.'

The floor was crowded now, everyone up at this late hour, and their movements were more and more restricted, to Alice's great delight. Hemmed in on all sides, they emulated those around them and clung, closer and closer, hugging shoulders, thighs and knees bumping, feet shuffling almost on the spot. 'I like this. This is better than all that jigging about.' Their heads were touching, their cheeks rubbed together, and Alice dizzily breathed in the sweetness of the girl in her arms, savoured her proximity. She could feel the delicate skin, and the brush of that silky hair against her lips. 'It's enough to make me wish I was a feller.'

Elsbeth's breath was warm. 'I like you just the way you are.'

15

The war seemed to be developing into something of a switchback ride as 1941 moved towards spring. The Easter holiday was the occasion of added cause for celebration with the news of the victory of the British navy over the Italian fleet at Cape Matapan, only to be followed a week later by reverses on land as the new German commander in North Africa, Erwin Rommel, began to demonstrate the tactical skill which would earn him the name of 'Desert Fox'. Gains which had been made only weeks before by the Allies along the coast were yielded as they were pushed remorselessly back towards Cairo, their forces weakened by Wavell's decision to send troops to Greece. It was all very far from Howbeck and its concerns, though they still heard the occasional night rumbles of the coastal anti-aircraft batteries, and the Home Guard paraded and drilled outside the village hall, their arm bands replaced by khaki uniforms, and, more gradually, broom shanks by Lee Enfields.

It was while the school was still on holiday

in April that Alice at last met Luke Denby. She tried, unsuccessfully, to overcome her prejudiced opinion of him. She could not help seeing him as some sort of dangerous gentleman seducer of Elsbeth's sweet innocence, or would-be seducer if Alice didn't look out for her and warn her to be constantly on her guard. It was doubly disconcerting therefore when in the flesh he turned out to be so affable and easy-going, lacking in any 'swank', despite the glamour of the uniform and his high social rank. But she couldn't help being vulnerably aware of her own rough edges of background and speech when she was with him and Elsbeth together, in a way that had never bothered her when she was with Davy.

'Luke's invited us for a day in Whitby on Friday. You and Algy and Doreen. And Davy can come along, too.' Friday was the last real day of the holidays, for school was due to start the following Monday. Elsbeth's tone sounded tentative, as though she was unsure of what Alice's reaction would be. And she was right to be hesitant, for Alice could feel her hackles rise, without any good reason for them to do so.

Alice made a noble effort to keep her hackles in check. 'Nay, lass. You never want a bunch of gooseberries tagging along on your day out. You haven't seen owt of the Brylcreem Boy for weeks, and he's off back to Scotland in a day or two, isn't he?' He had been moved north of the border for the final phase of training, which involved practising night raids over the Highlands and off the west coast, with live ammunition.

'Oh, please come! He wants us all to have a good day out. He's really keen. And so do I. Please say yes. He'll be awfully hurt if you don't.'

'Our Algy's never been in a car in his life. He'll probably chuck up all over the seats or summat.' But the big baby-blue eyes and Elsbeth's obvious desire for the communal outing to take place worked their magic on her, and, despite her misgivings, she found herself agreeing. The tight hug and smacking kiss on her cheek were reward more than enough, though her private unease was unabated.

In the event, it all went off very well, considering all the disparate elements which might have made for disaster. For a start, a CO and a bomber pilot seemed a volatile combination, while Maudsley Street and Howe Manor could scarcely have been further apart on the social scale. During the ride to the coast, Alice was untypically silent, virtually monosyllabic in her answers to the attempts made to converse with her. As she listened to the relaxed chatting of the other three adults in the unexpected luxury of the Morris Cowley, their refined accents made her uncomfortably thin-skinned and prickly.

'I managed to persuade the old man to let me give the motor a run. It hardly leaves the garage these days, what with the petrol shortages and all that.' Luke laughed and tapped his nose with a forefinger. 'Don't worry, though. I've got a nearly full tank. I have my sources!'

She had been on edge, too, at the notion of Davy and Luke meeting, but there was no visible tension at all. No reference was made to Davy's extreme and unpopular views, while he in turn questioned Luke about the various aspects of his job and training with no sign of embarrassment.

On Alice's knee, Algy stared wide-eyed out of the window, and maintained a silence that matched his eldest sister's. It was Doreen who startled Alice. She had recently celebrated her eleventh birthday, and Alice, examining her with a newly perceptive gaze in these unusual surroundings, realized how much she, of all the family, had changed over the past eight months. For one thing, her looks already indicated that in a few more years she would merit the description of a beauty, to rival Elsbeth's fairness with her own dark delicacy. She looked as neat as a pretty pin, with flaring flowered dress and over it a knitted and intricately embroidered cardigan, her thin legs encased in black stockings too new to be darned, and her feet in shiny, patent, buckled shoes. Everything, from hair ribbons to those buckled shoes, had been provided by 'Aunty Elizabeth'. It suddenly struck Alice that Doreen had changed almost into a new person, and under her very nose and unnoticing eyes. Even the girl's speech had been transformed. Her voice was softer, more contained, and the roughness of her accent had vanished. She was indeed a new girl, a budding 'little lady', created by the genteel spinster who had taken her into her elegant home. Alice felt another surge of undirected anger and unease. Outwardly she might be a new person, Alice thought mutinously. Inwardly, she was the same scheming, conniving, crafty little bitch she always was!

God knows what this war's doing to all of us, she mused. It's changing all our lives, whether we want it to or not. She found herself studying the figure in front of her, in the passenger seat: the lovely, flowing gold of Beth's hair, the way it moved, so soft and shining in the pale sun through the glass; the delicate beauty of the back of the slim neck, showing above the scoop of the dress line, the sweet little bump of the spine just peeping over the material. She imagined leaning forward, brushing her fingers lightly through that shining spun gold, lifting it, letting her lips touch that beautiful little downy bump, tasting the softness of that wonderful skin, breathing in its fragrance . . .

She felt Davy squirm beside her, on her left in the rear seat. His hip rubbed against hers, his shoulder nudged her. 'Come on, Algy, old son. Why don't you sit on my knee for a bit? Big lad like you, you'll be squashing your poor sister flat. Who's going to be first to see the sea? If you look out this side, it might be you!'

On Alice's right side, Doreen turned her neat, dark head with a superior smile, to indicate she was above such childish pursuits, but Algy was already wriggling free of Alice. Her legs felt hot in the corded breeches, and she moved them, savouring the freedom from Algy's pressing weight. She was disturbed, as always, by her day-dreaming about Beth and the effect it had on her, and she diverted her thoughts almost with relief, at least initially, towards Davy at her side.

He was a grand lad, and a *real* gentleman. But maybe she was being a bit unfair towards the lighter-haired figure at the wheel. Luke Denby looked different in his civvy clothes. Maybe he wasn't quite the dyed-in-the-wool lecher she had labelled him in his designs on Elsbeth.

A reluctant smile made the corners of her mouth twitch as she deflected her thoughts again towards Davy. After that one serious attempt at a kiss, he had scarcely touched her, apart from some companionable hand-holding during their walks. The only time he had put his arms round her had been on the dance floor. She found herself almost wishing he were not so thoroughly decent towards her. Mind you, she'd probably clock him one if he ever tried owt like that with her! And anyway, he was still mooning over that French lass he had left over there. What chance did a little rough diamond from Maudsley Street stand against a smart Froggie lass who knew about all sorts of things, including that funny religion he'd told her about whose name she couldn't even remember? And who probably always wore one of them posh Paris frocks and silk stockings, and not boots and a pair of riding-breeches that made her look like a Land Girl!

They parked in the station forecourt, and walked past the swing-bridge towards the twin piers at the harbour mouth, through the bustle of the fishquays. The rivermouth was full of the sturdy, squat masts of the fishing fleet, jutting like dark porcupine quills against the sunny blue sky and high white clouds. The boats were moored two and three deep beside the quay, and the stalls and the stacked boxes of the recently unloaded catch cluttered the quayside and roadway. Lorries with high wooden sides, horse-drawn carts and handcarts, added to the sense of lively organized chaos, as well as the crowds of buyers and sellers, through which the day visitors and holidaymakers picked their way.

Once they reached the west pier, the crowd thinned out, and Algy raced ahead excitedly onto the broad stone breakwater, with the lighthouse at its far end. 'Do they still show the light?' Alice asked, and Luke chuckled.

'What? To guide the Jerry bombers in?'

She felt herself blushing, and looked away at the sparkling, choppy sea. Stuck-up, sniggering bastard! She was glad of both her warm breeches and thick sweater when they moved further out on the pier. The breeze was stiff, much stronger than it had felt further inland. She turned and saw it flatten Elsbeth's summery dress against the slimness of her figure, outlining her legs all the way to the tops of her thighs and emphasizing the shape of her bosom, and she felt embarrassed on her behalf, and angry. Then the wind whipped under the hem and sent it ballooning, to offer a glimpse of pale limbs and the scalloped edging of a pretty petticoat. Elsbeth gave a girlish squeal of laughing distress and clamped her hands to her frock, holding it down.

'Spoilsport!' Luke called out, and Elsbeth gave him a maidenly reprimand.

'I should have worn slacks, like you.' Beth grinned at her, and Alice strove to curb that flash of irritation. She saw that Doreen was making the most of it, letting the breeze get under her skirts and aping Elsbeth in her mock consternation. Davy had gone racing ahead in pursuit of Algy, and Alice hastened after him, full of gratitude for the way he had made such friends with the little boy. He'll make a great dad, she thought, and immediately found the speculation oddly disturbing. All at once, she felt a reinforced sensation of awkwardness, of the strange and uncomfortable juxtaposition of this adult quartet, and her own isolated position in it.

Luke bought a little tin bucket and wooden-handled spade for Algy at a stall near the old battery. 'Must be pre-war stock. It's a wonder the government haven't grabbed them to make bits of tanks and things. Got to have a bucket and spade for the seaside!' he insisted merrily, and Algy gazed at him in dumb adoration when he presented them to him.

'Say thank you to Mr Denby!' Alice admonished severely, while Algy writhed in sudden shame.

Luke protested. 'Hey, come on! *Mr* Denby? That's not very friendly, is it? Luke, please. Or at least *Uncle* Luke, eh?' He grinned at the boy. 'Let's get down to the sands. Who's going to be brave enough to go in the sea?' He ran down the slope onto the beach, raced towards the retreating break of the waves and stood on one leg, already tugging at his shoes. Algy was ecstatic.

The others followed. Elsbeth quickly slipped off her shoes, gathered the flapping skirts of her dress in her hands, holding them high to show her white legs nearly to the tops of her thighs and ran to the shining margins of the water. She picked up her feet like a prancing horse, her toes pointing in high-stepping exaggeration, and screamed shrilly as the icy chill snatched at her ankles.

'Are you going in for a plodge?'

Doreen stared back at her sister with lofty disdain, and shook her head. She glanced at the capering figures in the shallows with disapproval. Alice noted how carefully she was treading over the sand, with its miniature banks of pebbles and dark seaweed strands. Her dainty nose wrinkled fastidiously.

Frightened of spoiling your pretty new shoes, are you? Alice kept quiet, but all at once the words of the old nursery rhyme about 'Curly locks' came to mind. No washing dishes or feeding swine for our Miss Doreen these days. All sitting on cushions and sewing fine seams. The little madam was going to find it very hard to fit back into the rough and tumble of Maudsley Street when everything got back to normal. Mind you, she wouldn't be the only one, Alice conceded, as she gazed at the sea's edge, where Davy was crouching low with Algy, making pot pies in the wet sand, and Elsbeth was hiking up her dress with one hand and dealing with Luke's arm which had snaked playfully round her waist.

★   ★   ★

'I've got something for you. A going-away gift. Something rather special. Just one condition, though. You must promise to let me see you wearing it.'

Elsbeth blushed, with her usual mixture of embarrassment and pleasure at his smile and his voice, as she took the plain box from him.

311

Something to wear. A jumper or cardigan, maybe? Perhaps even a dress. There was talk that the government were going to introduce some sort of rationing scheme even for clothing, with coupons similar to those allocated for food. She knew Mummy had been buying in a whole lot of extras, stockpiling against just such an eventuality.

'You shouldn't have,' she murmured politely, beginning to pick at the lid. It was a shame that so many things were in short supply now. In the old days, his gift would have been wrapped in pretty coloured paper, and tied with ribbon. She got the package open, and gave a cry of surprise, and delight at the beautiful smooth white silk folded within. She felt the blood invade her cheeks as she realized the import of what the sheer material and its colour meant. A nightdress? Or . . .

'Have a look then!' Luke urged, his tone still hearty with his laughter, though perhaps tinged now with just a little uncertainty. 'Take it out.'

It? Them, surely, she corrected confusedly as, steeped in blushes now, she unfolded the beautifully fashioned, delicate garment, with its thin satin straps, and bodice and legs edged with lace. Cami-knickers, of amazing daintiness — and brevity!

She felt the cool flow of the silk over her hands, through her fingers, like liquid, and could think of nothing whatsoever to say, aware only of the heat of her embarrassment prickling throughout her body. She kept her eyes down, staring at them.

'I hope they're the right size. I had to guess — with a bit of help. They've been specially made. Parachute silk. The finest you can get!' His voice was a little over-loud, definitely a touch uncomfortable, even though he was struggling hard to hide it. He waited a fraction, in expectation or hope that she would say something before he continued. 'You do like them, don't you? You're not offended or anything? It's just that silk's so hard to get hold of these days, even if it's artificial — and there's not much else you can use it for, is there?'

She cleared her throat, made a brave effort to meet his gaze. 'No, no! It's lovely, really! Thank you so much. I — I'll keep them, for best.'

'No chance of me getting my wish then? To see you in them?' His voice was tense, despite his efforts at levity. 'At least promise me you'll think of me whenever you do wear them.'

'Of course.' And that raised her blushes yet again; it sounded such a fast remark to make.

He almost snatched the garment from her and tossed it back into the box. 'I think of you a hell of a lot. Most of the time,' he said, his voice low now, and vibrant with his intensity. It wasn't really a lie. She crept into his thoughts at the oddest and most unexpected of times, when he was chatting up other girls, with the crew in The Eagle in Oban. Even when he was he was in bed with Kathy, in the shabby upper room of the flat, where she took him — and others, he well knew — for their intimate private meetings whenever he could arrange them.

He had half-convinced himself he was in love with this kid, this eighteen- no, nineteen now, since a month ago -year-old virgin, though it was the challenge of her naïve innocence as much as her fresh loveliness that inspired him in his pursuit of her. He tried to tell himself he was not so wicked or so weak, that there was always Kathy, and plenty of other girls and women besides, who were willing to satisfy his sexual craving. He wasn't really trying to bed her, he assured himself. Especially lately, when he had been in Scotland and far removed from the temptation of her desirable youthfulness, he had entertained noble aspirations to do the decent thing, call off his pursuit of her. But they did not last, fled the field at his first resighting of her, the first touch of his lips on hers. 'Let's call the whole thing off', the song said, but he was powerless to do so once he was back with her. He would even fall in love with her, if he had to.

'I'm crazy about you,' he insisted, on the afternoon of his last day at home. He had waylaid her on her way back from school, on the second day of the new term, and stuck to her side in spite of her confusion all the way through the hall, mercifully clear of gym slips, for the privileged, privately educated pupils enjoyed far lengthier holidays, and up the stairs to the sanctum of her own spartan room.

'You shouldn't be in here,' she almost whispered, faintly enough to encourage him in the hope that the weakness of her protest might stem as much from her own struggle against her desire as her sense of decorum. He was further fortified by the way she surrendered herself to his embrace, and even lifted her mouth to meet the undoubted ardour of his kiss. She was trembling, felt delightfully fragile and slimly yielding in his arms. Newly fired by both a desperate awareness of time running out and the urgency of his body, he bore her backward over the worn rug and creaking floorboards, to fall heavily down on the counterpane of the narrow bed, which squeaked even more loudly.

'Oh God! I love you, Beth! Can't you see that?' he moaned, his body heavy upon her, pinning her down in the springy hollow of the mattress beneath. His mouth was against hers, so that his speech was slurred, his breath hot over her, then it moved as he burrowed his face deep into her neck, his mouth open like a ravishing vampire.

A shudder like electricity shot through her frame, and she squirmed, thrilled and terrified by it. The cold air was on her limbs as he swept the thick skirt up off her legs and she felt again his hard fingers tugging at the fastening of a suspender, clawing at her bare thigh above the stocking-top: the thick, workaday lisle stockings whose ugliness she vividly pictured now, even in the extreme of her panic and confusion, whose unattractive-ness she did not want him to see. It came as a further shock to her, in spite of that electric jolt of physical sensation at his touch on her bare skin, that she did not want this to continue and she found herself fighting, really resisting, kicking and heaving against him and trying to scratch at his hand, to tear it from her. She was sobbing wildly.

And then he was gone, rolling off her, and she was struggling to sit up, and pull her clothing down over her limbs, and he was glaring down at her as if she were the one who had suddenly gone mad. 'For Christ's sake shut up, you little fool! You'll have the whole place up in arms!' He drew in a ragged, sobbing breath, fighting to gain control of himself once more. He moved away, glanced in the small mirror on the wall, ran a hand through his disordered hair, adjusted his collar, straightened his tie. 'I've tried to tell you how I feel.' He spoke quietly, his tone sounded oddly like someone who had been deeply and unjustly offended. 'I'm sorry. You clearly don't have anything like the same kind of feeling for me. I was wrong — I thought you had.' He had his hand on the door-handle, turned back towards her. 'We'll be posted soon after I get back. We'll be operational. Assigned to a squadron. I don't know where. Might even be overseas. I'll let you know. If you're interested.'

He did not know how close, in the next seconds, he came to achieving his goal. She almost called him back, felt the words rising to her lips, felt her body lifting towards the door. Instead, she fell back once more, limply onto the pillow, and sobbed bitterly for long minutes, thinking of the fury of his passion, her shivering response to that assault, his fierce kiss on her neck.

She bathed and dressed in one of her prettiest cocktail dresses, spent time on her hair, brushing it out, staring at herself in the mirror. She tied a light silk scarf about her neck. It might look a little affected for the informal supper in the Denby drawing-room, but it was pretty, and it hid the faint smudge of a bruise where his kiss had branded her.

His cheerfulness was forced, his face aglow with whisky. Elsbeth could see that his parents were both touched and saddened by his gaiety, with its hint of *Morituri te salutant*. She felt distracted, her mind was racing furiously. Above all, she felt burdened with a tremendous sense of guilt. She couldn't shake it off, no matter how many times she told herself she had nothing to reproach herself with, that he was the one who was wrong in making her feel this way. How could she give up all her principles, everything she had been brought up to believe in, to satisfy his needs — basic, bodily needs? If he truly loved her, how could he ask it of her?

But he might never come back here. She might never see him again. The thought made her cold, she felt her skin pucker in a shiver of pure horror. She felt such sadness at the thought. Maybe that was a kind of love after all. She *was* fond of him. No! More than that.

She dismissed the terrible feebleness of that word. She had been *fond* of Flossy, the terrier that had been the household pet for most of her childhood. He deserved more than that. Far more.

She found she could hardly follow the conversation, and her distraction was apparent to everyone, including Luke. 'I think I'll have an early night. Must be with school starting. I feel worn out. Anyway, you three want to be alone together, on Luke's last night.' Oh God! That sounded awful, what a crass and absolutely stupidly unfeeling thing to say! She almost apologized for it. Luke was looking totally sickened by her announcement. She waited until she could get close to him, over by the drinks-trolley and the coffee-tray, and bent close until their heads almost touched. 'I'm wearing your present,' she whispered. 'I'll keep it on. In case you want to sneak along later and see it. *My* gift to you. I hope you like it.'

★　★　★

She was shaking, her teeth chattering. She kept her woollen dressing gown on, over her brief underwear, and sat with her lower limbs under the bedclothes, and still couldn't stop shaking. She felt sick, her stomach churning distressingly, so that she wondered if she should go along to the lavatory at the end of the corridor. That really would make the whole thing a farce. She was seized with a chilling fear. She had no idea whatsoever of what would be involved. Well, that was stupid, of course she had some idea of what . . . what had to happen, between a man or a woman. But she wasn't a woman. Not at all. She was a girl — a *little* girl still, closer to the nursery than the boudoir. Perhaps he wouldn't come — but of course he would. She had invited him, like any flagrant hussy, to her bedroom. She was sitting in this scrap of silk and lace, flaunting herself, warming the very bed, where . . .

Where what? What would happen? What would it be like? What would she have to do? How could she make sure there were no terrible consequences, no baby which would grow inside her after he had left her, maybe for good? She had a terrible but powerful superstition that somehow she was assisting in his death. But how? By letting him take her virginity, perhaps carrying his seed inside her? Or by refusing him and sending him away unfulfilled, his mind consumed with his longing for her? She must leave it to him. Leave matters, leave herself, entirely in his hands. She was making herself his, to do with as he liked. She was sacrificing herself, surrendering herself to his will. She found herself wishing it had not come to this. She had brought it on herself, by her decision to go down to the drawing-room, to make that fateful advance, to offer herself to him in that whispered illicit bargain.

All at once, she found herself remembering another night entirely, a dark winter's night, which had begun in similar uncertainty and confusion. The night she had shared someone else's bed. She remembered that strange excitement, the tingling she had felt, in spite of her embarrassment; the undoubted thrill she had experienced in lying beside Alice, feeling her body fitted intimately against her friend, the feel of the arms about her waist, the hands on her breasts that had stirred her so shockingly, so lovingly that she had just wanted to go on lying there, wrapped together, for ever and ever, amen.

16

Alice was concerned at Elsbeth's absence on the morning of Luke Denby's departure. She could not help linking the two events, nor the great swell of hurt and anger they occasioned. What on earth was the lass playing at, making out that she didn't have any feelings for the squire's son, when clearly that was not the case at all? Why couldn't she be honest with her? They were supposed to be best mates, weren't they, so why couldn't Beth admit that she was sweet on Luke and have done with it? After all, what does it matter to me who she falls for? Alice told herself, only to follow it immediately with another question, whose answer, as always, she shied away from. Who the hell am I kidding?

Edith Bowen started to flap as soon as she arrived, tardily as usual. 'Where is Elsbeth? Surely Miss Laverton will call to let us know what's wrong? Was she feeling all right yesterday? She never said anything to me.'

They got the children in from the yard, and went through the morning hymn and prayer, and story. 'Could you look after Class I?' Edith asked Alice. 'Let them copy the letters.

And Jess, could you go up to the school and see Miss Laverton? See if she can tell us why Elsbeth isn't here.'

Jess Corbett was soon back, pink-faced and puffing with responsibility. 'She didn't know Elsbeth wasn't in.' She looked across at Alice. 'She asked if Alice could nip over to Big House and find out what's wrong. She doesn't like to ring them on the telephone.'

'Aye, right-oh.' Alice pulled her coat back on, over her overall and dungarees. She didn't bother tying the headscarf over her tight curls, in spite of the fresh, April breeze. She felt a certain reluctance at her quest, despite her anxiety. The silly bitch had probably skived off just to say her private farewells to the Brylcreem Boy. And if that was the case, she'd give her a right earful, as well as a good boot up her pretty little backside!

She was hoping she would meet a penitent Beth scurrying down the drive, but she saw no one as she approached the front of the house. She noted that there was no sign of the black Morris Eight that Luke Denby used, so he must have got himself away. She could hear the raised voices of various teachers, with their piercing cut-glass accents, coming through the open windows of the wing which St Anne's had taken over. From one room came the collective chant of pupils mouthing what was clearly some foreign tongue. Clever little sods! Wonder what they'd make of Lister Road, these spoilt little nobs? But there was no real malice in her speculation.

She went up the steps and entered the front hall. She saw a plump figure she recognized — one of the village women who worked as a cleaner here, in place of the uniformed resident staff of former, more gracious days. Alice enquired about Elsbeth, and the woman shrugged, nodded towards the wide staircase. 'Dunno. Nobody left in t' dining-hall. The rooms are all up there.'

'Yes, I know where her room is. I'll just pop up. Thanks.'

She tapped on the closed door of Elsbeth's room, and waited tensely. She tried the handle. The door was bolted from the inside. She called sharply, keeping her voice low. 'Beth? It's me! Al! What's up?' She heard the faint creak of bedsprings, then the sound of the bolt being withdrawn. 'Good God! What's wrong, love? You look terrible!'

'Thanks a lot!'

But it was true. Beth's face was puffed and creased, the area around the eyes darkly swollen. Her nose shone, and she sniffed as she turned and made her way back to the tumbled bed. She was bent forward like a crone. Her nightdress was hanging loose and shapeless, badly creased at the back. The material was thick, more suitable for the chill of winter, the little sprigs with which it was decorated adding to the incongruity. Alice felt the pathos of the forlorn figure, noted the thinness of the pale limbs, and the slightly dusty look of the narrow soles of her feet before they disappeared under the blankets again. 'I'm not well.' The voice was a croaky whisper. 'I feel dreadful. Tell them I can't come in.' She kept her gaze averted all the while. Alice was convinced she did not want to meet her eyes. Why not?

'It's not your time-of-the-month, is it?' The curse, Beth called it. Not a bad name for it, Alice reckoned, and a darned sight less unpleasant than some of the luridly disgusting terms the loud-mouthed youths of Maudsley Street, and no doubt their yokel cousins, the farmhands of Howbeck, used for it. At least it was something she and Elsbeth could refer to with minimal embarrassment in each other's presence. It was a fair indication of how far their friendship had developed, for when they had first come here Elsbeth would have cringed at the mere breath of acknowledgement of its inconvenient existence.

Elsbeth shook her head. She was still avoiding looking at Alice. 'Some sort of bug, maybe. Or a cold. I'm all stuffy, and my head's throbbing.'

Her voice still sounded hoarse, and Alice was full of worried sympathy. 'Look, I'd better call in at Doctor Ryder's. I'll see if I can get any Beecham's Powders. The school must have things like that here. Isn't there a school nurse? I'll go and find her.'

'No. I'll be all right. I just had a bad night. I need to get some sleep.' But her voice caught, almost broke, and Alice moved forward anxiously.

'Here. Let me feel — you've probably got a temperature.' She bent over and reached out her arm, to place her hand on Elsbeth's brow. She was startled at the violence with which the girl jerked her shoulders away, and pulled her head clear of any contact with Alice's palm.

'No! No, don't — I might — I don't want you to catch anything.' Her voice faded, she half-turned away towards the wall, as though in dismissal. 'I'll probably be all right by tomorrow. Tell Miss Laverton I'm sorry.'

She sounded even closer to tears. 'It isn't owt to do with Luke, is it?' Alice pressed bluntly. 'With him going?'

'What are you talking about?' The blotched face swung back, gazing fully at Alice now with a stricken look. 'Don't be so stupid!'

Alice bridled. 'Stupid, am I? *You're* the one who's stupid, if you ask me! If you're that sick you can't get out of bed, you need seeing to. And if you're not sick, why the hell have you been up all night? Blubbing your heart out, by the look of you! You're in a right state. Anyone can see — '

'Oh, just leave me alone, will you?'

It was a screech, and Alice was shaken by it. 'Fair enough, kidder. If that's what you want!' Her lips pressed thinly together, she turned, strode towards the door.

'Al!' The call was even more urgent. Alice turned back into the room. Elsbeth was sitting up in bed. Her face was tragic, she was holding her arms out in stiff entreaty. She gave a moan of profound despair, flung herself down, burying her face in the thin pillow, and her body shook with the wrenching sobs that tore through her.

Alice raced across, dropped to her knees by the bed, her heart thumping with alarm, and flung her arms across the heaving shoulders. 'My God! What is it, sweetheart? Tell me, whatever it is.' But for a while the wretched figure continued to convulse, the anguished sobs muffled by the pillow. Alice pressed her face to the tangled, limp, yellow locks, tried to lift the shaking frame clear of the pillow, to turn her so that she could hold her securely in her mothering embrace.

At last Elsbeth *did* turn, her face ravaged, wet with tears and mucus, her lips slack, and her streaming eyes reflected her pain. For a few seconds she was fighting for breath. When she spoke, the words came out in tortured gasps, punctuated by her sobs. 'Oh — Al! Last night — I — Luke — he came here. Came to my room.'

'What!' Alice felt a coldness, a fearful, gripping revulsion, seize her like a physical sensation in her own breast. No, please! she found herself praying frantically. The hate for him burned over the shock. 'The bastard! He can't — we'll have him, I don't care how rich he is!'

She was holding Alice tightly, and she felt the girl struggle in her embrace, a hand on Alice's neck, to pull herself up close, to gaze at her. 'No! No! It wasn't like that! I asked him to. Told him to come. I let him . . . '

Alice was staring back at her, in even deeper shock, her mind spinning, refusing to take in the import of what the weeping girl was saying. That she had let him — all the obscene words for the act raced at lightning speed through Alice's reeling brain. She didn't know, couldn't think of, any decent words for it. 'You let him . . . do it?'

'Yes, yes!' Her eyes, palely awash with tears, were locked on Alice's now. Then a great shudder seemed to pass through Elsbeth's entire frame, and Alice felt the shivering form sag limply in her embrace. 'It was *awful*, Al. Horrible!'

The confused nightmare of images, of sounds and sensations, raced yet again through Elsbeth's consciousness. The almost paralysing effect of his touch on her; how she had lain, stiff and as uncooperative as a plank of wood, while he fought with increasing desperation to drag and roll that absurd, awkward little covering of silk and lace down off her breasts, over her hips and legs; the stunning shame of being naked in front of him, and the even worse shame of his inappropriate attempt to alleviate it. 'I see you're not a peroxide blonde then!' he had said, when the sandy little tuft of her wiry pubis was exposed. But that was only the beginning.

There was some shameful kind of thrill at his kisses, at first; even the touch of his mouth on her breast, her sensitized nipples, its touch trailing over her skin. But then his hand was there, between her legs, on her sex, and she had a sudden urge to scream, to thrust him away, to scream at him, 'Just do it!'

But when he did, it was all just unimaginable, hard, brutal pain, and pounding invasion, and she felt as though she were fighting him helplessly, that he was, indeed, raping her, despite her complicity, the appalling shame of her frog-legged submission to it all. For a while, the pain overrode all the other feelings, fused with the gaping wet horror and the rank smell of their coupling. But then he was kneeling, free of her, and she saw the obscenity of the long, pale, opaque, shining thing, hanging from *his* 'thing'. She knew it wasn't part of him, or her, knew that this was why he had whispered frantically, as part of her earlier nightmare, 'It'll be all right, baby. You'll be safe.'

She turned away, drawing up her knees, on her side, away from him, and it wasn't until later, when he briefly left her then came back with a towel, that she had seen the smear of blood, and the stickiness on her thighs, and the small patch of blood in the circle of wetness on the sheet.

How could she tell any of this, least of all to Alice, her one dearest friend? She gazed up in mute anguish, wanting only to hide in those loving arms, to share that warm feeling of safeness, of belonging. But the shocks of the eventful night were not over, in spite of the bright morning light striving to filter round the edges of the heavy curtains into the still deep gloom.

Alice's arms were withdrawn, so suddenly that Elsbeth's head fell back on the pillow.

Her world exploded in a new and different pain as Alice's hand was drawn back and delivered a cracking blow to the side of Elsbeth's head, rocking it to one side, then the other as the knuckles rapped against its other fair temple in the returning, back-handed blow. Elsbeth's mouth gaped, the sob caught in what might in other circumstances have been dubbed comic astonishment, before the tears flowed again.

Alice stared down, as startled at her own reaction as her victim, whose head was still ringing, and whose hand had come up to massage the throbbing side of her face. She lay staring up, making no effort to defend herself, awaiting the further onslaught almost with resignation. 'I'm sorry!' she blubbered softly.

Alice's fists were already clenched, about to launch an attack altogether more robust and less girlish. Instead, she gave a wail of contrition, once more scooped up the supine figure and cushioned her to her chest, smothering the damp face with her kisses and her tears. She rocked her back and forth, and murmured, 'Oh my baby! My poor baby!'

★ ★ ★

In the days that followed, Alice learnt a little more about the incident. It was abundantly clear that Elsbeth did not want to talk about it, would prefer to erase it from her memory, or, equally impossible, would have liked to roll back time and withdraw her fatal acquiescence. But certain things had to be established, and quickly. Alice's own knowledge of sex, completely theoretical as it was, had been garnered through her upbringing at a social level where delicacy about such subjects was rarely a consideration. 'He used a Frenchy?' Such distinctions in their upbringing were aptly illustrated by Elsbeth's blankly bewildered look, followed by a tide of redness flooding through her features, of such depth that it indicated both her belated understanding of the question and the addition of a new word to her vocabulary.

Though the episode still made Alice's flesh crawl and fingers curl with the murderous desire to inflict all kinds of dire injury on the perpetrator of what she could only think of as a terrible crime against Beth's innocence, it had undoubtedly brought the two girls to an even closer level of friendship, and something sweetly, indefinably, more. Alice was far more tenderly perceptive. The fact of Luke's using a contraceptive merely marked him down in her reckoning as the corrupt seducer she had always suspected. Coming along to Beth's room, sneaking in in the dead of night, ready 'armed' for the fray — what further proof could there be of his wickedness? The dirty, evil bastard! She wanted to howl it aloud when she saw the drawn misery stamped on Beth's face at the memory — but she didn't. She bit her lip and swallowed down her rage, even though it blazed away inside her.

Because Beth would have none of it, stubbornly stuck to the notion that she alone was to blame for what had happened. 'It was *my* fault. I asked him, invited him, to my room.' She even confessed to Alice about the underwear. 'I wore it for him.' Yet further damning evidence in Alice's book of his lecherous intent. Elsbeth's eyes, their blue still faded from her grief, gazed at her solemnly. 'Do you want to slap me again?'

The faint mark of Alice's blow was still visible above the left eyebrow. 'Come here, you daft ha'p'orth!' she said roughly, and hugged her, squeezing her tightly to her. That was something else they could do a lot more of now, and Alice was grateful for it. They hugged and held hands and embraced much more freely, and Alice was sad only at the fact that Beth had had to go through so much before they could express their feeling for each other.

Elsbeth was so convinced that divine retribution would ensure her pregnancy that even Alice's nerves were taut with anxiety for her. Accidents *did* happen, in spite of man's best-laid plans, so that when the cramps and discomforts of Elsbeth's period came along on time, along with the early May mildness that was almost a herald of summer, Alice was as relieved as the recipient. 'What next?' she asked her edgily, unable any longer to deny her deep concern. She knew that Beth had already received at least one plump letter from Luke since his departure.

'He's feeling really bad about it,' Elsbeth confided. 'Full of apologies for what happened. Blames himself for everything.'

Alice bit back on her temptation to express her wholehearted agreement with his assessment. Instead, she voiced thoughts which were far more painful to her. 'How do you feel about him? Really? Are you that keen on him?' It hurt, deeply, to acknowledge that the answer must be yes, otherwise Beth would never, surely, have allowed him . . . let him into her bed? Beth gave her that look, so helpless and uncertain, that both soothed and irritated Alice at the same time. 'He's gonna want, you know, to carry on, like, isn't he? Where you left off.'

'No! I couldn't!' The words were out, without any hesitation this time, and again came that helpless look, a little shake of the blonde head. 'I don't know why . . . I know it was a big mistake. A terrible mistake.' Her eyes filled with tears again, but she drew a deep breath, stopped herself from crying. 'I can't explain, even to myself. But I just felt . . . he seemed so sad. And he's going to be in such danger. He'll have finished his training in a week. He'll be going out . . . on bombing raids. There's so many that don't come back. The government don't tell us how many . . . '

'He'll be back soon. And he's gonna want to know. Are you his girl — or not?'

Elsbeth's face had a hunted look. She gave a little shake of her head. 'Not like that! Not again!'

'Does he want you — properly, I mean? Does he want to marry you?' Alice curbed her irritation once more at the helpless flash of appeal she saw, the shake of the head again, the utter confusion. 'Do *you* want to marry *him*?' The expression scarcely changed, only looked more hunted, and Alice had to turn away from that liquid gaze, and its power over her.

It was a relief in a way to have her thoughts diverted towards another problem, brought about by her pursuit of her private suspicions concerning the Big Swede and Bob Symmonds. Davy Brown had found himself getting more involved — at first only because

335

of his liking for Alice and his need for her friendship. And after Gus Rielke's spirited acceptance and defence of him, to prove to her how wide of the mark her suspicions were. It didn't take Davy long, once he had been accepted, reluctantly at first, into at least a nodding acquaintance with the regular drinkers at the Oddfellows, to learn that there was after all something not quite above board about the big foreigner, though far from Alice's wild conception that he was a spy in their midst. 'Old Gus can fix up most things. Fags or baccy. A bottle of booze, anything you want.' So that's what he was involved in? The black market. And no doubt that was his connection with the unsavoury Symmonds, and the locked shed up at High Top, the tyre-marks in the fields.

'You can forget about him being a Jerry spy. That's what he's up to, a black marketeer,' he told Alice.

'Oh! And that's all right, is it? Fiddling and making money on the side, when poor folks have to make do with nowt?' Davy's seemingly easy acceptance of the illicit trade angered as well as disappointed Alice. 'I thought you of all people would be against that kind of thing, given all your highfalutin ideas about what's right and wrong.'

The colour in his face told that her shot

had struck home, but she got little satisfaction from it. She liked and admired Davy for his principles, and the extent to which he had been prepared to stand up for them. 'The profiteering's all part of this war, too,' he answered stiffly. 'There's plenty of rich people getting a lot richer from it, and they don't have to break the law to do it. You can't blame little folk for trying to make a few pennies on the side. Most of them round here are quite happy to take advantage of what Gus can do for them. And probably that scruffy tyke, Symmonds, as well.'

She shrugged, and grudgingly held her peace, though she could not rid herself of her nagging dislike of the Big Swede and her scepticism of that bland, hail-fellow geniality. She grinned appeasingly, and thrust out her hand at Davy in a peace-offering. 'Well, let's not fall out over yon big bugger, eh? I take it you're backing out of the job as my little spy down at the Oddfellows then? Still mates, though, aren't we?'

Davy took her hand, and held onto it, squeezing it hard when she tried to withdraw it. He smiled wryly. 'I don't usually say this to a mate, but you wouldn't swap this for a kiss, would you?'

She punched him hard on his upper arm with her free hand and he released her. 'Not you an' all!' she muttered softly, and he raised his eyebrows in surprise.

'Don't tell me I've got a rival?'

He was staring at her keenly, and she shook her head, gave a loud laugh to dispel her unease. 'Don't be daft! I've told you, I can't be doing with all that carry-on! I'll be an old maid, me, that's for sure.'

'As long as I know I've still got a chance.' His face showed the warmth that lay behind his lightness.

'As much as anyone else, sunshine, and that's the truth!'

★　★　★

She was involved very directly in the grey world of black market when Davy came to seek her out as afternoon school was finishing the following Friday. She was in need of some diversion. Elsbeth had received another letter from Luke, full of passion and longing to see her again. She hadn't read it to her — 'I don't want to know!' Alice exclaimed before her friend had even offered to do so. He had been posted to an aerodrome down in Lincoln-shire, had been on his first two 'missions', though he couldn't tell her where, and was hoping to get three days' leave early in June — only two or three weeks away.

The blue eyes, which had at last lost their washed-out dullness, misted with gathering tears, and Alice was torn with that fierce twisting of love and fury in her gut. 'It's bloody blackmail, that's all it is! He's using it — all the flying and stuff — to worm his way back into your . . . bed.' She managed to substitute the word for one of far less delicacy, then gave a groan of hopelessness and grabbed at Elsbeth and planted a swift kiss on that beautiful mouth — a kiss that was returned, thankfully, with equal eagerness.

The war news, too, was bleak. Though far from the sun-dappled quiet of the dale, London had received another severe air onslaught a few days before. Even parliament had been bombed, the front pages full of pictures of a blazing House of Commons against the night sky. 'I'm heading up to Big House when Beth is ready,' she told Davy, beaming at him in welcome. 'You can walk back with us. Skiving off early, as usual?'

'Not at all. I'm on my way back from Barker's. Been clearing ditches. Plenty waiting for me back at the manor. What I wanted to see you for was to invite you for a drink tonight.'

She looked at him in some surprise. 'Oddfellows on a Friday? What's the occasion?'

He winked at her. 'Don't blame me. It's your old mate Gus. He's got a present for you.' He laughed and spoke over her outburst of indignation. 'I've no idea what it's about. Not your birthday, is it? Anyway, he insists on handing it over himself, won't trust me to pass it on to you. I said I'd try to get you along. I think you should come, in view of all you've had to say about him. He's making such a big thing of it. There'll be a big crowd there. Everybody's agog to find out what he's on about.'

She looked at him in consternation. 'What's he up to, Davy? Why's he want me there, at the pub?'

He shrugged. 'Dunno. But it'll be worth coming along to find out. And I'll be there to look after you. Just don't forget, you're with me, right? Don't be swept off your feet by these gifts, whatever they are. You want me to come up to Beck Side to fetch you?'

'Nay, lad, there's no need for you to hike all the way up the hill. I'll be down for seven. Just make sure you're there waiting for me or I'll kill you! I'm not going in there to face that lot on me own!'

Gus Rielke's face was even redder and more widely grinning than usual when she faced him across the bar. She had a sense of expectation, even among the group of drinkers gathered and grinning, too, in anticipation of some fun. At my expense! Alice thought grimly, but she disguised her unease, and took comfort from Davy, staying close by her side. 'A liddle present for you, my dear! Just to show my appreciation of you, which I don't make de bones of, ya? I would give it in private but I know you don't agree to meet with me.' He nodded at Davy beside her. 'And I know young Davy here gonna knock my block off if I go anywhere near you. Maybe you change your mind when you see my present, though. Fit for the princess. You like, I hope.'

Vera Rhodes was still upstairs, ready to make her carefully groomed appearance later in the evening. The Big Swede ducked underneath the counter and produced a parcel, carefully tied with a precious piece of thin silk ribbon. Worth accepting it even for the ribbon, Alice thought, annoyed at the blush she could feel rising, in spite of all her efforts to appear quite relaxed and playing along with the jokiness. She opened the package, very much aware of all the eyes turned on her. She gasped, felt the cool smoothness of the beautiful material, saw it shine under the light above the bar. It divided in two; two small pieces, and the crowd erupted in a chorus of shouts and laughter and piercing whistles, as she revealed two pairs of panties, exquisitely made, the elastic at waist and legs delicately gathered and pleated. Her face was beetroot, burning with humiliation, and her body tensed. She wanted to turn and run, to fling them back in his grinning face, to mouth the string of oaths that hammered in her brain.

'I hope they fit, ya? Real silk. You never see that nowadays.'

Her lips were compressed. She managed somehow to force them into a grimace of a smile. 'Thank you, they're very nice. But why me?'

His laugh boomed out. 'I think right away they suit you. Soon as I see them. You can try on, if you like.' He made a grand sweeping gesture. 'The Ladies out back.' The laughs burst out all round her again.

'It's all right. I'll wait till I get home, thanks. These are real silk, eh? You're right. You can't get hold of that anywhere, these days.'

He tapped that broad nose of his and winked at her. It felt as though he were touching her, and she shivered with revulsion. 'Don't you worry, Alice. I can get many things. Stockings, the make-up. Scent. I'm your good friend, ya?'

Davy was looking ill at ease, clearly not

sharing the amusement of the others around him. 'Better wrap your present up,' he said to Alice. 'Not the sort of thing that should be on show in the public bar, eh? Now, can we have a drink, eh? A half of bitter and a sweet sherry. No! I'll get these, thanks,' he said quickly, as Gus began to make his offer to stand them the drinks. 'We'll take them through to the Best Room, if that's all right.'

'Sure. I put the light on for you. Make yourselves at home.'

Nothing could shake that grin, it seemed. They moved through the laughing drinkers, out to the corridor and the chilly room where a few small iron tables and chairs were set out. They were the only occupants. 'Did you know about this? *These!*' she corrected bitterly, gesturing at the loosely wrapped small parcel.

He shook his head apologetically. 'I should have known it would be something like this, though. I'm sorry.'

She smiled almost fiercely, with grim determination. She lifted the flap of paper, exposing the silk knickers, and passed her fingers over them. 'I've seen summat else like this recently,' she said. 'Luke Denby bought summat similar for Beth not so long ago. Parachute silk, he said. He's probably right. Bit hard on the poor lads that might be relying on stuff like this to save their lives, eh? Mebbes poor old Luke himself, one day. He's started bombing raids, you know.'

'You're right. It's no laughing matter, is it?' Davy's face was solemn, and full of regret.

She put her hand over his on the round little tabletop. 'Don't worry. I'll have him for this, the slimy sod.' And from the look, and the reassuring nod Davy gave her, she had won her ally back, she thought.

17

It was greed and overreaching ambition that brought about Rielke's downfall in the end. 'Business' was booming, and expanding. The word 'spiv' was coming into common parlance, as what had begun as fairly amateurish private enterprise and favouritism became more organized and large-scale profiteering. Shortage of manpower meant that local police forces were stretched to their limit and beyond, while the blackout and, particularly in the towns and cities, houses standing invitingly empty while their occupants hid in shelters, several streets away if communal, and, if not, usually conveniently (for the thieves) a garden's length away from the residence, greatly assisted their burglary. A proficient, intricate network grew up to dispense with these hauls.

Gus had contacts from the days before his sojourn in Howbeck, far away from the dale, in the ports of the north-east coast, like Middlesbrough and Newcastle. And he made new 'friends' in those places, who had the resources to take advantage of the favourable climate for criminal activity. Trade grew brisker, and Gus became more deeply and willingly involved. Goods were moved, concealed in remote places like High Top, before they were 'redistributed' to meet the growing demand. The shed and the unused sheep dip became inadequate to hold the amount of items passing through. More of the dilapidated outbuildings adjoining the farmhouse were used, more shutters and padlocks and guard dogs were required. Bob Symmonds's share was modest enough, though not to him, and he was more than happy with the notes stuffed in the back pocket of his filthy overalls, his wife pleased with the growing pile shoved into the bottom of one of her stockings and kept under the lumpy mattress. With one of the ever more frequent night deliveries, came a brand new Silver Cross perambulator for the new baby, not that there was much opportunity to perambulate with the infant about the rutted tracks or moorland surrounding High Top Farm. It made her feel good, though, and was an elegant resting place for the babe, by day and by night.

Vera Rhodes was not so happy, in spite of the plentiful supply of beer and spirits and tobacco that Gus ensured. 'Don't you think you ought to go easy a while?' she cautioned plaintively. She looked back with fond regret to the time over a year ago when he had first arrived in the village, so dependent on her generosity, and her welcoming bed. Now she was lucky if he spent three of the seven nights of the week in it.

Gus's associates relied on him to provide the means for an increasingly important aspect of trading — 'meat on the hoof'. 'You're in the right place for it,' the smart businessman in the bespoke, pinstriped suit smiled, handing out his gold-plated case for Gus to take a cigarette. Even if Gus had been unwilling, he would have been foolish not to co-operate, knowing what his associate knew about him.

Bob Symmonds was an essential cog in the machine of this particular activity. Sheep-rustling was not unknown, but the scale on which Gus's associates wished to develop it was. It was all night work, and tricky, too. It required speed, local knowledge and skill, in a swift round-up and getaway, in the dark and over some rough terrain.

They kept as far away from Howe Dale as they could. It was time consuming, for they had to scout out a suitable location, in daylight, to learn the layout of the land and to work out in detail the route of the escape, the link with the road where the transfer of the captured animals to another vehicle would

347

take place, to transport them northward to the distant city and their slaughter. The trouble was, the fewer people involved in this sensitive line of work the better. Shifting fags and booze was one thing. Rustling livestock, 'robbing their own', as many locals would put it, was definitely another.

'We've got to be able to trust them,' the Big Swede warned. Even young Alfie James was roped in to help, the first of the mistakes which would bring their enterprise crashing down.

It was almost mid-summer, and the hours of darkness were much diminished. One night the transporter failed to turn up at the coast road where the venerable, wooden-sided truck waited. Gus was at the wheel, with Bob Symmonds beside him and Alfie squashed against the window. Patch, the working dog, lay whining among the booted feet. The sheep kept up a steady, nerve-racking bleating and coughing, crammed in the body of the truck behind the cab.

The sky over the sea was furrowed with long streaks of reddening light. Gus's stream of profanity, despite its rich mix of languages, produced no tangible result and did not alleviate his tension. He had to decide quickly. A dash up the road, in the new daylight, through the busy traffic into the seaport where he could make contact with someone who might know what the hell was going on — or wasn't. Or . . . safer to risk the rougher but shorter ride back to the Tops and Symmonds's farm, and pasture their booty there until some new arrangements could be made.

Symmonds took it well enough. 'We'll have to put 'em in t'ould byre fust,' he said phlegmatically. 'Get rid o' the markings. Put fresh'uns on afore we let 'em out.' Sometimes Gus wondered if it was simply lack of imagination that made Symmonds so stolid, or if it was a more serious mental incapacity.

They made the return journey without incident, and Alfie was roped in to help with clipping and scrubbing to remove the coloured dye which denoted the animals' true owners. They daren't simply shear away the fleece that bore the marking, for the identical newly bald pale patches would be a devastatingly clear proclamation of foul play. But they snipped and clipped and soaked and scrubbed, in a solution powerful enough to burn and blister their skin if any of it seeped through the gloves they wore. Which it did, in Alfie's case, and his skin, younger and tenderer than his more senior accomplices', suffered. By the time he woke from his truant day's sleep, his hands and forearms were covered in an angry red rash, which itched and then stung abominably. Mrs Symmonds sacrificed a generous amount of the baby's zinc and caster oil ointment, and covered the worst of the affected area with some old sheets torn into strips to make bandages. It greatly eased the discomfort, and Alfie was delighted to claim another day off school, spent taking it easy in the warm June sunshine. He was on hand to help load the newly acquired mini-flock into the wagon which called to collect them the following afternoon.

The rash was still visible the next day, when he was forced to return to school. The district nurse took a look. 'Dunno,' Alfie grunted, in reply to her questions as to the cause of the mysterious 'spots'. One look at him and his unsavoury clothing sent her eyebrows soaring eloquently, but she decided he did not need to see the doctor, and gave some ointment that was scarcely different in substance from that used on Baby Symmonds's even tenderer parts.

Still smitten by his feelings for Doreen Glass, now more unattainable than ever in her emergent 'little lady' reincarnation brought about by her adoptive 'auntie', he confided something approaching the truth about his infliction to her. With typical insouciance, Doreen let slip his confidences to Alice. She pounced on it quickly and was at once on the scent, badgering the hapless Alfie until she had wrung at least half an explanation out of him.

'We have to know what it was you were messing about with,' she lied convincingly, and cunningly. 'It could be something infectious, like. You might have to be kept off school for a bit, in case you pass it on.'

Alfie tried not to let his grubby face light up. 'Well, it was this stuff they put on the sheep, yer know. To mark them.' Alice pressed for more, and was successful. 'We were cleaning off the old stuff. Changing it. We had to cut the wool an' then wash 'em in this stuff. Like disinfectant. Then dob on another colour, different paint.'

'We? Who else was doing it? They've not been infected, have they?'

'Naw, it were only me. There was just ould . . . Mr Symmonds, and the Big Swede.' His voice faltered. All at once, he had an uneasy feeling that he had said too much, far too much. He sniffed, tried to look as winning and innocent as he could, long shot though it was. 'Er — listen. You'll not say owt, will yer? About Symmonds and the Big Swede? They mightn't like it.'

'Eh?' Alice pretended to look puzzled, and shrugged nonchalantly. 'No, right-oh. Not if

351

you don't want me to. It's only you we're bothered about, Alfie. They're nowt to do with us, are they?' She almost felt sorry for her deception at the clear look of relief on his face, but any qualms of conscience were soon stifled by the excitement she felt as she thought of the revelation she would make to Davy just as soon as she could track him down when school finished.

★　★　★

Davy had changed his mind about the black market. Or rather he had re-examined his conscience after Alice had reminded him of his 'highfalutin ideas' in her usual impetuous, bull-at-a-gate way. He had an idea it was getting somewhat beyond the minor scale of the local grocer and butcher, with his 'little bit under the counter' for his favoured customers, or erring slightly on the generous side in weighing out the four ounces of butter which was the individual ration for a week. Luke Denby had told Davy in confidence of Gus Rielke's usefulness. 'He gets me the odd can of petrol, so I can keep the old buggy running. Old Barr would do his nut if he knew! He guards the estate's store as if it was the Royal Mint. Keep it under your hat, old boy, eh?'

Davy thought immediately of that covered-in sheep-dip, and the drums hidden up there. The locked shed. You could hide a hell of a lot of stuff in a place like that. A darned sight more than you would need to do a few little favours for your mates, in a little place like Howbeck. Yet everybody spoke so well of the affable foreigner. He was a hero after all, had risked life and limb to escape from the Nazis, to get himself over here. And lamented long, loud and frequently that his medical rating rendered him unfit for active service.

Like me, Davy thought, with a touch of gallows humour. He had been downgraded when he was released from prison to a category C-3, which had helped greatly to reduce the severity of any subsequent punishment which might befall him. In fact, it had offered him what might be interpreted as an almost honourable compromise, which he had been grateful enough to grasp: acceptance of conscripted employment in agriculture, and the post of labourer on the Denby estate. His health grading was no lie. Physically and mentally he was brought low by the abuses he endured during his brief enough incarceration in the famous, or infamous, London gaol. Three months: an eternity of no hope for him. He had suffered a breakdown. That was the term they had used on the medical certificate, which had been instrumental in securing his early release, along with his parents' unceasing efforts on his behalf. He had been just about ready to cave in altogether. They could have shipped him straight off to the nearest front line, and he would not have had the will any longer to resist. But he would have been worse than useless there. He was treated with far more humaneness than he had come to expect. He was given time to recuperate, to shelter in the loving, uncritical warmth of his home, before being sent to Howbeck, and the life that had, if anything, helped further to restore him in body and spirit.

The Big Swede's cheap shot at embarrassing Alice in public had been the chief motivating factor in converting him not only to her way of thinking but making him enlist more actively in her private cause. He took it even more personally than she did. It was typical of her that she should have that initial, fire-breathing burst of fury then shrug her shoulders and notch it up as one more score against Rielke. Perhaps Davy was a little too sensitive for his own good. But he failed entirely to see the sniggering funny side of the incident in the pub. He could feel himself hotly blushing, at least mentally, at the revelation of those dainty silk knickers, and the lip-smacking lechery that lay behind it, however jocular. 'He fancies me!' Alice said lightly, when she had calmed down a day or two later. That got under Davy's skin, too, for he was forced to recognize that *he* fancied her also, good 'mate' or not.

But his fancying was a vast world away from Gus Rielke's animal sexuality. Everyone knew the Big Swede was wallowing and rutting in another man's bed — and who was to say only one? Davy's idealism had taken some hard blows in the few years of his adulthood — he had given it one or two severe dents himself, he admitted, during his spell in London, and then his year fighting in Spain. But he did at least acknowledge lust for what it was, and was not proud of his few lapses. His growing feeling for Alice Glass disturbed him because it meant so much more.

He had confided in her about Lou, had been glad to talk of his love. There was a kind of recapturing the flavour of it in the telling, like looking at the few snapshots he had, and had proudly shown. 'She looks real nice,' Alice had contributed, with typical generosity. Davy had failed in his efforts through the Red Cross to make contact with Lou, or to learn anything about her. But he had managed to get in touch with someone of her faith — a middle-aged lady who lived near Leeds, and had promised to try to find out from Baha'i believers news of the family. *Some of us have connections with the Paris community*, she had written. He was waiting to hear more, had promised to meet up with the lady in Leeds, when circumstances might permit.

He loved Lou, even though she had made it plain that she could not return that love, that she had already promised herself to another, someone he didn't even know, and didn't want to.

But now Alice had come along. Al! He couldn't bring himself easily to call her by the boy's name she inflicted on herself, even though she reprimanded him with a sharp jab from her knuckles that left a bruise on his upper arm. His feelings for her were as tender as his battered arm, even if she did insist she couldn't 'be doing with all that carry-on'.

He moved decisively off the fence one humid evening in July. The clouds had been building up, in swollen, darkly bruised masses, and the lightning started to flicker, the thunder to rumble in the threat of a heavy storm. It was the wrong time for a downpour as far as the arable farmers along the dale were concerned, for their crop was high and golden, within a few weeks of harvest. Davy felt restless. There was an air of tension, and waiting. Uncertainty on all fronts. Hitler had moved against Russia, and several people spoke wisely of Napoleon, and hoped, even though the German force was rolling up new territory in its rapid advance through splendid weather. It had just been announced on the wireless that an Anglo-Soviet 'Treaty of Mutual Assistance' had been signed. 'That's a laugh, that is,' one of the more worldly of the drinkers in the Oddfellows observed. 'Thought Winston were all again, them communist buggers.'

'At least it'll take their mind off us,' Gus said, the broad smile spreading automatically as Davy came to the counter. 'Half of beer, my friend?' He filled the glass, stood it on the stained wood. The liquid looked darkly turgid, with scarcely a bubble on its surface. It would be almost lukewarm, Davy thought, with an inward grimace. He had noted Gus's use of the first person pronoun. For an instant, Davy was ashamed of the way it had jarred.

'How you do with your little friend?' The sandy lashes flickered in that wink, Gus leaned forward, putting his red face close, his freckled, hair-covered arms folding before him. 'I bet she let you see more of them pretty panties than *I*, ya? You lucky feller, for sure.'

Davy's heart started to pound, the anger within him acid-sharp. Right! He leaned forward in turn, until their heads almost touched. He lowered his voice to hardly more than a whisper. 'Listen. Speaking of expensive things, I need to start putting some extra cash by. You don't have any extra work you could put my way?' Now it was his turn to wink, and he did so, feeling more than a little ridiculous. 'I don't mind what it is. Know what I mean?'

'Sure. I keep you in mind, Davy.' The big hand reached out, caught hold of Davy's sleeve. 'You don't worry. I let you have something. A loan. You pay back later. When you can. I find something for you soon.' He moved away, digging in his pocket, then beckoned Davy close again. He held his fist closed, thrust some crumpled paper in Davy's hand, pushed the hand away from him. 'Put it in the pocket, ya? Nobody see. Don't worry, you pay me back soon.'

When Davy sorted out the scrunched up notes later, he counted out eight pounds. Did that mean he was already on some sort of illegal payroll? 'I'd better not spend any of this,' he told an excited Alice. 'It would take me weeks to pay it back on what I get!'

'You're a grand man, Mr Brown. Come here!' She snatched at him, and darted her face forward to kiss him swiftly on the cheek.

'Is that all I get?' he growled. He made a playful grab, and she squirmed away out of his hold. They were both caught by a sudden embarrassment, which seemed to take them by surprise. 'I'm only doing it for you, you know.'

She tried to strike the right, light note, but they were both aware of the slight tension, and her keeping a small distance from him. 'I know. Don't think I don't appreciate it, 'cos I do.'

The call came around the end of the month, just after the school had closed. This time, faced with the long summer break, the Lister Road evacuees had departed, almost *en masse*, for their home town. 'I'll be back in a few weeks,' Alice told Davy. 'But you can write to us if owt happens. Be careful, eh?' She grinned and held out her hand.

'Don't you dare!' He caught hold of her shoulders, drew her close, and their faces came together. He felt the softness of her lips, then the way they remained clamped tightly together, the stiffness of her as she endured the kiss. He released her with a resigned laugh, masking the keen disappointment he felt. 'Now don't swoon away.'

She was blushing. She reached out with her right hand, and let her fingers just brush against his cheek for an instant. 'I won't. But you take care now. I mean it.'

She couldn't stop thinking about him, and his kiss, even in the noisy chaos of the train journey to Middlesbrough, until she caught sight of her neatly dressed young sister in all her finery, and the deep sadness of those soulful brown eyes. 'For God's sake, our Doreen! You're going home to see your family, not being carted off to gaol! At least try to *look* happy, even if you don't feel it!'

★   ★   ★

Davy had never considered PC Rowe, the village bobby, as a possible ally. He was far too close to home, too comfortably installed as part of village life, to rock any boats. He even knew all about the time honoured custom of the lock-in at the Oddfellows, and visited the pub only to make sure the front doors were securely fastened, and no chink of light showed, before accepting his pint 'on the house' and downing it in the back passage before wending his law abiding way homeward to the police house. The longer the arm of the law from the village the better, Davy had decided.

He took the chance of a visit home to arrange a meeting with the detective inspector in York, with whom he had had dealings concerning his own troubled history, and whom he had found to be impartial, and, latterly, sympathetic, after Davy's release from prison. Now Inspector Holden listened to him and took him seriously. 'You're right. The village bobby's not the man for this. You keep your ear to the ground. We'll get all the details from you about this foreign chappie, and I'll see what we can dig up. He's got to be registered as an alien. He should be on our books as well as down in London. I'll try up north, too. Newcastle. Mind you, it'll take a few weeks, I dare say. You know the old saying. There's a war on.' They smiled at each other. 'But if you need to get in touch quick, call this number. Once you're through it should be safe, even from any nosy operator, or the village postmistress.' He escorted Davy out into the August brightness, to the steps of the police headquarters. 'You've done the right thing, lad. Your duty.' He patted him approvingly on the shoulder.

★　★　★

The man in the suit quoted a price so high that even Gus, practised deceiver that he was, could not hide his surprise, or the desire which quickly followed. 'That's the price we can offer per beast. But we have to have them

361

now. Within the next four days. We need a score, at least. You interested?'

The Big Swede's mind was racing. It was tricky. He could never organize a raid in time. They had just completed a delivery, had covered the areas above Castleton, couldn't do another run that side. But how could he turn down an offer like this? The price was up by a full fifty per cent. And think of how much this would enhance his status with these city boys: the big men who ran the rackets, and made the real money. 'Yes!' he answered confidently, far more confidently than he felt. He nodded emphatically. 'Sure thing. You leave it to me and my lads. Wednesday, all right? Pick up at Leeholm. Make sure they get there before dawn, ya?'

Even Bob Symmonds's dirty, unshaven features lost their habitual scowling impassiveness. 'I don't like doin' it on t'own doorstep. Bit risky, like.'

'But it's just the once. And for this money! We can do it if we careful.'

'Well, we could pick up a score, between Aygarths and Barkers, I suppose. They'd be the best bet. Best not waste time lookin' elsewhere. Got to get them away straight off, though,' he added worriedly. 'No cock-ups wi' t'wagon. I daresn't have them hanging about my place.'

'We'll be all right. I take on some extra help.'

Bob Symmonds's face screwed up in suspicion. 'Who's that then?'

'The young conchy feller. He already been asking me. He need the money.' He chuckled. 'He already owe me plenty.'

Davy had been detailed to help with harvesting, and it was dusk when he called in at the pub. He was hot and sweaty, and his skin liberally grimed with the long hours of labour, but he was looking forward to the two halves he would enjoy before the bath and supper and bed waiting up at the stable block of Howe Manor. 'Ah! Davy! I am glad you come in. Come for walk out back. I want to talk.'

Vera Rhodes stared coldly as the pair left through the back door into the yard and the vegetable patch. Was this another he was dragging in to his various bits of devilry? She was getting seriously worried about it all. He'd come unstuck if he didn't put the brake on it soon. She was getting right fed up of him, even if he was making enough not to have to sponge off her any more. In fact, she almost regretted his new-found indepen-dence. She had far too much time in her lonely bed to worry about him — and to miss his undoubtedly necessary presence beside her there, she had to admit.

'I got some very important business to take care of Wednesday,' Gus said, when he and Davy were safely away from the building, strolling down the cinder path between the rows of vegetables. 'They don't lock you up in that place? You get away late, don't let nobody see you. Meet me here, out back. At eleven.'

The lorry didn't even use its slitted headlamps as it ground up the long hill out of the dale, climbing above the grounds of Howe Manor, to the narrow road which led further west, over towards Carlton. 'You stay here.' They dropped him at the highest point, above the line of trees where the Timber Corps had recently been encamped until they had drastically thinned out the wood before moving on to forests new.

Gus had brought him up here the previous evening, before sunset, to point out the road back to the village, and the narrow track snaking over the moor to Carlton. 'You watch out both ways, for any sign of anybody coming up, heading back over east, towards High Top. Got to be car or lorry. You see anything, anything at all, moving, you take torch and flash. Two. Three. Over that way, ya? Somebody watching for signal. You got to let us know in plenty time. And then you run. Go through trees. Nobody in there now. Wait

364

by the hut, then go back to village. Don't let nobody see you. This important, Davy, understand? You do good tomorrow, I find plenty jobs for you. Make plenty money.' He slapped Davy's back encouragingly. 'I know everything go fine. We do this many times. You stay till two o'clock. You have watch, ya? Then go back to your bed. I see you Thursday night, in pub.'

Davy had given Inspector Holden a description of the two secret caches at High Top Farm, and had studied with him the large scale OS map of the Howe Dale area. 'We need to catch them on the job. Then we can have a look at what they've got tucked away. We don't want to give the game away until we've nabbed them fair and square!'

Left alone in the dark on the lonely moor road, Davy hoped this would be that time. He had phoned through on the number the Inspector had given, sadly aware that the information he had was little enough. He didn't even know what the night involved, except that whatever was planned was due to take place somewhere in the direction of High Tops moor, and that his part in the operation was to act as look-out on the far side of the dale.

He should not have been surprised, Davy thought later, that the whole thing had been a bit of a shambles. A police car had discreetly approached and dropped him off again at Howe Manor. Its occupants wouldn't countenance his playing any further part in the adventure. 'You're our undercover man,' the plainclothes sergeant smiled, rather sneeringly, Davy thought. 'Wouldn't do to give the game away.'

Next day he learned that a lorry had been discovered, but was abandoned off the road before the police could get near. It was full of bleating, panic-stricken sheep, which, it turned out, belonged to the Aygarth flock, and to Norman Barker, a neighbouring farmer. The abandoned lorry had false number plates, its ownership could not be traced. Of far more moment was the sensation of the Big Swede's unexplained absence, a cause of voluble distress to the landlady of the Oddfellows. 'How am I ever going to manage without him?' she wept, when, after a further two days, there was no sign of him, or an explanation for his absence. There were a few behind-the-hand sniggers and sotto voce suggestions, and even volunteers to replace him, though not within the distraught Vera's hearing.

Any immediate justice, apart from the discovery and confiscation of the many assorted items on and about High Top Farm, was of a rougher kind. Sheep stealing had been a hanging offence in bygone days, so some believed Bob Symmonds had got off lightly. He was missing when the police searched his premises, but he was found later in the day lying by the roadside on the edge of the village. His swollen, badly beaten face was hardly recognizable, he had several broken ribs and a fractured knee-bone, as well as smashed hands and broken toes. He was naked, and there was hardly an inch of his stunted frame that was not darkly bruised and agonizingly painful. A blunt instrument was diagnosed as the weapon. Two Indian clubs, a popular means of exercise, had been wielded with brutal efficiency, 'by assailants unknown', the official report erroneously stated.

18

The scandal of the Black Market cell right in their midst marked a kind of watershed for many of the inhabitants of Howbeck. 'Things'll never be t'same agin!' folks told each other, with a sigh and a shake of the head. Davy had anticipated a backwash of resentment against him when it was discovered, as it inevitably would be, that he was one of the prime movers in the downfall of Rielke. And, by a process of association, much of the ill feeling might be directed against Alice. However, the thing that greatly blunted the hostility of the villagers, and instead made a number of them uncomfortably aware of just how welcoming they had been to the treacherous foreign interloper and the little 'favours' he had so often done them, was the nature of the crime which had been his undoing. Sheep rustling, and from the very community which had taken him to its bosom so readily, was unforgivable.

Davy couldn't help feeling sorry for the unsavoury Bob Symmonds. He had certainly borne the brunt of the swift summary 'justice' dealt out. He was in hospital in Scarborough for almost two months, and was then sentenced to a severe eighteen months in prison for, among other things, being a 'receiver of stolen goods', found in plenty on his run-down farm. He had the good sense to remain 'unable to identify' his assailants, not that it would have made his sentence any lighter had he named names. His wife stolidly and unshakably maintained total ignorance of the contents locked away in the various outbuildings. She was not evicted from High Top. Mr Barr decided it would be extremely difficult in these times to find another tenant for such an unappealing spot, and the older offspring of the Symmonds could hardly make a poorer job of it than their father, at least until their call-up. And Mrs Symmonds had the comfort of the lumpy stocking over which she slept each lonely night.

However, there was one who took no trouble to hide her animosity towards Davy, and that was the landlady of the Oddfellows. She had a lot of fast talking to do. Accompanied by her act of outraged innocence, it failed to save her from the wrath of officialdom, and a substantial fine for dealing in 'contraband'. She was fortunate not to lose her licence, but she did not see it that way. The torrent of abuse she sent in Davy's direction, even though it was delivered in a low tone, like a hissing serpent, made him decide he would have to forgo his nightly two halves for a long, long time to come. For ever, possibly, for the dramatic episode of August '41 brought him to another life-changing decision.

He felt he was personally deeply involved in the Big Swede's exposure and disappearance, and Inspector Holden, at the headquarters of the North Yorks Constabulary, welcomed his interest. The inspector had been right in his estimation that it would take time to investigate the man's history. But eventually, when the incomers from Margrove were seeing for the second time the splendid beauty of changing, autumnal hues in the trees around Howe Manor and the woodland above, the truth about the Norwegian 'Big Swede' emerged. The nationality was correct. He was, indeed, from Norway, but his daredevil escape from the Nazis and the wounded hip were from the realms of fiction. He *did* have a connection with the sea. He had jumped ship from a merchantman in Newcastle about the time of the outbreak of the war, and had made his way down the east coast, to work for a while at the inshore fishing around Yarmouth. The trail had turned cold, after some dodgy dealings and queries about the Registration of Aliens. He was still listed as 'missing' down there.

'We're trying to trace some of the goods we found up at that farm, work our way back through the chain. Newcastle have some ideas. There's one or two 'big fish' moved up north recently. But he had seaman's papers still, apparently. They've got the idea he might have signed on, maybe up there or Shields, or even Middlesbrough. Or Hartlepool. Easy enough these days, with crews hard to get. One thing's sure. I doubt you'll see him up in the Dales again, so I wouldn't lose any sleep over him.'

He wouldn't, he assured the inspector, with whom he had struck a note of rapport. It was Inspector Holden who first brought up the idea that was to bear such significant fruit. 'You know, like most jobs nowadays, we're crying out for recruits in the force. A bright feller like you, you could do a lot worse than sign up.' He held up his hand quickly. 'I know your views about the war and all that, and I can understand them, even if I don't agree. But keeping law and order on our streets is vital, in war or peace. And I tell you, lad, there's some right villains taking advantage of the situation we're landed with. And not just your Gus Rielkes and his racketeers. There's some real nasty thugs crawling out of the woodwork just now. We need all the help we can get.'

'But they wouldn't take me, surely? With my record? Prison — I mean that would bar me straight away, wouldn't it?'

'Not necessarily. A criminal record, in normal circumstances would, that's true. But what you were up for — that's different. Standing up for your beliefs. You could start off as a special constable. Just a few weeks' training, then you're out on the beat. And like I said, a bright lad like you, no telling where you could go. There's our branch. Detective. Some challenges there, I can tell you.' Davy felt the first stirrings of excitement, of positive response. 'I can find out for you. Make some enquiries. I know we're short handed here, for a start. But it's the same all over the country — down in London, all the major towns.'

It was a very long time since Davy had felt such enthusiasm. It was a worthwhile job, and one he could, in all conscience, he thought, undertake. 'Keeping the peace', even in war, was an honourable occupation. All at once he experienced an eagerness to make a new beginning. Working in Howbeck, useful as it had been, had been merely marking time, part of that sense of recovering he had been going through since coming out of prison, and striving to come to terms with the horrors he had been subjected to in there.

There had been times when he had thought he never would recover from it. This was a new start — new hope.

Suddenly, he thought of Alice. Her bright young face, that cheery, accepting smile, her wholesome, direct goodness, came up before him and stopped him short. He was fond of her. She had come to mean so much to him, he looked forward to seeing her and being with her, sharing his time, his thoughts with her. She was *dear* to him. He would like very much for her to be part of his future also.

And then he remembered Lou. That special quiet calm she had brought, an ethereal quality that seemed to be wrapped around her, and to touch all who came into contact with her, the quiet but complete conviction of that new faith of hers, which was the utter centre of her, unshakable. It had made him feel unworthy — but not when he was in her presence.

He loved her. But she had never loved in return, not that way. Another kind of love, and yes, a very beautiful love, but not uniquely for him, the way he had wanted it, her, to be. There was someone else, someone she was prepared to marry. So Davy could never have her. He had known that when he left France, even though he had tried to cling to some hope. Since then, he had not been able to learn anything further of her. Except that the Baha'i sources he had got in touch with feared that the declared adherents of the faith might well have been rounded up, as some had been in Germany, and sent to those detention camps about which so many disturbing stories were beginning to circulate.

Meanwhile, there was Alice. Maybe he wouldn't have to leave her. Not permanently, anyway. He would go ahead with the application. Howbeck was not that far away, not if he joined the York force. And who knows? Perhaps he could persuade her to move, too. She liked him. He quickly erased the thought of the social difference between them, that gap which she would so often emphasize. What nonsense! She was a grand girl — or *lass*, as she would say. How would she feel about becoming his fiancée? How would she feel about spending the rest of her life with him? He was shaken by his desire for her to say yes. He wasn't certain that she would, but there was a chance, and today he suddenly felt anything was possible.

★   ★   ★

Change was in the air all right, Alice acknowledged, and it was more than just the hint of a nip in the air of those lovely, misty autumn evenings, that made her throat tighten and her eyes prick with sudden tears behind them, when she gazed out over the fading shades of the valley and the slope up to the moors. The numbers of Lister Road evacuees had been reduced drastically — fatally, it had turned out, for their continuation of this little branch in exile.

Back in Margrove, life had reverted to the weary succession of nights disturbed by the sirens yet with no more threat of nearby danger. People got up grumbling and went to the shelter, or the cupboard under the stairs, and shuffled back to their cold beds in the early hours at the all clear, still grumbling. For them war was broken sleep, and queuing, and shortages, of clothes now as well as food — and for some of the young women, now that conscription for twenty-year-olds had come in, it meant excitement, even glamour in new places and independence, money, and other hectic pleasures they wouldn't dream of writing home about. The families of the evacuees realized how much they had missed their kids, especially their youngest. 'I want our Algy back home,' Maggie Glass persisted. 'The bairn belongs here. And our Doreen, too!' she added quickly. Algy grinned. Like most six-year-olds he lived in the present, and the present was good in the summer, for his mam made a great fuss of having him back again. Doreen was more thoughtful and silent, and kept her own counsel, even when they teased her about her new clothes and the 'swanky' way she talked.

The result of all these reunions meant that when the Lister Road contingent reconvened in September, the pupils were down to twenty-four, well below half their original number. And of those, only four Class I infants remained. Miss Laverton delivered the bombshell without preamble. 'We'll be closing down here by 'tattie-hoyking' week,' she announced, using the local parlance for the week's break in late October when many schoolchildren earned money on the farms picking potatoes. 'Howbeck School can cope with any of our pupils who are staying on here. There's a possibility that Edith may be kept on, offered a post, if numbers justify it. For the rest of us it's back to Margrove.'

Alice put on her brave face to hide her bitter disappointment. 'I've got to register in December anyhow. Get my call-up then. I can always find summat to tide me over for a couple of months. I'll miss it, though, this place. I've really enjoyed it here,' she confided to Davy. 'And me mates. You and Beth. I was hoping we might have been able to stay on here. At the school. Miss Laverton thought it might count as war work. I wouldn't have minded.'

Davy was more nervous than he would have believed. His palms were clammy, his heart-rate accelerated. 'Listen, Alice — Al. I've got a place in York. With the police. How about — I mean, we could see each other. And write. Then, when I've finished my training . . . the pay's not that much, but . . .' He saw the tense expression, the set of her brow and lips. 'I think a lot of you, Alice.' He battled against his own sense of failure. 'Couldn't you . . . you're very special. Could we . . . could you have that sort of feeling for me? I've felt like this for quite a time. The more I've been with you, got to know you.' He took hold of her, desperately, felt the wooden non-resistance of her, the closed lips as he pressed his kiss upon her mouth, and was aware of a profound sadness, knowing that she didn't share his need.

She was awkward and brusque, but her eyes shone with tears. 'No, Davy. I've told you, I don't want any of that. I'll always be your mate. Always be glad to see you, and hear from you. Friends, eh?'

'Maybe you'll change your mind one day?'

She shrugged, gave a sad little grin. 'Maybe.' She spoke out of pure kindness, but even as she answered, she felt false, knew she never would.

She had to accept, shameful and shocking though it was, there was only one person she could ever feel like that about, and it was a love that could never be acknowledged or spoken about to anyone, least of all the object of her passionate attachment.

Beth had endured a miserable summer, and Alice had suffered just watching her suffer. Luke Denby had found it impossible to believe that Beth would not welcome him to her arms and her bed again. Her initial reaction, he guessed, was to be expected from such a narrowly brought-up provincial little ex-virgin. He tried to woo her from Lincolnshire with a passionate pen and romantic declarations of undying love, the romanticism conveniently heightened, he hoped, by the impossibility of making any long-term plans or commitments, given the danger of the times, and of his particular occupation. *I can't look beyond today, my lovely darling, you must realize that.* His first forty-eight hour leave from the new 'drome in late June had seen him speeding home with high if less than noble aspirations, so that Beth's startling repudiation, her chalk-faced rejection and almost hysterical tears really shook him. And hurt him, too, for it made him hit out and be cruel in turn. 'I might have known! I thought after all that's happened between us that you were grown up. That you'd moved on from the simpering schoolgirl pictures your mummy was so proud of. I reckon you're in the right place here.' He jerked his head savagely back towards the wing of his ancestral home which housed St Anne's. 'With all the other gym slips and inky fingers!'

Elsbeth had been away in Margrove for his next visit home. The phone calls and letters had stopped. So had the invitations to those informal suppers in the drawing-room, though Elsbeth couldn't help feeling an added sense of injustice at the way the Denbys cut her off so abruptly from their marks of favour. 'I thought she was worried about me trying to steal her precious boy off her,' Beth grumbled to Alice. 'You'd think she'd be pleased we're not seeing each other.'

'Good riddance to bad rubbish!' Alice said decisively, and took the sweetly torturous chance to give her another squeeze and hug, and a kiss on the lips. She had not intended to say anything to her about Davy and his intimate confession of his feelings, but she found herself, embarrassing though it was, gruffly confiding a brief account of his admission.

379

'Oh, he's a good man!'

Alice couldn't help feeling a stab of disappointment at her friend's seemingly enthusiastic reception of her confidences. 'Don't be daft! You know I can't be doing with owt like that. Yes, he's a nice enough bloke. He did his bit as far as the Big Swede was concerned. I wish him all the best. I hope it works out for him. I'll miss him.'

'What about me? Will you . . . ?' Beth paused, her blue eyes big and solemn as she gazed sadly at her.

'Eh?' Then the colour mounted to her face as Alice realized the import of her words. Back in Margrove, their old world, the gulf which had kept them separate for almost ten years would be firmly in place once more. The unfathomable gulf between Maudsley Street and the detached houses two miles away, behind the park. 'It's not the end of the earth,' she tried gamely. 'We can still meet up now and then . . . if you want.'

It was Beth's turn to blush, and Alice knew at once she had been keeping something back. 'I'm not going back to Margrove. I don't want to go back to Lister Road. I wasn't much good there.' She looked up vulnerably, as though she anticipated some sharp reaction from Alice. 'It's so nice — I like it so much here.' Her voice took on a hurried, almost muffled quality, as though she were confessing something shameful. 'I've been offered a post at St Anne's. You know — the school up at the manor. Assistant mistress, in the junior classes. They'll take me on. I might even be able to stay on when I register, in March.'

'Good for you, kidder!' It came out harder than Alice wished, but she couldn't hold back, she felt the sharp sting of real hurt and loss. 'Back where you should be, really. Not with us Lister Road tykes!'

'I was hoping . . . listen. Isn't there any way you could stay on in Howbeck, too? At least till December?'

'What could I do here? Not unless you can persuade them nobs of yours to tek me on as cook and bottle washer. But they've already got their own skivvies up there, haven't they?'

The miracle occurred only two days later, when Alice was feeling really down in the dumps. And it was her beloved Beth again who brought the news, who had indeed been the instigator of it. She was too brimful of happiness and excitement to draw out the drama as she had planned. She couldn't keep it in, she flung herself at the amazed Alice, almost sent her staggering at the force with which she grabbed her, swung her round. 'Oh God, Al! Marvellous news! I was talking to

Mr Barr! You know! He said he'll take you on. The estate needs another labourer, with Davy going next week! You'll be just like Evelyn and Beryl!' They were the two Land Girls. 'But wait! I haven't told you the best news of all! They're moving out. Into the main house! We can have that little flat they're in, over the stables! Can you believe it? Oh, I'm so happy!'

She had flung her arms around Alice's waist and whirled her in a crazy, capering dance. 'Whoa!' Alice said, still struggling to comprehend Beth's enchanting gabble. 'Just hang on a minute! Don't I get a say in all of this?'

Beth's eyes widened, her face twisted in a parody of alarm. 'Oh no! Please . . . you've got to . . . tell me you'll say yes! *Please*! I couldn't bear it! I thought you'd be over the moon! Just like I am! You will stay, won't you?' She seemed to have stopped breathing as she waited, her lovely face a picture of breathless anticipation.

Alice's heart was drumming. She felt the throb of happiness, and profound thankfulness, released like a dye through her veins. 'I think I'd better, kidder. Somebody's got to keep an eye on you, Miss Hobbs!'

★　★　★

And two weeks after that, it had all happened. Davy had departed; Doreen was staying on in Howbeck, too — Alice suspected darkly that Miss Ramsay had virtually bought the rights over Doreen's young life, at least for the duration of the war, and maybe it was the right move, after all. Doreen was as enthusiastic to be taken over as her benefactress was to assume such a prodigious responsibility. 'She'll go far. I'm putting her in for a scholarship for the girls' grammar in Whitby. I'll give her all the financial support she needs.'

'So she's going to live happy ever after, as they say,' Alice murmured wryly, on that momentous first night, in the lamplight of their shabby, snug haven over the old stables of Howe Manor.

'And so are we,' Beth whispered. Her voice was unsteady, and her heart was racing, but not with the great unknowing fear with which it had throbbed only a hundred yards or so from this spot earlier in this eventful year. There was a nervousness still, and ignorance. But it was she who stood and shrugged off her dressing gown. The lamp was behind her, on the shelf which served as a crude bookcase. Through the low spill of its light, her slim body showed in dark silhouette against the thin satin of her best nightgown. 'At least until December. Take me to bed.'

Alice took her hands, stood up and drew her close. There was no need for words at all.

We do hope that you have enjoyed reading this large print book.

Did you know that all of our titles are available for purchase?

We publish a wide range of high quality large print books including:
Romances, Mysteries, Classics General Fiction Non Fiction and Westerns

Special interest titles available in large print are:
The Little Oxford Dictionary Music Book Song Book Hymn Book Service Book

Also available from us courtesy of Oxford University Press:
Young Readers' Dictionary (large print edition) Young Readers' Thesaurus (large print edition)

For further information or a free brochure, please contact us at:
Ulverscroft Large Print Books Ltd., The Green, Bradgate Road, Anstey, Leicester, LE7 7FU, England. Tel: (00 44) 0116 236 4325 **Fax:** (00 44) 0116 234 0205

Other titles published by
The House of Ulverscroft:

SILK STOCKING SPY

C.W. Reed

Travelling alone from India to England in 1940, newly married Cissie Humphreys is captured after her ship is torpedoed. Given the choice of prison or collaboration with the enemy, she works for their propaganda service led by Lord Haw-Haw and falls in love with Sean Munroe, an IRA rebel. Now a secret agent, Cissie accompanies Sean on a spying mission to a fishing village on the North Yorkshire coast. But before long Cissie alone must face the consequences. Now her only chance of survival is to act as a double agent for the British. Where will it all lead?